**Matthew Crow** was born in North Shields in 1987.

During his teens, Matthew moved to London to work freelance writing articles and reviews for online blogs, magazines and national newspapers. He quickly secured a literary agent and his debut novel *Ashes* was published by Legend Press in 2010.

Matthew is one of the most exciting young authors on the literary circuit. He currently lives in Newcastle-upon-Tyne.

# My Dearest Jonah

## Matthew Crow

Legend Press
Independent Book Publisher

Legend Press Ltd, 2 London Wall Buildings,
London EC2M 5UU
info@legend-paperbooks.co.uk
www.legendpress.co.uk

British Library Cataloguing in Publication Data available.

ISBN 978-1-9082482-5-1

Set in Times
Printed by Lightning Source, Milton Keynes, UK

Cover design by Tim Bremner

Legend Press

Independent Book Publisher

Praise for Matthew Crow:

It was more than a blowjob, Jonah, you pig – we were in love!

PS. Due to circumstances entirely unforeseen, I am in the process of imminent relocation. My new details will be forwarded forthwith. Until then I would appreciate a swift and appropriate response. V

Dear Verity,

I am truly sorry if you interpreted my previous missive as in any way accusatory. I can assure you this was not my intention and for any upset caused I apologise. That is not to say I entirely condone the recent tangent you seemed to have happened upon. From your description these men sound more reptile than human and their line of work appears - in print alone - questionable at best. That said I have faith in your morals and strength of character (though how I worry for them all the same!) and for what it's worth your burgeoning affiliation has my acceptance if not my approval. With that I hope we can carry on our correspondence as normal, or at least allow regular service to resume.

This morning in the cafe that same old man sat alone once more in his preferred window seat, his ledger placed at a perfect right angle with the edge of the table, his left hand resting gently on top as though swearing oath. A gold pen rested to the left of his cutlery as rigamortis took hold of two untouched waffles, which formed the altar of his arrangement. Behind him two girls chatted in church tones, every so often craning their necks in a bid to disguise the regularity with which they perused his limited actions.

Unusually for mid morning, two trucks were parked in the driveway along with a long black car whose appearance brought on that insatiable itch of *déjà vu*. I ignored it and sipped my coffee despite it still being a little too hot. The measured pain as it passes my lips is a sensation I have grown to enjoy. After all these years - and believe me when I say it is many since I was considered a child by even the most mature of acquaintances - the adult thrill of enjoying hot, caffeinated beverages is still one I hold dear.

Eventually he stood up to leave with the languor of those

unemployed through choice. I can't say I wasn't a little relieved. His presence made me feel observed and vulnerable even with my back to him. I have no basis for my prejudice, it was simply ever thus.

The waitress kindly raised the pot of coffee but I declined her offer. The old man, making no attempt to neither hide nor excuse his uneaten breakfast, packed his ledger into a wide pocket of his coat and proceeded to the counter where, as per usual, he produced an immaculately crisp coupon from his top pocket.

As he left, the girls who had been eavesdropping with all the subtley of a sledgehammer began a panicked fumble to collect their belongings. They threw down a handful of crumpled dollar bills and trotted off into the daylight, inexplicably enthralled by the obsessive routine of that geriatric loner.

The waitress placed the coupon in the till (for all its one-off-small-town-intonations the coffee shop is, in fact, part of an ugly conglomerate. Look to page six of your newspaper today, I'll bet my last dime there's a perforated voucher for free waffles when you purchase their bottomless java bucket).

"Poor old Levi," she muttered, ostensibly to herself, though loud enough so that I, the only remaining customer could hear. "Richer than God and tight as a duck's ass."

I nodded and left.

Two men looked up at me through the tinted windows of the long black car as I emerged from the coffee shop. They shared a glance before driving away. I know I've seen them before but can't quite say where or when.

Like you I've been feeling forlorn of late. I don't know how long you have to be somewhere before it begins to feel normal, before you start to feel as though you belong. I've lived here for longer than anywhere else bar one since the age of eleven, yet can't seem to lose that feeling that I'm a latecomer to a party, and no matter how many drinks I take I'll still be playing catch up with the masses. You can feel a town's routine, its ebb and flow, the way the light moves across the water throughout the course of the day, the dip and peak of pedestrians on Main Street, the general consensus on so-and-so; how She used to be pretty until she lost the weight, and how He was always a little too involved with the softball team during his tenure as coach. These things are the familiar, they provide you with a framework, an empty hook on which to hang a life. But to feel involved, to feel part of the machine you observe from the periphery, is a skill that seems to be forever out of reach.

Despite this, I have decided to become the driver of my own fate. And, you will be pleased to hear, have formulated the most basic of plans.

You see, this morning's mutterings of disgruntlement rolled through the cafe like tumbleweed as I went head to head with the ceramic over two final drops of coffee. The same whispers that had been heard yesterday morning, and the morning before that and, were my memory what it used to be, no doubt the morning before that too. The latest bone of contempt has for some time now been the building site, which has hung like limbo for over a year. Two schools, a small church and a nature reserve which houses, we are told, a butterfly so rare that its existence is still questioned by many zoologists are being demolished in favour of over two million square foot of soulless concrete and glass. 'Everything you could need under one roof!' the flyers read when they were sent out during the formative stages of the mall's fabrication.

A stout Virginian with a silver tongue and the Midas touch promised to give this town the elixir of life in the form of cut price denim and chain restaurants. The day he arrived, the storm that had already claimed three lives and two pickup trucks subsided, and the sun began its long and strenuous programme of recovery. Rumours were spun so fast I often wondered whether or not their orators had written them in preparation, and had merely been waiting for a blank canvas onto which they could smear them. Apparently he was an orphan who owned his first pair of shoes at thirteen and his first bank at twenty-three. Others pointed out with glee that his moneyed ancestors had pressed their initials onto the declaration of independence. Were I a betting man I'd say the truth lay somewhere in the middle.

In the beginning we were in his thrall. His rhapsody was infectious and soon every hard hitter in town was investing in what appeared to be a licence to print money. Of course within four months the bombastic demigod performed a non-too-glamorous midnight run. Two cranes, half a city's worth of scaffolding and the dusty remains of two schools, a small church and a nature reserve were all that was left of his promise. In his hotel room they found a pair of spats and a half drunk bottle of whisky. He has become our most cherished legend; sightings of him are more frequent and detailed than those of Big Foot himself.

All wasn't lost though. Soon a conglomerate from upstate heard the news and, checking facts against figures, decided that such an investment may in fact be a hit. Before long it was *Virginia be damned – think local and you can't go wrong.* So the landed gentry now continue to slowly construct a reality upon the skeleton of a stranger's fantasy, and in the time it seems to be taking animosity has crept back into the common accord like acid reflux.

*We've give them our God and our education,* is the general consensus. *There best be some mighty fine bargains to be had in their place.*

My plan, if you can apply such a grand title to such simple actions, is to take a walk out to the building sight tomorrow. I'm not a proud man, nor am I workshy, and if there's one thing that project seems to be in need of its labourers.

I think I've talked for long enough, tonight at least. By now the rooster outside is filling his lungs and a milky residue is beginning to swirl in the sky like the first drops of cream in well-brewed coffee.

God I hate morning.

I hope you are no longer upset, Verity, and that your next letter will intone as much. I hope, too, that for your sake you're in control of whatever situation you have gotten yourself into, and for what it's worth you're forever in my thoughts.

If possible - and not too much to ask - please keep your fingers crossed for me tomorrow. As well as financial reasons (a pressing matter in themselves) the solitude of unemployment in an alien town is beginning to take its toll. I sometimes forget where my thoughts stop and the real world starts. Only yesterday I walked into the town's general store and instinctively went to open a beer straight out of the fridge. It's the company I miss. Nothing quite as grandiose as camaraderie. Even an occasional pleasantry with a day-to-day face should just about do it. And sadly it seems that paid and regular employment is the only way I will achieve this small luxury, at least for now.

Thank heavens we have one another, is all I can say.

With love,
Jonah

Dear Jonah,

Four days ago I woke to total darkness.

I pounded for what seemed an eternity; though common sense suggested no answer was forthcoming. To my side I felt an object whose texture seemed familiar yet without the appropriate senses to hand its specifics remained uncertain. It was about the size of a withered bunch of grapes and vaguely lifelike, with a coldness running through like a tiny prosthetic limb. As time lapsed the air became thick and gelatinous within my grave (and how certain I was that I was witnessing my own burial), until finally a moment of calm took over. I remained immobile, cocooned and oddly safe. Echoes of an outside world entirely separate from me played on like I was falling asleep to a movie I was desperate to see the end of. My memory of events is foggy at best. My one moment of clarity came when I searched for your face in the darkness. It wasn't there. Even if it was I'm not entirely sure I'd have known. I could see you a dozen times a day and, quite frankly Jonah, pass you as though a stranger.

The surprise of my surroundings seemed to repeat itself a number of times - each time with the same thump of fear like a blow to the stomach - as to suggest that I was slipping in and out of consciousness with an alarming regularity. When I awoke one final time I pressed my cramping feet against the solid mass above me and pushed with all my might. I felt the invisible texture - metal, I had concluded, hollow, but coated in fabric - give an inch or two with each press. I felt the shape shift beneath my feet and heard something to my right move out of itself, like a bullet from a silenced pistol. There shone a glimmer of light to my right-hand side that disappeared like a shy ghost. Another kick. Another tease of light. My desperation mounted until I was pressing upwards, back arched, with every ounce of power my body had.

The trunk of the car flew open and an arid warmth surrounded me like fire. The tears from my eyes flowed freely but were extinguished on impact by the sting of heat and the sandblast of the desert around me. I crawled out of the car, knock-kneed and gelatinous, before hitting the ground in a withered mass of limbs and gravity where I unfurled gradually to my body's own timing, like a crumpled receipt in a wastebasket.

I scanned the endless horizon; sterile and scorched in every direction, with barely a cactus to observe my ordeal, and then found myself crawling frantically back inside the trunk of the car, no longer so sure of the possibilities or even the benefits of an outside life. The roof of the trunk I kept gaping at all times, like I was the commanding tongue in a dislocated jaw, eager not to let a change in wind and an obliging mechanism yank me screaming back to the point at which I awoke.

Two large, solid furrows flanked my buttocks and a slight discharge had begun to seep from the roof. Brown, Jonah, like drying blood, and almost exactly the same colour as the scarf you once sent me, which I treasure to this day. Wires hung frail and uncertain; stripped bare at the point of insertion from what must have been decades of shoddy workmanship. The overall impression was that this car had been solely maintained for situations such as this; the quick and effective removal of hazardous waste, i.e. myself.

I suspect I would have remained in that car for the rest of my natural life, until sand and starvation petrified my corpse into some ancient ruin, had it not been for my natural curiosity and an ever prevalent gag reflex. Were that the case my previous letter would surely have been my last; a fact that would have been high up on my list of regrets.

With little to occupy myself with save the swirling sand dance that stung my exposed ankles I felt that same object pressing against my leg. It reminded me of something though still I couldn't claim what. Leaning forward - tricky, given the excitement of the preceding events I was only just beginning to realise the severity of my physical condition, which was unpleasant at best - I went to pick it up.

I screamed Jonah, God knows I screamed. First just the once. And then again with the force in which I threw myself against the back of the trunk causing the roof to slam down onto my already tender head. The third time I screamed at the thought of being held captive next to something so awful. I kicked the roof open, easier this time, thank God, and fell back onto the sand, this time my insides retching until a steady stream of bile, intersected with occasional fragments of tortured food, began to mix with the dust and form a sour smelling gloop not entirely dissimilar to breakfast oats.

It was a hand. Human. This in itself was apt to induce shock. But the true horror was that I knew it to be Eve's. My sudden ejection from the car had caused it to bounce upwards and hang grotesquely across the bottom lip of the trunk like the final strand of linguine of a giant's feast. It had been severed above the wrist, allowing perhaps three or four inches of that sweet, slender arm to change so suddenly from its once glowing china white to a crueller hue – older, almost, and damaged, like a well thumbed novel left out in the sun. Her fingers were still splayed, with each nail painted a sophisticated purple. Around the wrist the bracelet was wrapped - gold; cold and mocking - as much a warning to me as anything else.

I steeled myself over the next half hour. The only indication of any real timescale was the increasingly lingering prickle of heat at the back of my neck. I had been granted the dignity of my clothes, a gentlemanly final touch that no doubt saved my life, and eventually managed to prize the bracelet from Eve's severed limb.

Your apology was characteristic and appreciated Jonah, but in hindsight I fear slightly misplaced. Your original misgivings were perhaps more acute than my blinkered notion of events. That said I ventured onto this path not as innocently as I would have led you to believe. Honesty, above all else, is what I prize between us, and I know you do too, yet for the past few months I have been inhibiting this unspoken code, yet plan to rectify said misdemeanour if only you'll grant me the chance. J was not simply a gentleman with a shifty eye and a questionable entourage whom I met in the coffee shop, nor were my dealings with him strictly of the heart or flesh. There was calculation, on my part and his, and I fear that they are far from over. I had planned to tell you this all along, though feared...

well, I just feared, Jonah. You're the only unmoving positive I seem to have ever had. The thought of losing you pressed heavily on me and so I perhaps omitted certain details which I felt might displease you. And now feels as good a time as any to begin to fill you in on the previous two months which culminated in me being left for dead in the trunk of a car with only my best friend's severed hand for company.

But first things first.

I write to you now from a peeling back room in the type of motel where married men show poor young girls the real value of money, and where accented drug dealers begin empires that will go on to terrorise communities for years to come.

"How you wanna pay, lady?" asked the man on reception. "We do hourly, nightly, or by the week."

"By the week should suffice," I said in my haughtiest tones.

I had, in my blind panic, managed to secure a change of clothes, yet still the grubby marks of the desert and the not-quite-cleaned traces of blood clung to my flesh. The thought of my scent is enough to make me hide my face in shame even now; three showers and nigh on twenty hours of sleep later. The only reason for choosing this particular establishment was that other than requiring a safe and distant place to recuperate, my appearance would have caused little stir. Even as I checked in (false name, indoor shades) a recently married couple began touching what I can only describe as third base on the waxy sofa beneath the neon vacancy sign as their young child shot a pellet gun at the wall.

"Sign here, here, and here Miss Neave and you'll be in room 147. Pool view."

"Perfect."

I used to adore these hotels as a girl. Real life plays out like cabaret in hotels like these up and down the country. The sort of life you don't hear about, and the sort of life you do. We were next door but one from the beauty queen and the talk show host the night before the story hit the papers, and I got my first period in our en suite at the Coconut Grove Nebraska. I lost my virginity to a janitor in the laundry room of The Flamingo Park Lodge Wyoming. Those single-serving packets of fabric softener still send a shiver down my spine.

What else is there?

I have the bare essentials. A bed, a desk at either side, two lamps, one of which works, the other provides a mild electric shock and so not worth the effort for the flickering illumination it emits. The heating kicks in at regular intervals which I can neither control nor tolerate, and so am left to pace the room in just my underwear as having to hand-wash my clothes is proving particularly arduous and increasingly risky (there has been no indication as to a repeat delivery of tiny soap discs). Everything is here, I suppose. I daresay I could live the rest of my life in this tiny room, so functional and sterile. It's not entirely dissimilar to the lives most other people live. Only the square footage would mark it out as in any way eccentric.

However, there are downsides.

The strip lamp above the bathroom mirror acts as a cruel reminder of the fallibility of the human form. Each time I step out of the shower the floor-length stretch of reflective surface seems to capture me at my least attractive, my many imperfections unavoidable. I look both huge and tiny all at once in that mirror with that light on, and as such have taken to showering in the dark.

The less said about the room service breakfast the better.

The bed itself is not entirely unsatisfactory, though the unmistakable human stench - the faint top-notes of sweat and sex that are replaced in classier establishments by chemical neutrality - seems to seep through each and every fabric. It crawls from the dewy walls and up from the carpet so worn as to be almost redundant.

Worse still is that all I have been gifted are the twin atrocities of daytime television and a pocket bible to occupy myself with. Someone has stolen the New Testament. Ripped it clean out like a coupon. Did I mention that? Whether an act of calculated rebellion or simply wanton destruction I do not know. All I can say is that having been forced to spend forty-eight hours and counting with nothing but myself for company, it feels like a personal attempt on my sanity to deny me of such stimulus. I find myself loathing the perpetrator regardless of his or her intentions and ache only for the thrill of Lazarus' rise.

And so all I have is you. Your letters (another essential I was able to secure) and the thought that somewhere, something good exists in my life. For now that seems enough to get by on.

The sun was at its fiercest when I began my trek. Sand blistered my feet and I swear that each time I'd reach a landmark I had set myself - pass a stone I'd had my eye upon, or a winking shard of glass - the expanse would stretch once more before my eyes like a cartoon corridor. Overhead two vultures swooped in and out of one another with an ugly wisdom. Even when so weak I could taste death on my tongue like vinegar, the beauty of the desert was not lost on me. That enormity gets inside of you. Sizes and shapes stop mattering when you have nothing to compare them to. When it is just you and the world. The scrape of my foot against a clump of rock became deafening, yet the pain that had wrapped around me seemed to stop mattering. It was as if my feet said, 'we're getting out of here, with or without you.' And so I became almost dead, led by the same strength that must enable most women to give birth. Attempting to make tangible the hideousness of the situation - to even think it could be quantified via such lowly mediums as tears or tantrums - seemed as ridiculous as it no doubt was.

So I walked.

And I walked.

My footprints disappeared behind me. The car resigned itself to volatile vaults of memory. The severed hand already on its slow return to nothingness, like the opposite of birth.

God I was thirsty.

It grew dark and then light and then dark again. The speed at which the cold arrived like a net cast out to sea seemed almost rude. But I didn't stop.

On the second morning the landscape became more varied. Mounds appeared where before there had only been flat, and with each step the terrain became increasingly rugged, like the drawings of a heartbeat under attack. A tyre lay decomposing, buried in the sand. I touched it and it felt precious. In the distance I saw two dogs. They were either fighting or mating, though I was unable to tell which. As I drew closer a small cluster of buildings began to take shape: a gas station, a convenience store. I heard a wind chime jangle to the sweet soul of an invisible conductor. A makeshift bar. Two old men - toothless and gaunt - sat silently on a porch. Outlines began to rise like steam from a city grate. I heard the rhythm of my breath change and felt myself become fuller as their shapes began to calcify.

Just one more step.

The following events are blurry and those that remain clear I would disregard if given the chance. Suffice to say that I do not care to see in print what I had to do in order to secure a ride into the next functioning town (though I daresay that had I not offered it then it would have been taken nonetheless). It seemed a small price to pay at the time, though in hindsight I think the five dollars I later found stuffed in my bra may well have been adequate. I suppose we'll never know.

My trailer looked interfered with even from the outside. Nothing was particularly different, though were it to be granted the luxury of expression it would have held one of sheer indignation. As I walked towards the door, two boys wearing only their underwear played on the grass with cutlasses and swords. The smallest boy, Dylan, a redhead, eased the fervour of his attack as he saw me and raised his eye-patch.

"The bad men been in there, miss," he said with a mild stutter born of genetics as opposed to fear, a fact I had deduced from his mother some time ago.

I mostly kept myself to myself within the park. Though in the early days, before night time became such profitable currency, I would sit out on the porch during those balmy evenings and - on the rare occasion I had forgotten to take a prop-novel to avoid such instances - talk to Deloris next door as she allowed her broiling legs to soak in a bucket of cool water.

Her husband had invented a safety mechanism now used in every plug socket in America. Only in his excitement he had copyrighted the snappy name and not the technology, and so his prosperity was over before it had begun. He did not hold his misfortune with dignity, in much the same way some men can't hold their liquor (incidentally another flaw of his, despite almost nightly attempts on the contrary). When I arrived in this particular park just two years ago, on the exact date of my first letter to you Jonah, Deloris was a svelte young mother with a swing to her step that would make a grown man change religion. Now, just a few hundred days later, she looks like she belongs to the legs under which the cartoon cat and mouse forever wage war.

She was fast and easy with the truth, the way the formerly pretty and otherwise vacant tend to be. And so her life story was mine for the taking. I was so bored sometimes I'd stop listening. Sometimes I think she knew, and I honestly don't think she cared. When it came to my turn I'd feed in the tiniest inaccuracies - an unlikely embellishment here, a contradiction there - to see if she'd pick up. Either due to politeness, stupidity, or simply the fact that I was but an inconvenience to her stream of spoken thought I do not know. But she never did, Jonah. Not once.

Inside, each item that could have been broken by hand or bat was. My glorious television - black and white, bought for fifty dollars by the smoothest talking beggar I ever had the pleasure of meeting - was smashed in half, the empty screen lay in fragments across the carpet like glitter, its insides kicked in such a manner that the volume knob had embedded itself in my Rita Hayworth poster. My clothes wrapped around one another on the floor like lovers or victims of some terrible ordeal; a trouser leg penetrated the waistline of my most expensive pantyhose; the arms of a crisp shirt, torn, wrapped defiantly around a vest like a lioness protecting her cubs. My underwear ripped to shreds. The flimsy work surfaces were scuffed and doused in liquids and the walls were kicked through with holes, causing the light to streak through me like celestial arrows. My bed had been fully upturned and my make-up shattered into an iridescent pool on the carpet. But, most devastatingly, a single blow had split in half my most prized possessions atop the ornate coffee table I had bought for that sole purpose.

What they destroyed was you. Or rather they had tried.

I had collected you in the furthest corner of my bedroom. You're two short hairs plucked from the deepest recess of an envelope and now taped to a laminated card. You're a hurriedly cut out advert from the *Morning Echo* advertising the scheme on which I was first introduced to you, and a rejected visiting order which I submitted in secret only two weeks later; the arrival of which felt like the biggest betrayal of my life. You're a penny from a wishing well artlessly scooped up the day I posted said request in the vain hope some of its luck would bring us closer together. You're a bottle of cologne, whose name required a two day round trip to a perfumer in the city who, when presented with the sealed envelope and its mummified odour, proclaimed it to be the ghostly trails of the kind of aftershave bought by middle aged men from dime stores across the land. You're dozens and dozens of ink stained sheets whose very scent makes me feel grounded in a way that reality never quite has. Your words, your precious words, scattered across my bedroom floor like confetti the day after a wedding.

I wept when I saw what they'd done to you.

But you get no points for moping in this life, Jonah. So I changed tack. I fortified and solidified as if to save face. I scooped you up and threw you carelessly into an overnight bag, along with a few bare essentials and - after a brief scrabble on all fours like some feral child - secured my car keys before driving far and fast to the borders of the next town. My pockets heavy with memories - trinkets and ornaments of a past that I was able to discard so thoughtlessly in one brisk and tearful car journey - I arrived at what, to most in this godless settlement, must feel like the end of the world.

Oh, one minor detail. Having hurled you and me - or whatever was left of us - into the back of the car, and checking to make sure the children next door were safely inside, I returned to the apartment and lit a small rag atop the gas hob. Kicking over the tracks. Burning my bridges. Always moving forward. If you've taught me one thing so far Jonah it's that the past is seldom worth visiting. So I severed it at the root. Full stop. End of the line for that particular story, thank you very much. There were pragmatics involved, of course. How I would hate for them to discover a missed scrap containing your address, or for that matter something that could lead to my current whereabouts. But mostly the fire was a symbolic offering. The end and the beginning of myself.

Another land's dusk began drifting over me as I pulled away. The sky flickered a threatening red that grew and shrank around itself like embers. Only after driving for the duration of the rock and roll track that blared from the broken radio did I allow myself one final glance in the dirty mirror. Behind me all stood still. The children were inside, the lights shone constant through the plastic windows of the trailers. And in the middle of it all a tiny orange flame blew smoke rings to the heavens.

You see I've gotten into some terrible trouble. And I fear the effort that went into frightening me so wholly was more preview than main event. So now I am here Jonah, and how I wish you were with me. But you are not, and for reasons known only to you are not willing to be. I neither understand nor take pleasure in the situation but respect it nonetheless. But here's to honesty, and here's to change, and here's once more to the endless stream of one-glass bottles of whisky that have just about gotten me through this letter. I will tell you, of course, how I came to be in this place, but later.

For now I must sleep.

Love,
Always,
Verity

Dearest Verity,

Rejoice! I write to you freshly bathed and uncommonly exhausted.

Today was my first day at work. And it feels divine.

The gentlemen that I work with are a predictably clichéd group. Max, our foreman, barely opens his mouth when speaking. Occasional vowels prevail, but on the whole instructions are to be deduced from the direction in which he nods. And so I can only assume at this stage in proceedings that I am following orders as diligently as would appear. The two young boys in greased vests speak little, but often enough as to not appear rude. And the crane operators seem to have a hierarchy of their own; attention to which prevents cross-departmental communications entirely. Everyone is marred with dirt as though camouflaged; their sturdy fabrics worn and exhausted. One boy's jeans are so threadbare that the freckles on the back of his thighs could be counted with relative accuracy when the sun is at its peak.

Rolls and rolls of empty piping lie dormant at the lip of each rut. Tarpaulin sheets have a tendency to buck from their tethers and float up on invisible winds where they hover above hollow ground. The general mood is that we are in some small way acting out a theatrical version of a building sight. No-one seems to know precisely what he is doing, whether at this stage demolition or construction is our primary goal. But the unspoken agreement is that so long as we keep doing it then everything will eventually come together.

Emmet will on occasion loom large from the makeshift cabin from which he operates the administrative duties, and the length of time he spends in said cabin implies that the admin of dirt is a deep and involved process. He seems pleasant enough, and in all honesty I am still too overwhelmed with gratitude to be able to form any objective character reference. For now all I know is that he is the man who changed me. And for now it feels as though it has been for the better.

I took a walk out, as intended, to the edge of town, scraps of paper carefully written and folded inside each pocket. My clothes cleaned and pressed for the occasion. I passed the busy banks and the empty shops, past the broken water fountain and Maxwell, staunch and present as always, spouting his prophesy. He wore a white suit, as he had the previous day, and as he no doubt would tomorrow, and the day after that and the day after that, and bellowed through a cackling loudspeaker.

"... now I aint descended from no monkey, I didn't explode out of no black hole, so I asked myself ladies and gentleman, what am I? And then one day the answer came – I am but a thought in the mind of God almighty... "

I took the common response and ignored his urgency, passing by with a dipped head until he became little more than indistinguishable background noise.

I walked straight past the dozing labourers to the Formica office at the southernmost point of the construction. Dark grooves, hollowed in the middle from tentative digging, had marked out the proposed outline of the structure, containing an area so large I daresay it would require an aerial perspective to truly comprehend.

I knocked three times and, allowing what I felt to be a polite enough period, entered when no answer was forthcoming.

Emmet did not look up. He sat in his straight-backed chair, bulging and creased. A suit made in fabric so cheap it appeared reflective was topped - I kid you not - with a cowboy hat. You would have thought that anyone in charge of such a venture, least of all this one, would be eager to appear less like a cartoon Texan baron (or, indeed, less like the flighty Virginian, now rich from this very town's misplaced faith). But such is life.

There truly is nothing quite as strange as folk.

"How can I be of assistance, sir?" he said without looking at me, engrossed in the blueprints beneath his ham fists. On his desk there was a bound stack of twenty-dollar bills; crisp, as though freshly ironed.

Within an hour I was changed and digging with the others, on a salary I had haggled up by fifty cents an hour.

It's odd how accustomed you can get to constructing an existence around sheer frivolities, and odder still how uptight you begin to feel when real life infiltrates said routine. Today is a Wednesday. My day would have once begun with a lengthy stroll, followed by a breakfast of precisely one hour during which I would scan the free papers and process the day's news, conversing, if lucky, with a likeminded diner or waitress on various points of interest. Following this, the route back to my house would more than likely lead me to the convenience store, where I would buy non-essentials - when, in this lifetime, will I need a Swiss army knife? or, for that matter, three different brands of coffee? - before returning home and taking a light nap. After the nap - which always manages to spread out of its allocated boundaries like a child's attempt at colouring - I would locate my library books and return them, taking out no more than four tomes to last me the duration of the week. I would arrive home once more, still full from breakfast, and begin to feast on my words well into the night until the ink and paper became inseparable and I entered that filthy void between sleep and wake.

But not today.

I finished work at six and managed to make it to the library just in time, whereupon - though still in possession of the previous week's selection - I took out a further collection and walked the last mile and a half home, weighted with words and fatigue, arriving at a not entirely unreasonable seven fifteen.

I must say, however, that for all my selfish joy I was not only shocked, but frightened by your last letter. You worry me, Verity. How can a woman of sound mind allow such events to spiral into the uncontrollable? I know I am not entirely one to talk. But at least I was always the driver of my fate, my consequences always a direct result of my often foolish and always careless actions.

I suppose at this point I ought to be thankful for your survival. And I am, truly I am. Yet I suffer that strange dichotomy which must befall each and every parent whereby hearing of such incidents is only marginally more tolerable than suspecting them. I feel a knot that can slacken but never entirely unravel each time you tell me of your troubles. That is not a criticism of your (our) correspondence. But increasingly I feel helpless and hopeless. I want so much to assist you, to guide or nurture, but it's an impossible task as things stand. And so all we have are our words; the ink and ideas, which can ease the intangible yet, I daresay, would hold little value in the face of a problem such as your own. So tell me, Verity, how you came to be where you are. I can't promise I will help but I can promise I will try in my own distant way. Lord knows the difference a kind word can make, or an alternative perspective (your very offerings have dragged me from a dark that seemed so permanent I could have curled up and died on a number of occasions), and for what it is worth I will hold you dearly in my heart and my hopes. This is all I can offer, Verity, and I hope it is enough.

I kept my proposed plans for employment secret during yesterday's breakfast. Keen not to elicit any specific interest in my character or circumstances, nor encourage any scorn from my relatively new neighbours by accepting a job on some doomed and ill thought of project. Increasingly talk is veering towards the subject of the funding that has been cut in order to afford such a grandiose vanity project. I can't say I have an opinion either way at this stage, and can't pretend that for now if pushed for an answer, my loyalties err on the side of the development itself.

Unusually, a pretty young girl sat with Levi at his usual table. He seemed smitten yet inattentive towards his newfound companion. She, herself, seemed happy to sit silently in his presence, occasionally twirling a lock of her golden hair, or teasing her fingers across the string of pearls that spread up from the collar of her dress like some exquisite rash; the ashen beads dotting her throat like bullet holes. Where his breakfast usually sat his ledger now lay open, the ink indecipherable from where I perched at the counter. Behind the cash register Mary harrumphed, heavy footed and uptight. A patch of stitching to the right of her shoulder, mended a number of times over and each time with an ever so slightly different spool of black thread, had come loose. The pale flesh of her shoulder, rounded like the hump of a whale, poked out from the serrations in the cloth and caught embarrassingly on the lights that shone onto the counter. She placed my coffee in front of me with a subtle yet discernable bang before returning to the furthest reach of the counter, where she began the arduous process of wiping the crystal formations of sugar from the worktops.

I felt a tap on my shoulder.

"Hi stranger," came the voice.

"Morning," I offered.

"You must be Jonah," she said. "It's a pleasure to make your acquaintance."

I asked how she seemed to know my name. She chose to ignore me and took the swivel seat next to mine.

"Penny for 'em," she said, swaying to and fro on the seat.

"I doubt they'd even make that much at auction."

"I'm Aimee," she said eventually, grinding to a gradual halt. On the counter she placed a glossy magazine opened and creased at a central page. "This poor lady had a baby with hooves," she said, stroking the image of the disfigured infant. "Can you believe it?" She spoke as though we were long time companions, picking up form where we last left off.

"I'd question the source," I said, turning my face from the magazine.

"Say, what star sign are you? You're a Taurus, aren't you? I can tell a Taurus a mile off." She picked up the magazine and flicked to the rear pages, tracing the text with the tip of her finger.

"Don't know. Even if I did can't say I'd pay much attention."

"Of course you know, everybody knows their sign."

"Not me."

"Well, when's your birthday?"

"Couldn't say."

"Oh," she said, placing one hand on my arm. "Don't be shy, I won't judge you. Age means nothing these days, it's how you act... "

"I'm not embarrassed, I don't know my own birthday, fact."

The girl looked puzzled for a moment, scanning my face for a twitch or smirk that might give away the joke. In fact I was telling the truth. I have no birth certificate, no driver's licence, no tangible proof of any particular start date, and am left with only the foggiest of memories of a time when ribbons and candles marked my celebration. I have a vague idea, of course, working forward or back from incidents when somehow my specifics were deduced, but on the whole I'm a mystery even to myself. I know little more than the fact that I've been around for as long as I can remember.

"I'm with Levi today," she said, girlishly, pressing at the pleats of her dress. Both conversation and magazine discarded as though they never happened.

"And what - " I asked perhaps more coldly than I had intended, " - could a man of Levi's years possibly have to interest a girl like you?"

With that she smiled and stood up, amused as though I had walked into the very trap she had so carefully lain for me. "Not what you think, stranger," she said, standing at the jukebox and selecting an old time love song which began to drift across the room like fog. On the spot, and to an empty room save her escort, the waitress, and myself, she began to sway to the sound of the jukebox, looking down at the floor yet somehow dancing for and only for me. "He's going to make me immortal," she said breathily, at which Levi stood up and placed his coupons on the counter. "Like you."

Levi walked to the door and Aimee followed dreamily, still breathing to the sway of the song. "Until the next time, stranger," she said as the door clicked and sealed.

The record dimmed to a whisper and then with a polite click and a bright red sign demanding further payment, the machine fell silent.

"Yeah," Mary said out loud. "God damn genius alright and never so much as a civil word. Damn fool." She looked at me and for a moment a wave crossed her face which suggested an apology was beginning to form, a wave she managed to single-handedly denounce before returning to the semi-snarl which she had worn, like a veil, all morning. "Sorry, sugar," she said, though her face made no such attempts at remorse. "I got problems that just won't quit. You just ignore me until you need some more coffee, honey, and I'll see if I can't fix me a smile."

"Not on my account," I added, standing up. If there is one thing worse than being unhappy it is being forced to suggest the alternative to an audience. "I hope you find an answer to your prayers."

"And you yours, sugar," she said without looking up, "... and you yours."

My duties amongst the site itself seem to be relatively straightforward. I turn up and dig, I tear out foundations, the chipped wood and petrifying fragments of whatever went before, leaving only empty ground to be filled anew and built into a structure which will be, in some small way, my own.

At the sound of a klaxon we cease work twice a day. There is the celebrated forty-five minutes for lunch, and a further fifteen minutes to be utilised as we see fit somewhere between three and four in the afternoon. During these periods we congregate into subsections around a pile of dirty chairs and make small talk about lives, which require minimal discourse at the best of times. Some of the men indulge in hurried smoking. I was never taken with tobacco, and so align myself with the family men whose wives insist on smoke-free homes and have consequently curtailed their addictions entirely. That is not to say they are a wholly health conscious bunch. At least two of my colleagues sip throughout the day from tarnished hip flasks, and the scent of the steam from several of the thermoses would be enough to send you spiralling over the drink driving limit. The breaks are a small mercy, I can tell you that. Were it not for the pleasure of mumbled introductions and a whole host of new characters to memorise and evaluate I could easily have begun to doze by early afternoon.

My first job was as a gravedigger, I don't know if I ever told you this. Four days after I left home for good I drifted into a backwoods town, starving and freezing despite the sepia promise of spring, and in a moment of almost hallucinatory desperation stumbled upon the parish where I intended to do little more than beg for the necessities that would allow me to see in another morning. The priest, a firm but kind man whose ordination was based solely upon his ability to read and his minimal criminal activity, asked few questions and agreed that once my strength resumed I would be taken on as a cemetery assistant. Oh such grandeur!

I was to aid the elderly gentleman who was at that point providing the entire town's eternities alone, and in turn would be paid by the grave at a rate so extortionate that were I not dazed by hunger I would never have agreed. Thankfully a combination of youthful vigour and the region's ceaseless smallpox pandemic meant that within two months I was earning more money than most of the town combined, and within six months was in possession of my very own automobile and a satchel full of dirty money which I used to propel me straight out of that hellish backwater never to look back.

Such memories remain distinct and clear whereas many - for example the entire purpose of last week, or the name of the street on which I lived previously - slip from my mind with alarming ease, and so I am used to the nature of the task at hand. For now the repetition and the hypnotism that comes with rote undertakings of a manual nature are a pure luxury.

Several hours have passed since I began this letter. Though in no small part due to excitement I have found myself distracted of late, particularly this evening. That same black car has circled my street all night. At first it remained stationary outside my living room window. The twitch of the curtains and the television's cobalt glow roused the engine to a quiet purr before the vehicle shifted towards the furthermost point of my street. They drove slowly until positioned at a distance I was unable to observe through the small square of my window. Though for all intents and purposes out of sight I could tell they were still there. So I went and stood out on the porch, clutching a coffee for warmth. The night air crystallised the bathwater on my stomach and arms and caused me to shake like a corn field caught in a breeze. The car's interior lights were dimmed. From the weak glow of the streetlamps yet to be shot out by disgruntled nightshift workers I was able to make out two figures. One tall man and a companion whose shapes could easily have been cardboard cut-outs were it not for the occasional movement as they turned to talk to one another. A bullet of light shot from the car's mirror as it was repositioned. It caught my eye and then dimmed as the engine began once more and continued down the street and around the corner.

Thankfully they're gone now, and if not out of mind then for now I will settle with out of sight.

Of all the men I work with, Harlow seems to offer the most promising chance of friendship. He is older than I, though by how much I couldn't say. He has a kindly face and an open manner.

He caught my eye as we sat down for lunch, he nodded as did I, and initially that was enough. Whispers of the previous nights' escapades rattled through the luncheon club. Younger boys bragged about various levels of speed and inebriation depending on their preferred method of relaxation. One or two of the recently married men spoke proudly of the latest vowel uttered by their offspring, or bemoaned the now constant fog of exhaustion that clouds their wives. I sat and absorbed it all, hungry but happy. Harlow noticed my lack of reserves and made his way over to where I sat. "The wife always gives me too much," he said, placing half a sandwich in front of me. "Twenty-seven years and you'd think she'd have got the balance right. Still, I aint complaining. Too much better than not enough, that's my motto."

I accepted the sandwich and smiled. Already our relationship seemed too advanced to offer an offensively formal handshake. "Thank you," I said. "I could just about chew the head off a shovel. It's been a while since I did a full day's work."

He laughed once and it felt like a gift. "Yep, I know that feeling. Nothing like an empty life to make a man feel halved. What's your name, buddy?"

"Jonah."

"Well I'm Harlow. And you need anything you come to me. They'll work you alright, but it aint that bad once you get used to it. Plenty of folk round here'd give their right arm for the chance on this site. You must be one smooth talker to have walked right into a post."

"I guess I'm just lucky," I offered, almost apologetically.

"Aint no such thing as luck," he said. "I seen you around town of late. You new to these parts?"

With this the hairs on the back of my neck stood up. "Yup," I said solemnly, taking a second and final bite of the sandwich. I have come to realise that whilst barefaced lies become accumulative and corrosive, minimising the truth - that is, to give of yourself precisely what is required without any further embellishment - is often the most effective way to conduct yourself.

"It aint a bad life round here. Plenty wants fixin', but plenty's just fine," he said, chewing through his crusts with one final wipe of his lips. He wrapped the sandwich foil into a tight ball and tossed it into a dustbin. "You take care, Jonah. And remember what I said. You need anything you just come to me. I'll be seeing you around."

After lunch it was an effort to raise the spade above my head even when empty, but the added weight of dry earth became excruciating. The sun had rose slowly throughout the day and hit its peak well after noon; it shone a fiery gold that caused heat waves not two feet from your face, making even the most redundant object appear uncertain as though a dream. The sweat dropped from my forelock and spattered the ground like I was haemorrhaging and the hours seemed to wade past you through treacle. The final klaxon, 'Tools down boys! See y'all bright and early!' was as welcome as the job itself.

"You got family round these parts?" asked Harlow who had caught up with me in the ant march back to town.

"No sir, just me," I said. "Yourself?"

"Yup, got me two daughters," he said, pulling a picture from his back pocket. It was yellow and peeling, and no doubt hideously out of date, but showed two smiling blonde girls as pretty as any father could ever hope for. I told him as much and he beamed. "They're good kids. God knows they've got their quirks, but both got good hearts," he said with a laugh. "Say, you like barbeque, boy?"

I nodded.

"Well the wife's having some friends round later on next week, why don't you swing by? Some of the guys from the site'll be there. Might give you a chance to make some new friends rounds here. Or at any rate decide who's worth befriending and who's not."

I accepted and we parted with the ease of long-time friends.

So that's that, I suppose. Funny how much things can change in a twenty-four hours. Romantic almost. I know this may seem silly to you. If the truth be told I take one step back from myself and realise just how damn silly it is to me too. I don't think a job on a building sight ever caused a grown man such happiness. But it feels like the beginning, like a catalyst, or perhaps even the beat of the butterfly's wings which spawns the hurricane miles and miles away. Undoubtedly I'm setting myself up for a fall here, but optimism is fresh ground for me and for now I'm happy wallowing blindly until an alternative presents itself.

Outside the raccoons are beginning to scratch and root for sustenance. I hear them scurry along the porch, tearing through my garbage, picking morsels from the litter and upturning all and sundry in the vain hope of survival. Usually I would make an effort to dissuade them, but tonight I feel generous, and so I let them feast as I prepare for welcome slumber.

Take care of yourself, Verity. This is all I can ask of you, and in return I offer my thoughts and my prayers. In keeping with our newfound honesty I would also like to know precisely how you ended up where you were, if it is not too much to ask, if only to abate my appetite for each and every aspect of you and your life which I find so fulfilling. I don't now what I did before it became the muzak to my own existence.

I have enclosed a small carving made from a log I picked up on the walk back from work. I whittled it down and smoothed the edges until it began to resemble the shape of a heart, somewhere between the cartoon Hallmark sentiment and the ugly yet vital organ on which it is based. The shape seemed pleasing, apt almost, though incomplete, and so I suppose you are the recipient of a work in progress. I hope you like it.

With all my love,
Jonah

Dear Jonah,

There was a bullet lodged in my front door this morning. How it didn't wake me I don't know. And whether by accident or design it has certainly affected the overall mood of my day. Suffice to say its appearance caused little stir amongst the occupants of this quaint little motel, and so I choose to take it as simply par for the course in my newfound residence, lest my mind run away with itself.

But first things first. Congratulations. If I know one person who deserves a chance in this life, whether second, third or fourth seems irrelevant, it is you. I feel as though all my prayers have been answered. As if by fixing you I will become solved myself. How likely this is I do not know. But one thing I know for certain is my joy for you and your newfound lease of life. I will raise a glass in your honour.

That is not to say I am without my reservations. People are not generally good Jonah, unfortunately I have come to find this out the hard way, and how easy it must be to take advantage of a lonely man with a good heart in a strange town. Aimee seems like the sort of girl who could be trouble. Beware lonely women Jonah. Their intentions are seldom noble. For what it's worth my advice is to stay far from her and her ilk, though I'd be the first to admit that my recent coterie would perhaps call to question my authority on associates.

Secondly, and before I forget, thank you. Your carving is beautiful and now takes pride of place on my bedside table. The jewellery box you sent me was left decapitated and dismembered on my bedroom floor, the throat of its chime severed mid sentence. I would still have taken it were it not for the pool of blood in which it lay. This, however, is more than an apt substitute, and is the first step towards what I believe they call 'nesting' in this barren womb of a space.

Did you ever collect as a child? I did. When I think of my youth it is not necessarily the obvious which strikes a chord; the endless summers or comfort foods that others describe with such precision you wonder if they happened at all. I think of my groups, my anthologies and assortments, which I acquired and documented almost religiously. There were the living things, my ants first, which were forgotten conveniently by my mother as we moved to another base, then my saplings, ordered initially by size then eventually by hue – the intensity of green moving from the glittering right to the pallid left. My worm collection lasted only until I was informed of their want to grow into two separate entities were they ever chopped in half. The detail now seems admirable to me - stoic and steadfast, almost romantic - but at the time filled me with such dread at the thought of a species able to multiply of its own accord that I took them as far as my legs would carry me and threw them in a writhing comet across the ravine. After that there were others. The glass shards I'd find on the railway lines as I walked home from another school, pebbles of obscure shape and size, shells when lucky, candles, bus stubs, lottery tickets, matchsticks, candy wrappers, tyre caps. All of my memories made flesh, lined like cavalry and displayed for my own pacification.

I remember, too, the weight of anxiety that each new collection would bring. These little traps I'd set myself. Each time the burden of responsibility would override any childish whimsy until I became physically sick with worry. Aged seven I was kept from school for three weeks with a fever which to this day I swear was caused by issues of or relating to my bottle caps.

Funny what you remember. I found myself thinking about that today.

For some reason there has been a more customer-friendly approach from the staff of this hotel, no doubt spurred by my delivery of a roll of banknotes to the front desk and a polite request to remain in the same room as long as it would afford me, after which I would happily re-feed my meter. So now sometimes twice a day my stocks are being replenished. Individual servings of alcohol and sodas, of sanitary products, of sewing kits and shoe polish (?) delivered with a smile and a nod from one of the unbearably gorgeous Hispanic maids. The individuality pleases and mystifies me in equal measures. Having made it so clear I intend to stay for the duration surely human-sized portions would be a better investment on the part of the establishment? Though there is something oddly satisfying about being given just what you need, no more no less, especially when you know that extra is but a phone call away.

The point being that I have become a hoarder of my packaging. Lilliput bottles, soap boxes, shower cap covers. Even the thread I unravel and hide so that the little plastic drums are mine to keep. I've arranged them into some variation of a house on the small coffee table beneath the window where I write to you. I have informed the maids - whom I am coming to know by name - never to discard anything they find on the table itself. They seemed to understand, though as I have not left my room in seven days and have no intention of doing so for the foreseeable future I envision no problems on that front.

I'm rambling. I know. And I can't put it off forever. It's just that I don't know exactly where to start. I think of Eve, of The Iguana Den, of the gold and glitter and the guns and the money that have made my life what it is today, and it all seems so obvious in hindsight. Like dog shit: so easy to step over when you realise it was there. But I didn't. I trod straight through it entirely of my own accord. And relaying the stupidity of my actions to you seems harder than everything that has gone before.

To pinpoint the exact moment I began to unravel so spectacularly would be like trying to retrace an earthquake. But I suppose that when pushed, the genesis of my quandary is undoubtedly J.

J wasn't his real name. It wasn't even his real initial. This fact remained hidden for the duration of our courtship. I suppose I never thought to ask. A person tells you their name and you take it as given. Though he was not the sole advocate of deceit. I came to play my fair share of the game, and so in some ways we were both as bad as one another. Bad, that is, within the confines of our relationship. Out there in real life he undoubtedly surpassed me in terms of sheer wickedness. There was no evil in J. Evil is innate. It could almost elicit pity if you thought long and hard about it. He chose his path. There was a moment where he hit the forked road between right and wrong, between life and death. He seldom chose wisely and within two months went from stranger to lover to murderer.

How's that for a shift in circumstance?


He caught my eye at the diner, which seems so remote on the horizon of my history that I can barely make out its shape. He caught my eye there, though how long before that I caught his I cannot say.

"Sunny side up, sugar?" I asked, moving to the farthest edge of the counter.

The weather never changes here. They say that about a lot of places. It's never true. Here it is though; the sand absorbs the warmth of the sun and magnifies it into a constant heat; forever pressing like a soldering vice around your head and ankles. Everyone feels heavy and leaden. No shirt unstained. It makes the days lap over one another like waves until before you know it years have passed by and you wonder how long you've been standing so still.

"Surprise me," he said.

I laughed and nodded, leaning over to look at the notepad in which he scribbled. He seemed amused at my interest though equally adamant to keep whatever he was writing out of view. His suit marked him out as an oddity. His hat pulled low over his face. That face. Jagged and gnarled, though noticeably young. He was gaunt in a healthy way, and as I would come to find out could shave at breakfast and be in possession of the most immaculate stubble before lunch.

In the distance two vultures shriek at one another over the same decaying carcass. I wipe my brow and fill the almost empty cups for the lizards and cacti that line the same stretch of counter day in, day out. Some are men. Some are women. It changes with the light. Some have wives. Some have children. Some have sheer silk suspenders clinging to their thighs beneath those battered 501s. None of them a question. None of them an answer. They simply hover until they are moved. Myself, I enjoyed the variation. The combination of the regular and the obscure. Mostly I liked the fact that it all stopped mattering the moment the door closed behind me. Jobs like that never followed you home. Never swirled around your head while you were in the queue at the grocery story, or filling up your car with gas. They never rang you five times a day. Never wanted to cuddle afterwards. Jobs like that disappear the moment you take off your name badge. I don't know why every girl in the world doesn't have a job like that.

J notices me playing with a child's puzzle that I found discarded in one of the booths as I wait for his bacon to crisp. "Simple things please great minds," he says, not quite smiling. "That's what they say."

"They have a tendency to be wrong," I reply, with an equally ambiguous hint of amusement. Funny, the one thing I remember about what has come to be known as Day One is that, at this very moment, all I could think of as I stifled my smile was 'so cool Verity, you've never played it so cool in your life... '

"Aint that the truth, darling," he adds, closing his pocket book and placing it in the lining of his jacket. I place his breakfast in front of him and am granted the donation of a slight smile.

"So, what brings you to this part of town?" I ask eventually. The majority of customers have left by this point and we are near enough alone.

"I got some business that needs fixing," he says. A gruff voice, each word a painful gift as though they were organs being donated for your survival.

"Well aren't you just the man of mystery. And unusually coiffed for these parts."

"Something - " he says, locating a tricky piece of bacon from his tooth with the fork of his tongue " - was taken from me. I'm here to oversee its rightful return."

"The plot thickens," I lean back against the hob and try to get a better look at him. Attraction is a funny thing. It can happen despite you. It was only at that moment that I was able to take in the overall package - the quirks and idiosyncrasies of his face and shape. I was impressed, Jonah, no two ways about it. And what's more I could tell that in some small way he felt the same.

"You don't know the half of it, darling," he says, standing up. His breakfast remains half eaten. "I'll be seeing you around."

"Came for the eggs, stayed for the service," I say, taking his plate and the cash he has left on the counter.

He laughs, nods, and leaves.

I walk back with the thought of him playing like music. I go home and slump on my bed and feel the four walls of my house bob up and down like it's nodding in agreement. I take a shower. Drink some beer straight from the can. Enjoy a cigarette in front of the mirror because I like the way the smoke curls and disappears like secrets from my lips. I lie on my stomach and imagine an entire lifetime spent with a stranger I have shared barely three sentences with. By the time I come to my senses the sheets are saturated and my wrist cramps painfully beneath my weight. I try three kinds of nail varnish whilst slightly drunk - one on top of the other - until the colour blends into a new, ugly shade somewhere between brown and green but with a sleek gloss finish. Then I shake my hair into a form not far from sexy and breathe out loudly while I spray it in place. Time for round two. Welcome to The Iguana Den.

What exactly The Iguana Den is I still can't say. Even once I became part of its insatiable mechanism I was not sure how or why it came to be. Initially I knew it as a legend. Then as a patron. Finally I became one of its most treasured possessions, as profitable as the watered down beer that they served by the pitcher.

Some nights I'd be so bored, Jonah, so bored and tired of life that I would dress myself up for no reason whatsoever, just to see myself change. Then I became more daring in my role. Dolled up in my finery I would stroll out into the night. Feeling the dark on my skin, the night air ripe with potential as I waited patiently for my knight in shining armour, knowing that I was at least dressed the part should some magnificent situation ever arise. Nine times out of ten I ended up dressed like some fallen debutante eating pie in the twenty-four hour cafe across from the Rialto. Tired. Alone.

This changed the night I met J.

It doesn't take much to alter you completely. And a brief encounter with a handsome mystery filled me with an emotion that I cannot quite put into words even now. It was somewhere between curiosity and fearlessness. As though I was unable to stop until I hit upon a change. So I walked past the town, past the familiar streets and the ordered traffic system. The road changed beneath my feet from asphalt to dirt track. My heels sunk and twisted. My shoulders flayed by the dancing sands. Far away, in the growing void, three men surrounded a tin can of burning garbage. I walked for miles and miles before I saw it. A blue streak, like a mirage. It flashed and disappeared before my eyes. I became transfixed and followed its taste, its sound, until I was standing outside a living legend.

It was everything I had heard the men describe in hushed voices across the counter and then some: a neon light in the dark. A ticking beat that moves round and round like a spider in tap shoes. Blood red smiles. All fours. Upside down. Blonde on blonde.

'Hey baby I can see your roots!'

'Then you aint looking right, precious.'

They drool. The living dolls.

It takes me ten minutes and two cigarettes outside those big double doors before I build up the courage to step inside. The nicotine and downtime enable me to slip into fantasy once more as to J's etiquette in such instances. Our arrival at any function would mark the beginning of the evening. We'd be the sort of glittering couple you always dreamt of being friends with: shimmering, assured, glorious.

I stub out my cigarette, breathe in deeply, and open the door.

An intricate web of red velvet and black lace disguise the fact that you're in a building at all. To enter The Iguana Den feels like stepping into the mind of some oversexed dandy, where you yourself become the fantasy.

I found myself in a small vestibule manned by an attractive woman wearing suspenders and little else. She greeted me as Miss and offered to take my coat. I obliged and handed her the garment.

"Twenty dollars entry," she said without wincing.

"There's nothing free these days," I said semi seriously.

"Nothing worth having," she said as she hung my coat on a padded hook.

I reached into my back pocket and produced a well-used bill. The main entrance led to a series of warrens and boltholes which held little interest amongst the majority of customers, most of whom were happily girded within a large room to my left. From where I stood I could see shadows float past seemingly devoid of bodies. Scattered applause and the occasional wolf whistle pierced the foggy atmosphere like the beam of a lighthouse. In the distance an old man pressed his lips firmly into the throat of a slender young thing who managed to open the door on which she leant and slip both of them inside in a pleasingly fluid manoeuvre. Initially I felt flustered and oddly too hot, but then the music from the main room began to take on a more rhythmic shape as my brain eased into its new environment the way you slip into a scalding bath. I felt comfortable, almost lethargic, and found my body moving to that distant beat which seemed to be playing from inside of me, guiding my every move.

"Welcome to The Iguana Den," said the lady on the door. I thanked her and began slowly walking towards the pulsing main room.

Along the corridor the chipped red paint held decaying photographs in gilded frames. Women in various states of undress glide up and down lubricated poles. Proud looking men grip young flesh in their papery hands. A larger lady - huge, in fact, almost the size of a cathedral - features in many. Her skirts are many and layered into an elaborate dessert of a garment. Her basque bulging across the weight of her generous and decorated chest and hair pinned tightly in an archaic nod to propriety.

The beat grew louder until it felt like it would pour from my mouth if I was so much as to attempt to breathe in. I stepped through the heavy velvet of the curtains and into the main room.

The tables are circular and the floor scuffed, somewhat at odds with the opulence of the entrance. The lights shine and flicker at orchestrated intervals in deep, primary colours making everything seem somehow tamer, as though you would be able to step from this room and dismiss everything you saw as a mere hallucination. Across the wall a long bar is manned by uniformed professionals who, as the saying goes, see all but relay nothing. Doors lead from every angle though no-one seems to go in or out. Suited gentlemen and plainclothes cops pick fruit at the machines that dot the empty space. Each table is occupied. Most sit alone. The stage takes the mantle at the front of the room; a round expanse speared with poles, from which two catwalks stretch like tentacles and are lined by the most expensive tables in the house.

I walked over to the first empty fruit machine and sat hard on the flat leather of the barstool. I dropped a dime and tugged lightly and the bandit's flimsy arm. The lights flashed and the pretend fanfare mounted as the salad spun before stopping with a jerk. Two apples and a cherry. Better luck next time. The lights turned out as I rooted in my pocket for a second coin.

"You play these games as much as I do you're bound to hit oil eventually," came a man's voice, light and inflected with a southern twang not dissimilar to my own.

"I play these games as much as you it'll take more than the one jackpot before I break even," I said to the slight gentleman in the bad toupee whose tux seemed over the top even in the most theatrical surroundings.

"Allow me - " he said, placing a penny into my slot, " - call it an icebreaker."

I pulled the arm of the bandit again and watched fortune spin out into another curious bubblegum flavour.

"Two plums and a banana. Why, sugar you're nothing more than an out and out tease. It's enough to drive an old dog wild," he said, riding his hand up the side of my skirt. "Now how much would it cost for a private view, my dearest?" he went on as his hand attempted to operate me like a glove puppet.

"More than a dime. That's given there's enough liquor behind that bar. Which I severely doubt there is," I snapped, pulling a coin from my pocket and slamming it onto the ridge of his machine. "That's for your troubles," I yelled, turning from him.

"And what are your troubles worth, sweetness?" he asked, placing the penny in the slot and pulling the bandit's arm. There were three pinging noise as the light of the machine pulsed whiter and whiter before the tin clank of coin fell cascading into the metal tray. "Looks like I'm in luck, darling. Care to taste my winning fruits?" he laughed.

"Quit jerking Carter and give me your seat," came a woman's voice.

The man stood up and presented his seat to the girl before walking off with pockets bulging with coins.

"Don't mind him. He's one of our regulars. Poor old Carter. Frisky as all hell get out but dead from the waist down. All you got to do is hug him a half hour and you don't need to worry about rent for another month." She was pretty and tall, and looked alarmingly familiar. Within a five-year bracket of my own age I would have guessed, yet more comfortable in her skin. The lace suspenders cut into her thighs, which were oiled and golden. And her hair had been teased into curls that made her face seem so angelic the peephole bra she wore came as all the more of a shock. "I'm Eve. You never been here before honey?"

"No, and I'm Verity. It's a pleasure to meet you."

We shook hands and laughed at the ridiculousness of the situation.

"You fancy a drink? I got friends and family discount in this place."

We sat and sipped beer while we poured easy small talk. She told me about her childhood, about the dirt roads and back alleys, about the parents so distant that she barely noticed when they both passed before her eighteenth birthday, and the various conditions that she had stumbled blindly into and out of ever since. You know that girl? The one you read about in the newspaper? The kindly hostess whose favourite customer left her his entire estate? Or the ageing pole dancer being hounded by the octogenarian oil baron's wife and children? Even the breezy cocktail waitress with the peek-a-boo roots who found herself clutching the bearer bonds of the aged philanthropist? They're all her. Each and every one. She said she never intended it to be that way, it just happened by accident then kept on happening over and over again. Of course the money never lasted that long. For every good man there were a dozen monsters, and so she seldom held her fortune for more than six months.

"Every time?" I asked, perturbed.

"Every time. Those rattlesnakes are the smoothest talkers of them all."

"Don't you mind? I'd be half mad or dead by my own hand if I lost the one fortune, let alone half a dozen."

"Not worth worrying about. Money always turns up. Love's the only currency worth crying over, and if that aint worth a gamble then I don't know what is."

It strikes me as sad, now, to be sitting here writing about her as though she were real, as though she still was. Sadder still that in all honesty I have yet to fully comprehend that she is not, and that there will come a point when I will have to leave this room and conduct myself in a world where Eve is no more; where she ends with the stained sheets I send to a comforting stranger some miles away; a fading memory; a hollow sound said so many times it becomes a dead weight on a numb tongue.

Nobody's mother.

Nobody's daughter.

So long as I keep writing it's as if she's here. But one day I will have to stop. And then what will there be? Nothing. A space where once something went. How can a person just cease? Where exactly do they go? It's enough to drive anyone insane if you sit down and think about it. I find more and more that this is the main problem with our arrangement, Jonah. Our heads are such lovely places to exist in that real life can't help but come as disappointment.

She told me that she'd been working there for almost two months by that point. Having fled an unfortunate situation with little more than a bottle of bourbon and a spare bra to her name it was the first place she came upon which required no identification and paid cash in hand.

"It's easy to hide when you're a different person each night. Aint that right, Prudence honey?" she said as a black beauty brushed past.

"That's the truth," said Prudence with a celestial boom.

"Just look at Alice over there," she said pointing to a leggy redhead performing the splits in front of a drooling Baskerville of a man. "This time last year she was chopping breezeblock for a living and answering to Carl."

I giggled at the sight of Alice, now bending backwards and exposing a scattering of shaving rash as Prudence strutted off behind one of the curtained doors.

"That over there - " said Eve, pointing to an immaculate and enormous man at the most prominent table, " - that's who we all call Kingpin. I'm still the new girl so I got nothing to base this on, but he's big around here. Been gone on some important business since I started but now he's back. We're putting on a real big show for him tonight I can tell you. Miss Jemima arranged it herself.

"Who's Miss Jemima?"

"If Kingpin's the head then she's the heart of this place. Been here longer than time and it shows, poor darling. She was good to me though. Taught me the tricks of the trade and one or two others. She keeps an eye on us girls," Eve said, draining her beer. "You ever think of dancing?"

I blushed and lit a cigarette. "God no. I wouldn't know where to start. I have trouble stepping out of the bathtub without falling over, let alone making one of those greased up sticks my own."

"I don't believe that for one moment. It sure was nice to meet you, Verity. You staying to watch us dance?"

"Why not," I said, feeling somewhat obliged.

"Well isn't that just fine!" Eve threw her arms around my neck and kissed me. "I hope I see you around. I got friends that are few and far between these days."

"I know that feeling," I said, stubbing my cigarette into the marble cup on the bar. "Good luck up there."

"I don't need luck, darling, I got my mother's tits and no shame." She gave her decorated rear a wiggle as she tottered off into the darkness.

The half hour before the show began seemed to grow more and more intense until the entire bar could have been popped by one careless open flame. Suddenly I felt awkward, alone and out of place. I pulled apart a napkin and lit matches in the palm of my hand. I blew out my candle, relit it, blew it out again and relit it one final time, deciding that a gentle glow may look more enticing to prospective company. I craned my neck to see if anyone might take me up on my silent offer, suddenly desperate for company. Most of the men were seated, their eyes glued to an empty stage. Some milled about the bar. A tall man in the distance caught my eye. He had something tattooed on his knuckles and a grey streak running through the entire length of his hair like a well groomed skunk. I raised my glass and he nodded once towards me. I nodded back. He turned slowly, maintaining me in his gaze, and headed towards the edge of the room.

I stood up and followed him all the way until he disappeared behind a creaking door. I hesitated for a moment and then entered.

The men's bathroom was empty and filthy. A warm musk filled the air and made everything illicit and irresistible. He stood alone in an open cubicle. I followed him inside and he locked the door.

I suppose when following strangers into public restrooms a person wants one of two things. I wanted the second. And within minutes that sweet, metallic smoke was coursing through my veins; lifting me to a place that felt the same yet different. A place where it didn't matter that I was alone, or that I had no idea who I was or what exactly I was doing. All I can say is that whilst not an experience I plan on repeating, for that night only I felt like myself for the first time in I don't know how long as I watched its magnetic dregs weep from my mouth towards the ceiling like tears in reverse.

We remained wordless throughout. He began by pulling a small cloth bag from his pocket and opening it onto the ceramic of the cistern, carefully arranging his apparatus like a practiced apothecary. He placed the rocks in the base of a long transparent tube, those filthy fingernails working the priceless jewels with more care than I'd ever seen a man of his size demonstrate. Finally, when he felt the arrangement complete, he lit it with a golden click of a lighter. He took a hit and handed it to me. I followed his lead and took a small breath and then a deep one before handing it back to him.

I slid down, dazed and blissful, as he packed his belongings and opened the door.

"Sweet dreams my little doll," he said, kissing me once as he left me reeling on the cold tile floor.

I did stay and watch for a while, Jonah. I was hypnotised. We sat transfixed by the movement of the bodies. Even the burliest men sat in rapture, like children being told their first story. Behind the main stage, where the curtains were white to reflect the changing lights, you could occasionally catch the shadowy outline of a grand figure of flailing arms and billowing skirts, hugging and changing the girls, ready for their next set piece.

Without prejudice I can say that Eve was the finest dancer I've ever seen in my life.

Some girls up there danced for money, others for sex, and most for attention. Eve danced for her life and she danced her life entirely. Each movement felt charged, like a choir's crescendo, that gave her the fallibility and grace, which the other girls lacked. Part of me fell in love with her that night. And all of me wanted to return to the den. The beating glow in the darkest corner of my hometown, like a secret spot that only I knew existed.

I walked back home that night reeling beneath the stars. With the joy of knowing that something was happening though I didn't quite know what.

With love and longing,
Verity

Dear Verity,

I begin by clearing out the detritus ignored by the previous God knows how many inhabitants. This in itself is a task worthy of reward. Sacks of hardening cement weigh down piles and piles of leaves and dirt, inside of which sodden paper and pieces of broken tools have amalgamated with various fluids and the occasional remnants of a decayed rodent. Even on the edge of my longest shovel it takes every ounce of strength I have not to gag when I exhume its stench.

It was Saturday morning, and I awoke with a start, sure that I was late for something before remembering that relaxation was now rationed, and as such it was my duty to make the most of it. By this point though, I was as alert as I'd ever be, and so in preparation for Harlow's garden party decided to tend to tasks long overdue. The function was twofold; on one hand I would begin to get my house in order in a way I never quite seemed to do when I had nothing but spare time on my hands, and secondly I would have something to discuss - perhaps even offer as an excuse for my otherwise empty day - come the time for socialising.

I was to construct a shed, ostensibly for storage, but that would also serve as my own corner of the world. Somewhere I would have to make the effort to visit, even if the effort did just amount to walking across my back yard. Perhaps somewhere I could write to you from, and carve shapes and familiarities from discarded blocks of wood. My mother, in one of the few memories I have of her, had a vanity mirror. Now, years later, it mystifies me as to how she came to own such an object. Our home was not what you would call decadent, in fact in hindsight I think it would qualify as a shack were prizes ever awarded.

Her secrets were kept hidden in those dusty drawers, so easy to open yet respected, on the whole, as sacrilege to enter without permission. Of course as we grew older, maybe eight or nine, we began to explore. My brother would lead the way. First just peeking; playing with the ornaments that dotted the desk beneath the mirror, feeling like trespassers in our own home. And then into the drawers themselves. The findings seemed unremarkable at the time: a photograph of a young man we didn't know, a stub of scarlet lipstick that smelt mild yet exotic, a half consumed packet of tablets. The first sip of alcohol I ever took was from a hip flask hidden in the bottom drawer as my brother poured its contents into my mouth and shrieked with glee as I lay on the cold floor, rasping for breath and holding my eyes tightly in place through fear they would fall clean out of my head. Even when they found her body that mirror was just about the only thing in the bedroom left intact. My father was sentimental like that.

The point being that I wanted somewhere just like that. And for some time now have been accumulating the resources to go about achieving it. The piles of smoothed wood have been slowly gathered from various sources and tethered to the side of my fence. Tins upon tins of treatment and fresh brushes sat on groundsheets in my kitchen. The only thing left was to build.

But first I had to remove what was left behind. So I spent my first waking hours getting stung and sweaty, filling waste bags with dirt and handfuls of other people's lives which they seemed so unwilling to deal with or carry with them wherever they went next. Though mostly garbage I did find a pristine axe-head, sharp as candlelight and engraved with someone else's initials. I placed it safely to one side after tending to my wound and will insert a new handle once I have completed the task at hand.

I raked and pulled at the twigs and thorns. Barbs caught on my hands and drew jewels of blood that stung and smeared onto my vest. And then I made my own little offering to the God of New Starts. In a giant tin can I stuffed the remnants of the rubbish and lit a match, before standing back and watching the fire spread like amber bloom.

I worked for four hours before realising the time. My glorious shed remains theoretical, I am sad to say, though the garden was by that point as flat and habitable as could be. I gave myself a fifteen minute break (how easy we become conformant!) as I observed the cooling bush now smouldering only dead smoke, and stared proudly at the tidy borders of my patchy yet trimmed lawn, before beginning the most pressing task of the day: my very own restoration.

My appearance has never been my strongpoint. Though I hold a certain sort of attraction to a certain sort of woman, often inspired by mass consumption and miserly standards, I have thus far relied on talk to take me where I wanted to go. I suppose I just have one of those faces, so easy to slip anonymously into a crowd; indistinguishable from just about any other human being in my age bracket. At times this has worked in my favour. Before the onset of video cameras I was hurriedly sketched by many an artist as some sort of all-encompassing Caucasian male, approaching six foot (I am, in fact, six foot one, and have more than once felt the urge to contact various authorities to insist as much, lest I be forever underestimated). The face of any man you've ever met, that's me. Though recently I have become more distinguished. Lines have formed where previously there was only skin. I am beginning to look like my very own novel; through the stubble - never too long, always suggesting greater things to come - and the ever so slightly bagged eyes is the implication of a life fully lived. This is not entirely the case. If anything it was a life lived several times over, and almost never correctly. I hadn't really noticed until today, it being the first time in memory I have truly felt the urge to impress face-to-face. All I could think was that no amount of time and detergent in the world will make me look anywhere near the person I want to be seen as. But there's merit in effort, as my mother used to say, and so it began.

I bathed and dried myself. Shaved for the occasion and felt bald and vulnerable without some small barrier between myself and the world. My hair slicked back into a dark sheen befitting some fifties teen in a prototype coming of age movie. It's all I know to do. Having spent my life either cropped to the skin or raggedly unkempt I am not entirely sure what a gentleman is supposed to do with his hair, so I comb it as close to my head as possible and simply pretend it's not happening. Pockmarks that line my cheeks and jaw are unavoidable and unchangeable, so I rely on the decency and embarrassment of others simply not to bring them up. It seemed the more I did the more anxious I became. Like with the rejuvenation of my backyard; the moment I began to break down the surface, more and more problems seemed to sprout up like pox on an infant. I began to wish I'd simply arrived as I was. Myself and nothing more. Though by this point returning to my natural state would have been as conscious an effort as the elaborate adaptation I had created, so I remained some skewered version of myself.

The trousers I chose were black and belted, bought one day when I had the drunken notion that I might, if presented correctly, be able to find an office job and scale the ranks to become a glittering corporate success. I chose a black jacket and white shirt, both unworn and both, once more, purchased with the intention of costume in a bid to masquerade myself into yet another unlikely role (bellboy and croupier, since you ask). To finish I added the one and only pair of black shoes I had in my closet whose leather was, thanks to my skill with a magic marker, almost entirely without cracks within fifteen minutes. That said it took another ten minutes and an eye-watering encounter with the scalding faucet to clear the ink from my hands.

And then I was ready.


I approached Harlow's garden, as instructed, though the gate, sidestepping the rigid front door like a lifelong pal. Even from the furthest edge of his street I could hear noises of happy chatter and quiet music. Drawing closer, sweet smoke and a mouth-watering trail of burning fat filled the air. I opened the door and stepped into the yard.

Complete and utter horror.

Every man there was in shorts and tshirt. The greatest effort had been made by Max, who in what I suspect was a substitute for any sort of personality had donned a garish Hawaiian shirt somewhat at odds with the overcast day.

Memory is funny old thing, but I swear even the radio paused when I entered.

"Well if it isn't my accountant!" Harlow hollered as I made my way urgently towards the centre of the party, hoping that by rushing blindly towards the nucleus of the action I would evade individual appraisals of my appearance. "What's the matter kid, you got a funeral to go to afterwards or something?" he continued in jest.

I felt a hand on my back and a large woman, resigned comfortably and contently to her own frumpiness, pulled herself into view. "How embarrassing for y'all!" she yelled at the men who had now all but returned to their offshoot conversations. "Being shown up by this fine young stranger."

Some of the men chuckled and raised their cans at the woman.

"Just shows how comfortable we all are in your company, Barbara darling!" yelled one of the men from work whose name I had not bothered to memorise.

"You must be Jonah," she said, still holding my arm in her hand. "I'm Barbara, Harlow's wife. I heard all about you."

"So long as none of it's true," I said, masking my mortification with an attempt at good humour. "It's a pleasure to meet you, ma'am."

"Ignore him Barb," said Harlow, flipping unspecified chops onto the bars with a rewarding hissing sound. "Me and Jonah's making fast friends. He's a grafter alright. And a fine new addition to *my* work force."

More cheering from the crowd, this time aimed at Max who, true to his nature, remained wholly nonplussed.

She flapped her hands playfully at the men, "Well you're certainly a sharp young thing, you look just like a movie star. Let me get you a drink. You want a beer?"

God did I want a beer.

She pulled a can from a nearby dustbin filled to the brink with ice and beverages and handed it to me unopened. I tore the can clean open and practically dove headfirst through the ring piece. "You need anything else Jonah just help yourself," she said, making her way across the garden towards the kitchen. "And it's a pleasure to meet you, my dear."

As the afternoon rolled on the majority of the men initiated a game of poker while the women tossed salads and clucked about life's minor difficulties behind the kitchen's screen doors. I have little interest in gossip and poker is a game I feel I've mastered, so took myself away from both groups and sat on an old swing set just behind the dying coals of the barbeque. Bananas wrapped in foil gently softened over the hot ash as a slight chill began to play like a xylophone across the amber glow of early evening. In nothing more than a bid to appear at least partially occupied I picked a piece of wood from the ground and with my pocket knife began to smooth its edges until it seemed manmade. It wasn't that I was avoiding people. I was thrilled simply to be surrounded, yet felt overwhelmed somewhat by my sudden thrust into a social life, and further perturbed by the ellipsis and elision that inevitably occurs between a longstanding clique, people with pasts, people with histories, people with lives that have interlocked and overlapped and acted as both witness and jury to each other at one point or another. I have never had this luxury. And as such am not entirely sure how to go about achieving it. I guess I've left it too late. Though maybe all is not lost. You and I seemed to lock into one another's existence at a time when most people were as established in their roles as ever they would be. But then again we had an incentive; that catalyst of a scheme which at least broke the ice and marked us out as ripe for company. Real life's trickier, I have found. And when faced with individuals I seem to spend so long deconstructing character and intentions that I inevitably miss the most obvious inroad and am forever resigned to acquaintance at best. This is tenfold when faced with large, established groups. So I take the loner's preferred method; separate myself entirely then wonder why it is I never seem to be the one holding court.

As I pushed the edge of the knife across the length of the wood, causing thin strands to curl and drop, a light hand appeared on my shoulder. I turned to look and no-one was there. Then I felt the swing to my right dip and the chains tighten.

"Hi stranger," she said. It was Aimee. Still dressed in white, only barefoot this time, and with just a hint of make-up barely noticeable to the untrained eye.

"What you doing here, Aimee?" I asked.

"Oh you know me," she said, swinging gently on the balls of her feet, her hands gripping the chain of the swing tightly. "I like to spread myself real thin," she laughed and then looked back at me. "You've met Daddy."

"*Levi?*"

She laughed and nodded towards Harlow. "Small world, huh?"

"You can say that again."

"How were the burgers?"

"Best meal I had all week. So you're Harlow's girl. Well I'll be damned."

"One of two. We're the twins. Identical," she threw herself backwards and pushed with her feet causing her to streak through the air. She swung like a pendulum before returning to my side. "For all you know you might not even be talking to me at all. I could be my other half," she laughed again and bounced the weight of her body gently towards me.

"Say Aimee, I like your Daddy, I like him a lot, so with that in mind I want to ask you a question and I want you to promise me you aint gonna get mad."

She giggled to herself and held me tight in her usually flimsy gaze. "You know as well as I do a person can't make that kind of promise," she said with uncharacteristic certainty. "But we've come this far so I guess you better go on and say it."

"You know what it is I'm gonna ask you. Why you kicking around with a dirty old man like Levi, Aimee? Good God. You're only a girl."

At this she shook her head lightly and those blonde locks tumbled across her face once more, making her expression distant and distorted. "He has what they call potential. He's going to give me things no-one else can."

"There's more to life than money you know," I said, gripping tightly to the swing's chains.

"That's what he says when he talks about you."

"He talks about me?" I asked. She stared to the ground and shook her head gently. "So then what is it?" I asked. "What keeps you following him around like a damn shadow? Surely there's more interesting folk you could be playing with?"

"All I ever wanted was to live forever. And he can do it. He's making me a character. He hasn't said as much but I just know it. He's stealing pieces of me each and every day. Aint that something special?"

"Harlow?"

"Levi... *the writer*," she said breathlessly. "They say he's a genius, you know."

"Can't say I did. I'm new to these parts."

"You'll get old soon enough," she said standing up. "For what it's worth Levi knows all about you. Says even he couldn't have invented someone as interesting as you," she ran her hands across my hairline and held my face up towards her. "You're a nice man, even if all these scars say different."

"A man can't help the scars he picks up," I said, becoming jittery at just about every aspect of our interaction – not least the proximity of Aimee's father; the man I was fast coming to think of as my one true friend in this town. "Don't make him good or bad."

"There's different sorts of scars," she said. As the long sleeves of her dress inched up I made out a small line, no longer than a slug and a fifth as thin, colouring her wrist like a bracelet. "These don't look like the kind of scars a man gets from just fighting back." She turned from me and waltzed carelessly into the house. Behind the window I saw her approaching Barbara who gave her a loving embrace and a small cookie, which seemed to enrapture her completely. Aimee twirled out of the door leading to the living room and out of sight.

"Don't mind Aimee," said Harlow, standing so close behind me he could have pushed me like a child on the swing. "She's a sweet girl, harmless, you just got to give her time." He sat down next to me and handed me a beer.

"She sure is pretty," I offered. "I spotted her around town. Never put two and two together I suppose. Older than I thought she would be."

"Them's old photographs I carry around with me. Stops me forgetting... more of a sentimental gesture, you understand. Something's worth remembering you hold it in your heart and your head no matter how many prompts you carry around with you. If you know what I mean."

I nodded.

"She wasn't always like that, Aimee. God knows we tried. It's her nerves, you see. Doctor's can't do anything about it."

"Doesn't seem to need curing to me."

"Course the wife blames the company she keeps. You say you've seen her around town. I know what people think. I know what they see. See her chasing after another stranger, strange old men, with

55

strange old habits. She can't help it, just the way she is. Never quite wanted to be herself. You ask me she's still just a girl playing fairytales."

"Worse things than holding onto your innocence in this life. Wish I hadn't been so keen to spend mine."

Harlow cleared his throat and took a sip of beer. "There's a difference between spending and having it taken over and over again, if you know what I'm saying. I just don't trust the sort of men who can't see that they're handling a girl as fine as china. Had it my way I'd take a gun to market and pick off every sonofabitch that came within ten yards of the little one. Only she's an adult now, on paper, which is all that matters in the eyes of the law, got to make her own mistakes. And I tell you, that girl makes mistakes finer than my wife makes Thanksgiving dinner."

"For what it's worth I'll keep an eye out for her, if I ever see her around."

As I spoke an aeroplane left disappearing fingerprints on the sky's canvas as it pricked the foot of a cloud. Harlow traced its ascent with a roll of his eyes before patting me on the back, and returned his gaze to the endless yellow of the cornfields that led to his yard. "That'd be good kid, that'd be good. Now… if there's one consolation it's Sylvia. You haven't met my other daughter. She was working today. Works in the city, have her working every hour God sends her way. Not that you'd hear her grumbling. I guess life's really down to chance."

"Some of us are luckier than others."

"Aint that the truth, kid," he said, draining his can of its contents. "Aint that the truth."

We were left in silence, immune to the faint clatter of background noise from the party's dying dregs. I could hear Harlow's breath, slow, steady, next to me. If I could have stretched that moment for the rest of my life I would have.

"That's a fine piece of work you got yourself there," came a voice from behind us. Caleb, a distant relative and - according to Barbara - a constant feature of Harlow's household made his way to the front of the swing set on which we rested. It took me a few moments and a brief glance towards my lap to realise what he was referring to. In my hands, against the blade of the knife, the wood block was now smooth and curved, like some abstract piece of fruit.

"Oh," I said. "Just a hobby of mine"

"Jonah's good with his hands. He's a frustrated artist," said Harlow, standing up and offering Caleb his seat.

"Frustrated something," I added.

"Ever thought of turning your hobby into some spare change?" asked Caleb, "I'm always after able craftsmen, and I'm sure Harlow'd give you a reference if need be."

"A fine one at that," said Harlow, sending a million inert mosquitoes up into the air as he prodded the white coals with a spatula. "I been faking Max's signature on references since you were knee high to a midget."

Both Caleb and I laughed. He reached into my palm, carefully avoiding the blade, and took the strange fruit from my hands.

"You think you could work to a larger scale?" he asked.

I shrugged. "Depends on what you had in mind. I'd draw the line at reproducing the Titanic but within reason don't see why not."

"Caleb runs the old funeral home on Sixth Avenue. Been in that family longer than the red in his hair."

"Buried four generations of pallbearers and counting. Say, you don't have any business you can pass my way do you?" He laughed at his own quip. It is a trait I have come to acknowledge that the more morbid a man's work, the more humour he is able to elicit from it. I bet my life's worth that doctors and gravediggers have more laughs than children's entertainers and street performers.

"Not this week, sir. Business can't be too bad for you though, it's not like it's a habit anyone's going to be quitting," I added

"What's that son?"

"Dying."

Caleb paused for a moment and then chuckled. "A habit. I like that my man. I like that a lot. So, what do you say? Fancy a sideline that'll never go out of business?"

"He pays good," said Harlow, covering the grate with a drum lid. "Or at least he will, now that he's poaching my very own house-guests."

"I'm sure we can come to some sort of arrangement. You in?"

"I'll certainly take a look. See if I might be able to help."

"Well that's just dandy. You come by tomorrow morning. We got some big business coming up. I'll show you the ropes and you can decide if it's for you or not."

"Here's to hoping," I said, raising my empty can towards his.

"To hoping," he mimicked, clicking his beer against mine.

I was one of the last to leave the party. I timed it carefully, you see. I wanted my presence to be noted, in an effort to show my enjoyment of Harlow and his hospitality. Though I was equally keen not to be the final few – those last drops of ketchup that simply won't vacate no matter how many times you tap the bottom and bash the side.

"Don't be a stranger," groaned Barbara as she embraced me by the front door, blushed from an afternoon of sun and wine coolers. "We're always open for visitors, any time, just you drop by."

I thanked her and kissed her once on the cheek as I accepted the cold meats and stale rolls she had kindly wrapped in foil as a midnight snack.

My street seemed more barren than usual as I walked the final stretch towards my front door. Porch lights beamed as moths grew closer to the flames, the lucky few jutting back as the heat scorched their wings whilst their more lethargic companions were caught flickering and hissing behind white shades; their shadows frantic and magnified. A cricket played a sad solo somewhere in the distance. The juices from the meat began to seep through their shroud and dribble awkwardly down towards my elbow. When I was able to take a closer look a trace of red had emerged like a wound across the now crumpled white of my shirt.

"Evening, boy," said Mrs Pemberton, rocking silently on her porch. The orange orb of a cigar was the only visible trace of her, like some shocked Cheshire cat.

"Evening, Mrs Pemberton," I said, stopping at my front door. Usually this would be the beginning and end of our interaction. I loathe her and she me. Neither with reason, I hasten to add. It just seems to have been an unspoken initial response that has remained unfaltering during my tenure as her closest neighbour. Despite this, and being in such fine spirits that very evening, I decided to grant her the courtesy of both my time and my good manners, though rationing both to the bare essentials. "Warm out," I offered.

"Been warmer," she said, making no attempt to move into the light. Her husband died three years into their nuptials and she has sat ever since, sour and Havishamesque, waiting on that porch. Waiting for what I do not know: for his return from the great beyond, I suppose, or perhaps for her own demise, and their ensuing reunion. Whatever her aim she is little liked amongst the neighbours I have spoken to. Though her age and longevity within the area have elevated her to a status of those whom we must respect.

"A welcome breeze, that's for sure. This time last year I could hardly draw breath."

"I like the heat," she said, her orange orb dilating with a quiet fizz. "Keeps my joints as they were."

"Well you take care Mrs Pemberton," I said, turning the key in my door.

"Awfully late," she said, just as I was about to step inside.

"Sure is. I'm pretty beat."

"Don't see you going out at night so often. Not for some time now anyway," there was a thump on the wood beneath her feet and a small black cat ran down the length of her garden and squatted beneath the car of the house opposite. "You haven't been courting trouble have you young man?"

"No, ma'am. Visiting friends from work. Had us a barbeque," I held up the aluminium meat as supporting evidence.

"I been on this street for forty years now and never seen a pick of trouble. I hope I don't start now."

"I'm not the sort of man to court controversy," I said, opening the door wider still.

"Mmhmm," she said, rocking back on the bows of her chair. "Some men been sniffing around your house."

For some reason my stomach turned slowly like a sycamore falling to soil. "My house?"

"Mmmhmm. Looking through your window. Been into your garden too, probably wanted to check your house wasn't burning down. I got three baskets of laundry ruined thanks to that fire. I hope you apply more thought to your surroundings in future."

"There were men at my house?" I asked again.

"Men, yes, two. How many times you need telling, boy?" she

said with a snap before returning to her dour tone, "I been sitting here for hours. I saw them clear as day. They don't see me though. I keep my lights off, for providence you see?"

"What time was this?"

"Yes siree, that stench won't be scratched from my delicates no matter how much I scrub. Lighting fires in broad daylight. Anyone'd think we lived in a slum."

"I'm sorry for any inconvenience caused, Mrs Pemberton," I said, fully aware that no further headway was going to be made on the subject, that night at least. "I'll happily reimburse you for any loss to your estate. Now if it's all the same with you I really have to be getting to bed."

"You go boy. And remember what I said. This is a nice street. Nice people too. Don't want no trouble."

"Goodnight Mrs Pemberton," I said, stepping inside and closing my door.

I looked out to the garden; the pleasure of the day now marred by such incongruous news. Nothing had been taken. Nothing destroyed. The garden lay as flat and featureless as it had been left. I pressed my forehead against the cool glass to get a further look but to my eyes everything appeared the same.

I do hope this remains the case. It seems that for the first time in my life I am beginning to fear change.

With love as always,
Jonah

Dear Jonah,

Being still drunk is so much worse than being hungover. If nothing else the latter is universally acknowledged; invoking, as it does, rolled eyes, ironic head shaking and the knowing smiles of those desperate to be seen as 'with it' enough not to judge. The former however requires an element of deceit; that strange notion that one must appear to be entirely sober despite alarming evidence to the contrary. In such a state one is inclined to forget that being sober is like so many things in life, whereby once a level of consciousness is applied it becomes satirised to the point of nullification. The symptom is always so much more telling than the cause.

I woke late and stumbled across the strewn clothes and empty cans that made up the base level of my trailer. The heel of the one shoe I had slept in snapped beneath my jaunty weight and I fell forwards, steadying myself in a painful crouch with both hands pressed against the edge of my coffee table, barely able to contain my own amusement. My uniform had been left scrubbed and clean, drying on the shower rail. This I only realised after my initial lather (pre rinse) as the fabric turned a darker hue where flecks of shower water had caught, and so I strolled outside while the shower still ran and hung them on the line that runs the entire length of my trailer.

"Verity!" yelled Delores from across the yard, "What in all the world?"

I put my hands to my head and then stared at my open palms as coconut scented suds ran down towards my wrists. "I guess I just wasn't invented for morning, Delores darling," I said with an attempt at ironic self mocking, holding onto the door frame for dear life as I walked back inside. Only as I looked down to slide the bolt did I realise that it was probably the fact that I was naked as God intended that had caused Delores such alarm.

"Lordy be!" said Ida as I straightened my hair in the glint of the coffee percolator, all the while wondering at what point hedonism became such a demanding creditor, "I've seen some things in my time but never have I seen a grown woman in such a state."

"And what state would that be Ida? Last time I checked there weren't no law against bad hair days," I turned to face her and the room began to spin. "Say, you seen my pencil anywhere? I always leave it on the counter."

"Drunk as the day is long," she hissed, handing me a pencil from the fold of her apron. "It's not right."

"And whatever gives you the idea I'm in any way incapacitated?"

She clucked her thick tongue and heaved her bulk across to the other side of the counter. "Barely stand straight for one," she said. "And your eyes been working to different beats since you stepped in here."

"Maybe I'm just struggling to contain my glee at the prospect of another full day."

"You know V... I do know what you're going through."

"I sincerely doubt that," I said, turning to lower the head on the grill pan.

"My sister takes a drink. Sometimes more than one," she opened her purse and placed a business card face down on the counter. "If you ever need someone to talk to. Just give it some thought."

I took the card without reading it placed it into my bra. Ida tilted her head with faux sympathy and I wanted to club her to death on the spot.

"I'll be seeing you tomorrow, Verity."

"Bye Ida."

"Oh - " she said, hovering in the doorway " - that boy was in at five o'clock this morning. Sharp as a pin too. Looked like he hadn't even been to bed. Ask me, you and him keep the same hours."

"What boy?" I said, pouring a sugar mound onto the counter and spreading it into a crescent moon with my thumb.

"Smart boy, in a hat, handsome. Said to tell you he'd been asking for you. Said he'd be back for the service at a later date."

She left and I was snapped into sobriety. I nearly melted all over that counter, Jonah, no word of a lie. Had I sat in silence for the rest of the day I'd have thought it complete. I turned to flip the bacon when I felt a stabbing pain in my chest and in a drunken fog momentarily convinced myself I was being taken to meet my maker.

I panted and gasped at the sharp shock, clutching my chest, which only made it worse. I opened my top buttons and went to massage the organ externally when I felt it beneath the fabric. From my bra I pulled the laminated business card Ida had given me. I flipped it over and, as my eyes began to attune themselves to the fine print, began to wish all over again that I had clobbered her when I'd had the chance.

High And Dry
Informal Friendship Circle for those affected
by Substance Abuse
Every Tuesday at 7pm
174 St. James' Avenue
Refreshments Provided

After that my day played out like a movie you knew you'd hate from the moment you sat down. Each second merely served to confirm the unavoidable: I should be somewhere else.

That night I walked alone again. As I crossed the already familiar route I traced the constellations overhead with the smoke from my cigarette. Thor's Belt never looked so seductive - a diamante tassel ripe for crumpled dollar bills - I thought as I rode that filthy Big Dipper down, deep deep down, into the hollows of The Iguana Den.

The moment the doors closed behind me a shiver trailed down my spine; I suddenly felt like Dorothy in glorious, incoherent Technicolor.

Through the velvet drapes I sauntered, already feeling like part of the architecture; as though my bones and skin would merge with the crumbling plaster were I to so much as lean against any one of the walls. Its dimensions appeared to have shifted, too. The vestibule now seemed longer, stretched like it was being viewed through the wrong side of a telescope. And the rickety, winding old staircase was to my knowledge a new addition. I quickly dismissed my misgivings.

The amount I had had to drink they could have been speaking fluent Chinese and I can't say I'd have noticed. Although it did seem to have a life of its own, within those four walls; a mercurial quality, like The Iguana Den itself were some great thespian that hurriedly took its mark each night especially for you. I bet no two people in that whole club saw the same thing once they stepped inside.

Also, it has to be said that even by my second visit, that gilded mask was beginning to slip ever so slightly. Of course it was still beautiful, still winged, beating, alive to the touch. Yet it didn't fare well to scrutiny. The Iguana Den was at its best from a distance, through the dark or a squint or, best of all, the frothy bottom of a bottle. That shabby charm became all the uglier the closer you looked. The wood didn't just flake; it was rotten to the core, the whole place disintegrating before your very eyes, fading like a dream. You could push your finger into the plaster of the powder room and see straight through to the gentlemens' facilities were you so inclined. The threadbare fabrics - velvet, lace - only just held themselves together, with a bleak propriety like mourners at a state funeral. Bricks would shed fragments of themselves in neverending hourglass sands straight onto the floor whilst cancerous spores that trailed brown mist when touched grew freely on the fittings. I once went to pick up my beer and found a cavalry of termites congregating at the corner of my table. I suppose all art becomes lessened when held to scrutiny though; zoom in on even the most beautiful painting in the world and you'll observe cracked brushstrokes or ugly clots of paint.

It was a quieter night. Early, too, which perhaps explained the slim pickings. Kingpin sat with his slight party. At the bar two men perched. One had only one arm and a hurried knot of bandage where the other should have been. Towards the back Eve sat, more conservatively dressed than before, with the shady outline of a gentleman nibbling the nape of her neck. I stood stone still and watched them from the sidelines. He took his lips from where they had been buried and whispered something in her ear at which she shot up and slapped him clean across the face. The attention of the room turned briefly. Kingpin rose slightly from his seat and Eve's suitor changed from furious to sheepish and slunk back into the shadows. She took a sip of beer and scanned the room. She noticed me and waved. "Well you're becoming more regular than us girls, and we're being paid for the privilege. Only just though. Sit down."

I did as instructed and she topped up someone else's glass from a pitcher of ale. "Thanks."

"Gets you, doesn't it – like a bad herb. Something about this place just keeps them coming back. I never seen such a regular group of faces in all my life."

I nodded. "You not dancing tonight?"

"It's my night off, and if I get my way I won't remember a moment of it. Want to join me?"

I bashed my glass against hers and she cheered.

We drank down the sharp dust of tequila. A bottle had materialised at our table and with it came a production line of various girls whom Eve introduced me to and then proceeded to deconstruct the moment they were out of earshot.

"That was Diane," she told me as a middle aged blonde walked away, wiping the taste of the spirits from the corner of her mouth. "Her husband used to beat her so she upped and left with his truck one morning. Now she doles out the punishments for paying guests, if you know what I mean. She's what Miss Jemima calls one of our speciality numbers. An acquired taste but particularly moreish if her regulars are anything to go by."

"Who's the guy at the bar?" I asked, pointing to the drooping one-armed man.

"That's Paul. Poor Pauly. In here every night of the year. He plays anything he can get his hands on. Or should I say hand, poor darling."

"How'd he lose his arm?"

"Paul likes to play, only his budget won't always stretch to the finer things in life, if you catch my drift. So he goes to Kingpin and borrows money. Only debt's a hungry dog, and Pauly seldom has the resources to make good on his promises."

"I don't get it," I said, pouring two more tequilas. I downed mine and grimaced as my insides filled and my eyes watered. Eve sipped her measure in one long, appreciative movement of her throat, barely breaking her speech as she did so.

"Kingpin has his fingers in a lot of pies, all unsavoury, which I'm sure will come as great shock to you. Anyway one of those pies is loans. Of course - " she said, lining up two more drinks " - often the boys don't have nothing to show for a month's labour. So he messes them up and extends their repayment window along with the interest rates. But he doesn't like to ask twice. And if the money still aint there he'll think nothing of taking creatively to make up the difference. Sometimes it's cars, sometimes it's televisions. Poor old Paul hasn't a pot to piss in, and in these situations Kingpin seems to take limbs as his preferred method of repayment."

I shuddered at the thought.

"Don't look so sad, honey. Those boys know what they're getting themselves into. It aint personal. It's just business."

"It's awful."

"It's life."

We knocked back two more shots and sat for a moment as the room wobbled and settled.

"It doesn't bother you?" I asked, lighting a cigarette.

"I don't let it. You get to choose what you do and don't feel if you walk alone, like me."

"Frighten you then?"

"I'm a smart girl," she said. "Once you've worked out the lay of the land you know where to tread. So long as you're careful around here you got nothing to worry about."

We watched as, with a fey reticence somewhat belied by her peephole bra, Prudence walked cautiously over to Kingpin's table carrying a bottle of something expensive and two glasses on a tray. She placed them down and whispered something in his ear. He glanced at her just once, pulling up the sleeve of his jacket to check the time on a large gold watch, before shaking his head and dismissing her with a wave of his hand before resuming his silence. Prudence walked slowly away looking forlorn, almost frightened.

"Prudence hasn't been herself for days," said Eve, noticing my unsubtle glances in her direction. "But it's none of our business until she makes it so. Best not to ask too many questions I find."

I waited in the hallway as Eve ran off upstairs to collect her bare essentials. I clutched the bottle for later and the banister for support until she came clomping back downstairs, all harangued and red. "God damn Shirley used the last of my lipstick. I never step outside without a fresh coat of lipstick," she said petulantly, kicking the foot of the staircase.

"Here," I handed her a miniature. "Use mine."

"Life... saver," she said slowly, stretching the crimson stick as far as it would go before drawing on her lips with my favourite siren red.

A commotion from the other end of the hallway began trailing towards us.

"Tell him I haven't heard such nonsense in all my days. I keep a tidy establishment with tidy rules. He has problems he knows who he can talk with... " came a voice, loud but wavering like a studio starlet of yore. More stomping. A great swathe of fabrics swished into view like a tornado made solid.

"That's Miss Jemima," said Eve, picking up her suitcases. "Let's say hi before we go. She's a real treat."

A young girl trailed behind her and as she stopped began to rearrange Miss Jemima's skirts, teasing the layers out into an even more outlandish trifle.

"Who's that?" I whispered to Eve, suddenly embarrassed by the situation.

"Calls them her ladies in waiting."

I lowered my face to hide my smirk.

A corset nipped her waist and pushed her breasts so that they practically merged with her chin, beneath which she wore a diamond the size of a child's fist. Her hair, like in the photographs, had been teased up into an old school bun, though strands caught and caked in the industrial strength make-up that cemented her face. She looked a hundred years old and beautiful with it. And then with a wave of a gloved hand the girl scurried off into one of the many doors that seemed to lead to nowhere.

"Eve darling, don't tell me you're up and leaving me already. My very heart would break on the spot!"

"We're just having us a slumber party. I made fast friends with Verity here and she and I are going to chase the devil with the bottle all night long."

"Ah," said Miss Jemima, "so this is the lady. It's a pleasure to meet you, my dearest." She held her hand to my face and pushed my jawbone to the light. "Well aren't you fine. You two could be sisters. Say you ever fancy dropping by in a more, shall we say, professional capacity?"

I laughed and looked to the floor. "No ma'am, I'm happy as a casual visitor as things stand."

"Verity's a woman of means as it is."

"Well isn't that just a pity," said Miss Jemima, her skirt quivering and shaking beneath her as though a separate being. "I'm very partial to a novelty act."

"Well I'll bear you in mind in case I ever fancy a change of career. It sure is beautiful here."

"Why thank you, darling," she said, taking a fan from her sleeve and wafting those rouged Baby Jane cheeks. "We do our best. You girls have fun."

"Oh we will. Bye Jemima darling," said Eve, leading me out of the door.

"It was a pleasure to meet you," I said, following suit.

"And you, my dear, and you. Just you remember what I said. Always a place for a girl like you in a joint like this."

"She's a doll," said Eve, walking fast ahead of me so that I had to skip each third step to catch up.

"One in a million," I said, sipping from the bottle. "Say, how long you planning on staying?" I asked as I arrived by her side and began to regulate my pace accordingly. She carried a small suitcase in one hand and a hat box in the other, both of which seemed to pull heavily on her arms.

"Oh don't worry about me. I just like to keep an eye on what's mine. Every worldly possession I have is kept safe in these here boxes."

I linked my arm through hers and went to relieve her of the suitcase at which she recoiled.

"No!" she yelled, before adapting her tone. "This one if you would, it's lighter."

I took the box, still linked by the arm, and she took the open bottle from me.

"To friendship!" she hollered at the dirty moon before taking a sip. She handed me the bottle and I held it awkwardly along with the box.

"To friendship!" I took a sip as we tottered off into the darkness, laughing at nothing in particular.

We drank and talked until my dim night-light's glow became redundant. Eve told me about Dylan, her current beau and - like the one before that and the one before that - the love of her life. Dylan had six tattoos and seven children by five women. His entire bottom row of teeth was solid gold. "Like treasure!" Eve swooned as she dragged the tip of her cigarette across her stomach and breathed in sharply at the sting. "He says that I'm going to be his lucky number six."

I lay back so that we were side by side on my bed, our feet resting on the tin wall above the headboard. "Where'd that come from?" I asked, gently pressing the bruise above her wrist.

She shrugged and fell silent, but, true to her nature, became deafened by the quiet. "Dylan likes things just so," she said eventually. "He only wants me to learn. He's a real gem."

"He should be shot like a lame dog."

"Don't ever say that, Verity!" she moaned, close to tears. "It's not his fault, he can't help it."

It was not, it transpired, the first time Eve had found herself in such situations. In fact it soon emerged as somewhat of a character trait. Eve enjoyed the kind of love that left you bejewelled with purple welts and red streaks as ornament to some intense unity.

"I just like it more when you can feel each moment as it happens, good or bad. Safe and comfortable never won no awards. Never set the world on fire. At least this way you always know he feels something. Which is better than nothing, don't you think?"

"Well I don't think it's right."

"Well you don't have to worry. Me and Dylan's going to be together for the rest of time, he just wants to make sure it's perfect. Forever's an awfully long time when something's not right. It's his way, and that's that." I shook my head and she rolled to face me. "You really want to worry for me, you worry about that rackety old building. The other week a tile from the ceiling fell onto Prudence in bed and cut clean through her mattress. Luckily she sleeps with her legs in two different time zones or else she'd have lost her main source of income, if you know what I'm saying."

I laughed and so did Eve. "You can stay here you know. I don't take much space myself."

"You mean that?" she said, sitting upright in the bed.

"Practicalities be damned," I said, stubbing the cigarette out into a saucer on the floor.

"Oh Verity, you're a lifesaver! You'll think you've got a live in maid or something. It won't matter that it's so small. I'll be so quiet and so careful you'll just about have the whole place to yourself." She lunged towards me and threw her arms around my neck. "Say, let me test my luck and go for one more ask," she said, pouring tequila into two coffee cups I had stolen from the diner, on what once seemed the rare chance I'd ever be required to serve houseguests.

"What would that be?"

"Dance with me."

I rolled my eyes and took the whole cupful of liquor in one mouthful.

"Miss Jemima takes real good care of us girls. And it's got to be more interesting than flipping pancakes all the live long day."

"I like flipping pancakes. Sometimes they even let me press waffles."

"Dream big!" sneered Eve.

I poured two final drinks and, with a shrug of my shoulders, clinked my cup against hers.

"Verity... was that a yes?" she asked leaning in closer to me.

"To decadence... " I rolled my eyes and swallowed the drink in one go. "To decadence!"

You asked me, Jonah, how I came to be where I am, and so there it is: I said yes. I suppose Eve hit upon something within me, highlighted, for want of a better word, the knowledge within us all that life could be so much bigger if only we said yes more often, if we dived feet first instead of eternally hesitating at the periphery whilst something grander plays forever out of frame. This has always been my trouble. I want everything but seem content to want. I want blonde hair. I want brown eyes and olive skin. I want to be able to wear strapless dresses without checking my tits every second like a leaking new mother lest I endure the horror of a rogue nipple in a public space. I want to be black. I want to be gay. I want to have known handprints on the thighs of my prepubescent skin from some drunken parent whose demise was the happiest day of my life. I want to experience the eternal whimsy that comes with a gilded upbringing. I want to be colour blind; to see the world but not hear it and hear it but not see it. I want to be confined to a wheelchair and irreversibly contorted into a spasm so acute that it makes fellow diners in any restaurant I m in feel nauseous and unable to finish their entrées. I want to experience spirituality so succinct I would kill, or perhaps die for it. I want bangs. I want to feel what the sweating virgin offering me bargain life insurance feels like each time I and every other sane human being slams the phone down on him with a fading obscenity. All these things I want but can never have. This is my problem Jonah – the enormity of life is so utterly breathtaking in its scope, I often think it such a shame that we only get to live it the once.

I was asked and I said yes.

I wonder just how many tragedies began with those very words.

With love,
Verity

Dear Verity,

I arrived early as to make a good impression. Sunday should, by rights, have been my day of rest. Though I figured that by this point in my life I'd had so long to rest that I was working in arrears, so didn't much mind the android chirp of my alarm at six thirty and the drone of my muscles as I got up and into the shower. Leftover smoke still clung to my pillow like perfume of some departed lover, so I bundled the covers in a ball and threw them into the middle of the kitchen floor to be dealt with at a later date. At such ungodly hours the thought of food flipped my stomach so I took a sip of water straight from the faucet (a perk of solitary living) and stepped out the door into the surprisingly chilly early morning light.

God's most devoted followers were already prepped and seated as the sun dissolved the web of dew blanketing the church's kept lawns. Maxwell stood at a distance spouting his zeal having become disillusioned with what he felt to be the wan passion of our given preacher.

'... so I implore you ladies and gentlemen, step out of the wilderness... step away from these lives of sin... you have to find something to believe in, and let it rule you. Only then will you be truly found... '

His cries became diluted by the bells of Sunday's first service, which began to thunder and chime as I made my way through the cornfields; discordant at first, just finding their feet, and then as if by magic the strands of a tune began to weave together until sweet music filled the air. I found myself powering forward to their faintly militant beat until I'd crossed the whole first field without realising it.

The Hare and Sons Funeral Parlour, Caleb's pride and joy, stood on a stretch of dead grass about a mile from the nearest residential street. Its faux gothic spires swirled up towards the heavens like birthday candle smoke. The lawn that surrounded it was yellow and fading and the front of the house was in urgent need of treatment. Caleb was removing dead heads from a hanging basket as I walked towards the house. He stood stout and unshaven in his stocking feet, wearing battered denim and a string wife-beater.

"Beautiful morning out," I said, offering my hand.

"Well aren't you the early bird. Bodes well for our imminent venture."

"Potential," I added, defiantly. "Still don't know if I'm up to the challenge."

"I trust my instincts," he said, tossing the shrunken heads of the plants into a dirt pile beneath the porch. "Come on round back let me show you."

We walked to the back of the house, past the stained windows of the service room, which glowed red and warm in the formative light.

"You want a coffee? I'll get you a coffee," said Caleb as we passed an open doorway to the back of the house. "Mary," he yelled without altering his pace. "Mary, two cups of Joe when you've got a minute," he shouted as we made our way towards the never-ending stretch of the garden. At the back of the house an ugly new addition had been tacked shoddily to the building like some hurried afterthought. Beyond it the gentle hills rolled down towards a small ravine, around which shrubbery grew in brilliant greens and reds. To the furthest edge sat a barn around which chips of various woods piled high and flew upwards on the breeze. "That over there's the workshop. That'll be part two of the grand tour," said Caleb, standing in the doorway, shivering slightly. "Come on in."

I followed him into the extension at the back of the house. It was a large room, white and utilitarian, with a gentle top note of fresh wood permeating the muggy stench of death. I itched my nose and looked around. Along either side of the room two rows of oblong boxes were lined in reverent symmetry. There were four either side creating a makeshift runway all the way towards the door to the kitchen. I remained towards the back as Caleb walked down the centre of the arrangement. Holding his hands out widely he pulled back the pall of the first two boxes. The crisp sheets billowed up and made a flapping sound like a flock of doves alarmed by gunshot. As they fell gently to the floor Caleb turned to me and nodded down towards two pristine coffins – one thin, heartbreakingly practical pine box, the other a more elaborate yew; smoothed at the edges and polished into a rich liquor of speckled brown.

"What do you think?" he asked, surveying his craftwork. For Caleb death no longer the held the dark eroticism it might do to you or me; its shimmering eternity merely a formality in his lifelong devotion to careful craft, to customer service and repeat business; to profit. Each fatality in a town where everyone was related to someone who knew someone was, to the sole funeral director, nothing but business, and good business at that judging by the assortment of vehicles parked in the lot beside the house.

"They sure are beautiful. Any of them... *occupied?*"

He laughed as the back door swung open and a dour woman in a plaid dress made her way towards him carrying a tray with two steaming cups.

"No siree, these babies are, how do you want me to put it, *awaiting their deposit,*" he chuckled. His wife did not. "This one here's our economy line, funerals paid for by the state or town collections you understand," he tapped the pine structure and it made a cheap, empty yelp of a sound. "This here's our executive collection. You want to be chauffer driven to St Peter this is the woman for you."

"Some coffee, dear," said the woman warily. "Careful, it's hot. There's milk and sugar in the decanter. I'll leave it on the edge here." She placed the tray down on the one and only bench in the room and walked away. Caleb patted her on the rear as she passed, causing her to jump and carry on with her business, seemingly immune to both his sense of fun and his touch.

We took the coffees and sipped them slowly as we walked towards the furthest edge of the garden, led by the pained cries of wood on metal. As the noise dipped we were granted a gilded silence. Caleb turned to face me and as his mouth opened to talk the shriek began again - loud and coarse - making it seem like malevolent spirits were leaving his body. " - od damn Rich!" he concluded as the sound stopped. "You want to look inside?"

"Let's do it."

Inside the workhouse lengths of wood lay unorganised on worktops.

Three circular saws took pride of place in the centre of the room where an older man stood, blowing dust from a six foot plank of mahogany.

"This is Richard, our only craftsman since Jacob went from employee to customer."

"WHAT?" yelled Richard through thick safety goggles, removing his ear protectors and placing them around their neck.

"This is Jonah. Given the word he's going to be helping out around here."

"Oh," said Richard, moving towards me. He wiped his dusty hands on his overalls, if anything more filthy than his palms themselves, and extended it to me. "It's a pleasure to meet you."

"Morning, sir."

"Can't say I won't welcome the help. Summer's a busy time. The heat gives the old 'uns that extra kick. Last year we were stacking them in the ground like pancakes."

Caleb rolled his eyes at me.

"Ask me it's irresponsible. Sooner they all get to grips with burning the better," Richard said, walking back across the workroom towards his current project, which he began sanding by hand with a square of paper.

"So," said Caleb, as we made our way towards the front of the house. "You think you'd be up for it?"

"Depends what my hours would be," I said. "Want to keep a certain standard at my new job, this'd be more of a hobby, if you don't mind me saying."

"Don't mind one bit son, anything I value your honesty." He took my coffee cup and placed it on the step of the porch along with his. "Harlow says you don't get out much... on an evening... weekends."

"I try to keep myself to myself."

"It's no bad thing. How about you start coming over on a Saturday morning. Maybe some evenings. So long as there's no service you can keep your own hours. We're deaf to the noise by now – forty years in any industry you stop noticing the evidence."

"That'd be fine."

"You can operate the saw?"

"Yes sir, was trained in... well, let's just say I had experience."

"Good. So you come by a Saturday morning, and any evenings you can make it. And we'll go from there. I'll give you the plans, the dimensions and such, the material will be sitting waiting, and we'll see how you get on."

"And payment?"

"Oh yeah, that too!" he laughed. "We like to look after our boys, you won't be disappointed. We'll start on a work to order scheme and see how we get on."

"Then it's agreed."

"So let's shake on it."

He held out his hand and we sealed our gentleman's agreement, Caleb enthusiastically, me slightly less so - suddenly confronted with the tiredness which had until that point been hiding itself in the camouflage of excitement.

"So long as you can stand Richard's jabbering I don't see why this won't be a fine time for all involved."

"'Cept the customers."

"'Cept the customers," Caleb laughed. "I like that... I like that a lot."


Mrs Pemberton twitched her curtains and shook her head at me as I mounted my own lawn, eager for a second shower and a light nap. I waved instinctively and she turned the blinds as far as possible, so that whilst she became invisible to me, I could still be viewed from an angle. Her slant was not out of character so I let it fade from my mind as I opened the lock and stepped inside.

Some things you can tell on instinct, Verity. From a doctor's stance a loved one's fate can be determined, no need to see his face - he has been trained in this kindly deceit - but the way he holds himself will give away everything you'll ever need to know. A clear sky in winter means nine times out of ten you'll be scraping the car with red, furious hands early next morning. And as cows take to their slumber it is fair to assume that a storm is brewing, silent and huge.

That I was not alone in my house became a similar instinct; as certain and vital to me all of a sudden as sight or sound. Perhaps one or two minor pieces of physical evidence penetrated my thoughts without me having realised it – the shunt of the back window, bent so suddenly that the hinges had re-set, or the laundry pile on my kitchen floor now a fair few steps from where it had been left. Yet whilst these were invariably true they were not what made me so certain of an intrusion. I just had a feeling that I don't ever want to know again; a cross between fear and violation with a distant back taste of guilt and the oddest, most pressing adrenaline I have ever known.

My skin became alive as though each of my senses was being filtered through its porous stretch; volatile and receptive to every rush of air that blew across me like sand across a desert. I moved carefully, low and slowly, like it was I who was breaking and entering. I heard a creak of wood, and a scuff. I pushed open the living room door and no-one seemed to be inside. I walked down the small corridor towards the kitchen. The bedroom appeared empty. Suddenly I felt the need to leave. My thoughts became unusually overlapping, clouded and unfamiliar like I was slipping away from myself, and all I could focus on was escape. The kitchen had been undisturbed save the window that still hung ominously opened towards my yard. I grabbed a knife from the kitchen counter and opened the back door as wide as I could.

The garden was peaceful. In the distance a sprinkler system hissed and a gaggle of girls whooped and splashed their way through its stream. No footprints were evident in the grass, though given it was as hard and dry as elephant hide it would have bounced a meteorite back to the heavens without so much as a dent. Around the open window a black fur had caught and suddenly I felt my whole body drop back into itself. It must, I decided, have been an animal. Raccoons were a problem in the neighbourhood, had been ever since I moved in. Surprisingly dextrous too, so I was told. In fact when each minor household transgression remained unsolved - a broken vase, dirty smudges in the hallway, a fresh pastry nibbled at the corner - they seemed to be the go-to guy for families hoping to put these small scale traumas behind them with limited fuss.

I laughed at myself, at my stupidity and vulnerability, at the sight of a grown man clutching a butter knife (only the handle had registered when I selected my weapon) for protection. I walked back inside and locked the door.

"Well I'll be," came the voice from behind me. "It is you."

I froze on the spot.

"Aren't you at least going to say hi?"

I turned slowly, hoping to God that he would have disappeared by the time I reached the source of his sound like a nightmare blinked from memory. This was not the case.

His face was less grotesque than when I had last seen him over a decade ago and when both of us were little more than children. The way I remembered him was weeping and oozing into a stranger's carpet, his skin hanging loose; blood pouring from his eyes like a holy statue. Michael had grown into his wounds, mercifully, though still they dominated his features and became all you could focus on. Now a man, the freckles of scars still dotted his cheek from where shards of glass and lead had showered his face. A small bald patch to the side of his head was an ugly silvery white. Most awful of all though was his eye – stretched and pinched to the side, it roved from within an angry slit that cut a deep ridge all the way behind his hear. He looked like he was fading, like a cartoon being erased by its frustrated artists. Had it not been for vanity and pride on my part I would have wept on the spot at the sight of him; wept at his image, at his unwelcome return, at the fact that only bad things could conclude from his appearance, and partly at my guilt over the destroyed face of a boy I had once cared for. I've never hated anyone the way I hated him at that moment.

"Well this is a nice house Jonah. A nice house," he said, sitting on my sofa. They had followed me into the living room where I sat, slumped and frightened in the armchair whilst they remained standing. "You must have stockpiled a secret stash without letting us boys know about it," he chuckled. His companion remained silent.

"Sit down," I heard myself say.

"*Thank you kind sir,*" Michael said with a jocular bow. The sleeve of his jacket had been ripped, his white shirt visible like muscle tissue in a black and white war movie. "Hope you don't mind the, shall we say... *elaborate intrusion.* You remember I always did have a penchant for the limelight."

I nodded.

"So, Jonah. How's life?"

"You've been following me."

"Say, is this house rented? I could get me a nice little house like this," he said, standing back up. He took the axe head from the table and began picking nicks of skin from his hand with the dullest of the two edges. "Nice little house in a nice little town. Maybe a nice little wife to go in it. I always did say I wanted a wife, isn't that right Jonah?" He turned to me. "I'm sorry, where are my manners? This is my associate Ed. Say hello, Edward."

The man, still seated, nodded towards me. He held none of Michael's maniacal energy. He was solid and slick; his hair greased back and his manner immaculate, like a praying mantis. The only indication of any wrongdoings was the tail end of a self-administered tattoo edging from the cuff of his sleeve.

"Pleased to meet you," I said, my voice a staccato inflection over which I had no control.

"What the hell's wrong with you, Jonah? You look like you've seen a ghost."

"I near enough have. How are you Michael?"

"Me? Well I'm just swell, friend. I'm just swell. Out on the open road you'll be pleased to hear. And the price of a cup of coffee! I tell you, it's enough to make you wonder who's the crook out there. Lot changes in ten years Jonah," he placed the axe head on the hearth and sat back down. "I hope my face doesn't upset you," he said with a wry, rictus smile. I shifted uncomfortably in my seat. "Now, now, don't you be getting upset. Let bygones be bygones. That's my motto. Go on, take a good look. I see your eyes darting back and forth, not knowing where to look. It's pretty aint it? Truth be told I forget all about it until I catch sight of myself in other people's reactions. Poor lady at the diner nearly fell to the floor when I asked for my pie."

I forced myself to look him in the eyes.

"There? That better? Now that the elephant's out of the room and I've forgiven you so admirably, how about you bring us some refreshments? Ed takes tap water, likes to keep a clear head you understand. Mine's a beer. I'm legal now too, have been for some time. Boy do things change in ten years - " he said leaning back in his seat as I stood up, dazed and somnambulant like the living dead, " - boy do things change."

"So this gentleman moves into my room," Michael continues, sipping from my beer as Ed sits silently, his water untouched. "And transpires he has a cell phone. I daren't ask how he got it in, let's just say the mouthpiece remains as far from his lips as can be, if you follow... " Michael guffaws and slaps Ed on the arm. "Anyway, I had enough of talking in that place, so I took to listening. Boy is it magic what happens when you start to listen. Ed has this down to a fine art. As did you, if my memory serves me correctly."

"How did you get out so soon?"

"Same as you, only I took the fast track. The platinum scheme. You start collecting, phone conversations, whispers, rumours. I found myself relaying these minor details to those with keys, and before you know it I was a free man. Honesty's a costly luxury Jonah. Given the choice between happiness and pride I'll take happiness any day of the week. How about you, buddy, how's life been for you so far?"

"I suppose... things are... *what the hell are you doing here Michael?*" I asked eventually, seeing no reason to acknowledge the charade of conversation when I wanted only one thing: his total disappearance from my life.

"Well well well, you have the house but not the hospitality my friend. Say, aint that a country song?" Michael threw back his head and laughed. "I was in the neighbourhood. Heard from someone who knew someone who knew someone that you were knocking about this neck of the woods and thought who'd be happier to see me than my old pal Jonah. Hell, we been making sure it was you for weeks now. See, there are a few practical issues with us being here. *Terms and conditions applied to my swift exit.* Didn't want to risk accosting the wrong man and finding our liberties revoked once more. It was made clear that a repeat visit would not go quite as smoothly by the some of the boys the day I moved out, you understand."

"Now you've seen me you can be on your way."

Michael stood up and began pacing the living room, arriving back at the hearth; the axe head back in his hands. "Well Jonah I won't lie, I'm disappointed. Here I've told Ed about my great friend Jonah, the kindest most gentle raconteur you ever will meet. I tell him what this man can't do with words is nobody's business, that you're clever, that you're kind. And Ed over here he insists on a road trip to meet this very legend. Only now he must be crestfallen. You sad Ed, sad at Jonah's unremarkable reception?"

Ed didn't respond.

"I don't want trouble," I said eventually, dragging each word to the fore with all my might. "I got a quiet life out here."

"Deadly silent," said Michael, opening and shutting a small box I had crafted on the mantelpiece.

"I just want to be left alone. Not too much to ask. It's good seeing you Michael, really it is, and I can't say I'm not relieved that you're doing okay. But you and I were different people back then, people that don't bear repeating. I think it's for the best that this is the end, don't you?"

There was a moment's silence.

"No," he said eventually. "I think we're going to stick around for now. Now, now, hey, don't be looking so worried. We won't cause no harm. Your secrets are safe with us, my friend. This is a nice setup you got yourself Jonah," he said, staring out of the window. "Type of life I wouldn't mind taking for my own. How about you go about giving us some pointers, meet us for a few drinks, then that'll be it. Like we were never here. Seems a shame to have come all this way for nothing."

"What do you mean?"

"Just a few hours of your time. How about Wednesday night? Beers. And before you start arguing it's our dime, that's a given. Yes siree, all we ask is your company."

"Fine," I said, standing, desperate only for them to leave. "Whatever you want. Just say where and when," I walked to the door and Ed stood up.

"Then it's a date!" said Michael turning swiftly. "Wow Jonah, it's sure good to see you. Sure is good, thought once we were pulled our separate ways that was the end of that chapter. It's nothing short of a miracle if I do say so myself." He walked to the door that I held open and Ed followed. "Wednesday night, we'll be in touch as to where and when. Until then we got us some business to attend to."

"I'll see you around, Michael."

"That you will my friend," he said as he walked out of the front door, followed by Ed's bulking weight. "That you will."

"Thanks for coming this weekend," said Harlow, the next day. I had removed myself from the lunchtime rabble and sat alone with a crust of bread in a dirt hollow just a short stroll from the action of the building sight.

"Thanks for having me," I tried.

"Sure did make an impression on the missus. Seems to think you're some kind of gentleman. Caleb's go okay?"

"Excuse me?" I racked my brain. "Oh, yes sir, giving it a trial run."

Harlow moved closer to me. "You okay boy? Haven't seemed yourself all day."

"I'm just tired."

"You sure that's all?"

"Yes sir."

"Well so long as you're sure. You ever need to talk, you know where I am."

"Thanks."

Harlow nodded and began walking away.

"Say, Harlow... " he turned to face me. "Thanks for having me at the weekend. I haven't enjoyed anything that much in as long as I can remember."

"Any time kiddo, any time."

That evening I arrived home to a handwritten note on my doormat:

*Howdy Pal,*
*Great to see you so well. As discussed Wednesday would suit us best,*
*if it's all the same with you. Let's say eight thirty at the old Tavern*
*on Main Street. We look forward to your company!*
*Regards,*
*Michael*

I folded the letter and went out to buy enough bourbon to stun the entire state football team.

Why did you write to me, Verity? What positive were you hoping to draw from a lifelong exchange with a convicted criminal? I often meant to ask you this, but suppose the time was never quite right. Initially I was wowed by the luxury of a personalised message from a sweet stranger; more so that it lacked the frenzied urgency that the spider scrawls of death row fetishists mostly suggested. And then before long it seemed too rude a point to raise, having become established in one another's lives so quickly. You lifted me in ways I never thought I could have been whilst I was inside. You gave me an audience, something to love and guide where once I felt so bleak. Yet still I am at a loss as to what exactly I was to you, initially, before we had even the vaguest idea of one another.

Sorry if this appears rude. It is not intended to be as much. Nor, I hasten to add, is this in any way a preamble to the severance of our relationship. I need you now more than I ever have before. I'm just curious, that's all, as to the nature of our ever-shifting roles. Am I your creation or are you mine? In truth I daresay it no longer matters, it is what is and that is that. Like I said, I'm just curious and wallowing once more in self-pity.

I look forward to hearing from you soon.

With love,
Jonah (Your Eternally Grateful Stranger!)

Dear Jonah,

Eve came rushing into the trailer in floods of tears and locked herself in the bathroom. I had been sitting on the floor, smoothing the corners of some of your oldest letters, readying myself to pen yet another note. The bolt of the door locked, a tap was turned on, and then one long, animalistic wail sounded out, followed by two solid hours of sobbing.

I let her be for a while until the reality of two girls and one bathroom became an issue I could no longer ignore. I considered the practicalities of a wide-necked bottle. I even gave thought to the flexibility and aim required to hit the sink. But vanity prevailed and so I was left with no option but to intervene. Keeping my legs pressed as tightly together as I could I walked over to the door almost doubled over in agony. I knocked. No answer. I tried again.

"You need in?" she said eventually, her voice cracked and distorted through swallowed tears.

"Eve, what's the problem, sweetheart? You can tell me. I could help."

There was a brief pause, then a reluctant sliding of the bolt, before the door opened with a creak. Eve stood, half naked and red faced, her eyes still streaming. "Oh Verity, I'd do anything for love... but I won't do THAT," she said, taking herself to the bedroom and wallowing deep within the covers where she remained, lachrymose, for the remainder of the day.

And with that Dylan was relegated to one more notch on Eve's increasingly whittled bedpost.

She had been gone since leaving for The Iguana Den the night before. The agreement I had made drunkenly seemed to still stand, and so after a brief phone conversation we found ourselves traipsing back across the sand flats in the lunchtime burn. Inside there were sounds of real life as opposed to the hushed tones of night owls and alley cats that I had grown accustomed to. Minus the benefit of mood lighting it seemed exposed, as though its clean white towel had been whipped away and all that was left was a less than perfect body.

Behind closed doors sounds rang out. I heard two girls shriek and then laugh. In the distance a dog barked twice then settled. A hairdryer blew suddenly and then snapped as though choked. A sixties pop record played through tinny speakers. In the main room of the bar, in front of the stage, Kingpin played poker with three men. They turned their heads instinctively at our intrusion though in no way attempted to acknowledge us. No sooner did they recognise Eve's face than they returned to the game at hand. Eve took my arm and led me behind the stage to where, she told me, the real magic happened.

Miss Jemima sat in front of the largest of the mirrors, carefully painting on two lips with a brush and red oil.

"My dears, what a surprise. And just in time. I don't like to be disturbed until my face is in place."

"Miss Jemima," Eve walked over and kissed her on the cheek. "You remember Verity."

"How could I forget?" She moved towards me and kissed my hand. "Such a pleasure to make your acquaintance once more, and what fun we're going to have. Follow me, dear," she said, leading us out through a side door. "Verity... that's an unusual name. You don't find too many Verities round these parts."

"No ma'am," I said.

It's true. My name is a cruel hangover from parents whose income was one generation removed from the very bluest of collars yet whose tastes, sadly, were not. I am all too aware that were I born into a dynasty of some sort - of old money charm and faded grandeur - it could conceivably bear some watermarks of hereditary celebration or even ironic humour. As is, it speaks only of the misguided notion that obscure and polysyllabic will somehow equate to success or, at very least, aspiration later in life. In such circumstances the opposite is almost always true.

"Come girls," she said. "We're working to a deadline."

Eve followed first, I trailed behind. As I stroked a hair from my cheek I felt something stick to my fingers. Looking down, the tips were coated in red blotches of her make-up, as though I'd been bitten by a viper.

We spent the next half hour rifling through costume drawers, deciding on colour, fabric and style. Eve tossed a threadbare feather boa at me and howled with laughter. I begin to enjoy myself despite any initial misgivings.

"I take it you're housed?" asks Miss Jemima, once my finery has been decided.

"I have my own place."

"It's real nice," says Eve, flicking a thong from the largest of the carved chests across the room at me. Two sequins had somehow stuck themselves to her neck making light bounce sharply into the eye of anyone who stared too long. "She's even letting me stay, we're our very own odd couple."

"I can't say I'm not relieved. We accommodate the fallen women where possible of course, though in my experience they're often fallen for a reason."

"I'm pleased to be standing on my own two feet, for now at least."

"And long may it continue. Come now, change into those there clothes and let's see what you're made of."

Back on stage the lights have been dimmed. The bar is cooled by its artificial darkness and the poker game carries on as normal. Next to the men, Prudence is stood, silent and solemn, barely an inch from Kingpin's side. Miss Jemima walks to the table and whispers something in his ear. He looks towards us and holds my gaze. I feel myself chill. His eyes seem to deconstruct on the spot, what exactly he is looking for I am not sure, but he seems to find it and with a nod to his guests they stand and leave the room followed by Prudence and we are alone once more.

From nowhere a slow beat begins to sound. Eve walks to the centre of the stage and begins a simplified version of the dance she performed the first night I saw her, every so often glancing in my direction. Miss Jemima walks behind me until I feel her skirts brushing against the bare skin of my leg.

"Eve can be... how shall we put this? Excitable to say the least," she whispered as Eve swung her hair around until her face was hidden. "I wouldn't want to feel like you'd been coerced. You think you're up to it, darling? Say now or forever hold your peace."

"I think I could be."

"Alright. Well now imagine a room full of people. Men. Braying, salivating, wild horses that you alone have to tease and tame all at once," she leans even closer, scanning for a reaction. "Still game?"

I pause for a moment as Eve winds to a halt at the base of the pole and spreads across the floorboards with the grace of an ice cube melting in the sun. "Absolutely."

She tells us that we're artists, mastering our craft. That the pace and rhythm must remain measured; each layer unfolding to the right beat, the pleasure of our audience maintained at all times before the final reveal. There are, of course, prerequisites of the vocation. The reveal itself must be of a certain standard. We must be toned and tight enough as to appear desirable, yet retain a certain fallibility which suggests that one could, if only in their wildest dreams, be in some way attainable. Yet despite this the insistence is that the prelude itself is half - if not three quarters - of the battle. It retains its own significance. Too fast and they've shot their load before they're so salacious they'd hand over the deeds to their homes just for one more inch. Too slow and they become bored, the bottom of the bottle holding more appeal than the folds of fabric and flesh shifting before them. You have to spin your web with care, she says, and select the perfect moment to catch even the most reluctant of prey. The spider dance is a ritual as old as time, the trick is patience, time, and knowing when best to strike. It is a skill only few acquire wholly, but those that do can live a long and fruitful life from skills of the flesh.

It comes to my turn and I feel my stomach churn. I walk to the stage. Eve has now taken to the front row of seats. She wolf-whistles but I do not turn around. Miss Jemima stands at the furthest edge of the stage, her corpulence nothing but a convex extension of the shadows in which she bathes. The music changes track seamlessly and I find my shoulders begin to shake slightly. I breathe deeply and force myself to relax into the repetition of the beat. A light catches my eye and for a second I am dazed, uncertain of both self and surroundings. I hold out my hands and grip firmly onto the greased pole.

I can't say exactly how long I was up there. I disappeared from my own head, I allowed my body and limbs to steer their own course. I felt the dip of my legs, the brush of metal on skin. A sharp scraping as my knees dragged across the floor. The only consciousness was a slight effort to synchronise any movements I made to the tune of the song. I twirled and twisted to the empty room. I thawed beneath those lights and, Jonah, I'm not ashamed to admit it, I began to enjoy it. The sounds stopped, my scant audience disappeared and it was just me and my body, moving as I pleased.

Then the sound really did stop. Silence crept over me and suddenly I became aware, mortified even. No reaction from my crowd of two. I wanted to die. I wanted to run and scream and cry. Then a pat, then another, and another. Eve began hammering applause from the front row and whooping with delight. The sounds buffered the shame I felt though still did not appease me as I had hoped it might.

She rose from the shadows, her features finding themselves in the glare of the stage lights. Miss Jemima walked towards where I stood, now shivering, sweating, beside the pole. She stopped in front of me and looked me up and down. "My dear, what exactly was that?"

I looked to the floor. Eve fell silent. I opened my mouth but could not bring myself to respond. Her hand stretched beneath my chin and lifted my face up, up towards the lights, towards her smile.

"That was magic, my dear," she said with a nod. Then, turning to Eve, "Darling, we've dug us a diamond!"

After that it was easy. Being watched alters you for the better, in this instance at least. If anything the glinting eyes act as guidance, the sounds direct you into places you didn't think you could go. I move to their noises like a lover and I like it Jonah, I like it a lot. If anything I resent the choreography, the allocated timeslot. My saddest moments become those when the track dips and my time is over and I am left to glide my way to the back of the stage, oiled dollars slipping between garter and thigh as the hollers mount and die behind me.

Miss Jemima spends most of the evening backstage preparing us girls and offering her own applause as we finish our sets. "Perfect, darling, just perfect," she swoons, kissing us again as glittered girls brush past to meet their hungry audience. "You're a master already, must be in your blood."

"That and bourbon, Jemima darling" I say, stepping out of my stilettos and wrapping a gown around my frame.

She laughs and goes to check on the development of Chastity, whose bruise requires a more elaborate blusher than Miss Jemima would usually allow.

The rumour mill, which seemed to propel The Iguana Den, must have caught Prudence in its mechanisms, as on my seventh day of employment she disappeared and was never seen again. My initial inquiries as to her whereabouts were met first with shifty indifference, though before long were stopped short with an urgency which I grew to realise stemmed from fear. I managed to console myself with the fact that her departure must have been the result of the same dirt road which led such a sweet girl into a life of glitter and oils for the paying pleasure of those who truly know better. Such roads rarely alter their course, I was told. And with that the discussion ended.

"I don't get how she could just disappear," I said to Miss Jemima one evening as she pulled my corset strings tighter and tighter, my breath stolen with each passing inch.

"Best you don't, darling. The world moves in mysterious ways. Ours more than most. Now don't you be troubling yourself, let me do the worrying – those boys want to see a lot of things out there, but concern isn't one of them."

So this is how I became Miss Jemima's star attraction. Before long there were more elaborate routines. Longer set pieces when I begged for extra time. Eve and I were occasionally brought onto stage as a double act. Two halves of a whole, slipping in and out of one another like Russian dolls. This gets the boys the most excited. It also proves the biggest challenge when it comes to Eve keeping a straight face. For all her talent beneath the spotlight on many an evening she would be scolded by Miss Jemima for her blooming smirk or her shaking shoulders as she ineffectively concealed a fit of giggles. I felt the same, though new girl nerves kept all traces of amusement hidden beneath an iciness, which I allowed to soften as I became more accomplished.

The first night Eve danced alone I was sat at the bar watching. A bottle of champagne and a crystal flute appeared and a shadow grew over and around me. "Hello," I said as Kingpin stepped to the seat in front of me.

"A welcome gift," he said, in a voice as deep and rich as the scent that seeped from his suit.

"Thank you kindly," I said, pouring myself a glass. "Won't you join me for a drink?"

He looked to the bottle. "I have business needs taking care of. Just wanted to welcome you to the club. I have an interest in all that goes on here."

"So I've heard."

"I like to meet the new arrivals one on one. Instinct's a valuable tool in my industry. Some of the girls, they traipse in trouble like dog shit and it's up to me to clean it up. You won't cause me such anguish, I can only hope."

"Not if I can help it. Why don't you sit down?"

"I'm a busy man."

"Powerful too, or so I'm told."

He smiles and straightens his back and seems to grow an extra inch. Across the bar, Peter leant against his carer for the night, a crutch held him steady beneath his one arm and carried the weight where his right leg used to be, from which I could only assume that repayment was an ongoing narrative.

"You don't want to believe everything you hear. Some things though, some things are worth bearing in mind."

"Well, " I say eventually, my mouth damp and my nerves whetted by the first flute of champagne. "It was a pleasure to meet you."

He took my hand and kissed it once. "And you," he said. And with that he was gone. All that remained was the chill that clung to my skin like old bathwater for the remainder of the evening.

And so this became my life. Days at the coffee shop, nights at The Iguana Den. Nothing but passing strangers that had disappeared before I so much as caught a second glance. Eve quickly became my only constant, as well as you, of course. That said, with all the sudden activity I allowed my letters to become more vague and varied, through shame, and also through sheer exhaustion. I don't remember sleep featuring too heavily in the months that led me to this grim motel existence. For my deceit and carelessness all I can do is apologise.

And, now, to beg. I fear for you almost as much as I fear for myself Jonah. More, perhaps. Were something dreadful to happen to me - for the horrors of the past few weeks to reach their gory conclusion - I would be as upset as one could be about their own death. Were I forced to live a life without you... well, I'm not entirely sure I could cope. The argument could go, I suppose, that due to the nature of our relationship whether you're outside or inside those barred walls makes little difference. And at first this may have been true (if anything, and this is a longstanding secret which I hope you won't judge me on, I somewhat relished knowing what a vital force I was in your existence during those formative months of our exchanges. That I was, through circumstance alone, as fundamental to you as you were to me) but now your liberation gives me as much joy as the words you send me. That you have become more yourself over the past few months pleases me in ways I can't put into words, and so shall spare you any such attempts.

When I first wrote to you I had taken so many sharp turns in my life that I was as lost as a person can be. Every relationship seemed to turn to dust, each new town, each minor job seemed to blend into the same beige stretch as the one before until all I could do was sit and cry.

So I packed up. I took a ride out and I rented the most inconspicuous space I could find in the form of the trailer I came to hold so dear. On the way I stopped at a gas station to fill up.

Inside I bought a packet of cigarettes, a bumper packet of aspirin, and a quart of vodka as well as the local rag as to not arouse suspicion (my theory being that only a person very much intent on living would seek knowledge of the day's events... though in hindsight how long their vim would last on processing said events is anyone's guess).

I am not telling you this to garner sympathy, nor to massage your ego. It is simply the truth. Even at the time I felt it no great tragedy. I'd had my fun with life, you see, enjoyed it in my own small way. I had left no worthy mark, experienced neither searing bliss nor crushing agony. I was prepared to discard it the way a child might a toy it has outgrown; with minimal fuss, simply moving on to whatever came next.

And so with my ammunition and a few dollars, I happened upon my trailer, which I moved into within the hour. I sat neatly, fussing over cushions and polishing scuffs in the tabletops until they gleamed. Then, feeling frugal, I decided to at least get my money's worth from the last newspaper along with a cool glass of vodka before embarking upon my final binge.

So I opened the paper and sipped at the petrol fumes of the cheap vodka. A small child had been reacquainted with his dog after two years of pining. A car dealership was entering receivership and two warehouses had been burnt to the ground in the run up, leading policemen to suspect foul play. Two robberies, three births and the death of an old athlete who hadn't made that much of an impression whilst in his prime were tacked together in the central section amidst notices for flower arranging courses and pets for sale.

And then there was you.

Or, to be precise, the advert for the pen-pal scheme.

So I started writing. I wrote and I wrote until I'd exhausted each scrap of paper I could find in my purse. My pen ran dry. Do you remember how messy my writing was towards the end? How my final paragraph was on the waxed innards of a candy wrapper? This is why. It was all I had. I walked to the front desk and asked them to post my letter and, returning home, drained the vodka and awoke nearly twenty-four hours later.

I still have the aspirin, incidentally, they're collected with the rest of you.

So this is it, Jonah. I still can't tell you why I wrote. Perhaps subconsciously I had hoped that in the inevitable interim between posting and receiving any sort of response I might re-evaluate my flippancy towards my own mortality. Perhaps you simply caught me at my weakest. Perhaps I just wanted to speak with someone whose life had been lived, wrongly yes, but undoubtedly on their own terms. I doubt it though. All I can say is that for some reason I wrote, and for some reason you answered. You, Jonah, only you. And since then everything seems to make perfect sense.

Please don't meet those men, Jonah. For me.

Back at the cafe Ida was far from blind to my now constant lethargy.

"Girl, you're burning that candle at every end and then some. You aint no whippersnapper no more, if you don't mind me saying."

"I'm doing just fine. Tired is all."

"Hmmm… "

The situation was little helped by Eve's presence. "Say, Ida, you got yourself a gentleman friend at present?"

"No, miss. I have not. I am married to the Lord and find it taxing enough," she'd say, burying herself deep in tasks which required minimum effort at the best of times.

"Must get awfully lonely at nights though, what with the many wives the Lord has to tend to," Eve would persist, pouring avalanches of sugar into the coffee I'd sneak her for free.

"I can bear a lot in this life young miss, but blasphemy is where I draw the line," Ida would say, growing redder and redder.

"Oh Ida I didn't mean to cause offense, to you or the good Lord. I was just thinking out loud."

"Loud's right. Thinking I'm not so sure of."

Eve would desist momentarily as she wiped her grin with a napkin, "Ida, what does the Lord think of dancing girls?"

At this Ida would mutter a testament passage and remove herself to scrape the fryers or count change, jobs she usually resented with all of her heart yet seemed to favour over Eve's flippant manner.

"She loves it though!" Eve would protest on the days I became uncomfortable with Ida's growing unease. "Bet it's the most fun she's had in years."

"It's her way and that's that. Just because it's different to you doesn't make it wrong. Just let her be. Show the lady some respect, she was here before either of us."

"Poor bastard," Eve said, swivelling on her seat to steal a glimpse at the sparse clientele. "Before us, this town was nothing but dust and shadows. We make it what it is, Verity, and high time we got some credit if you ask me."

It was on the hottest day of the year that I saw J for the second time. It had been the quietest, too. Even after lunch Ida had cashed up barely a hundred dollars, and most of that was in tips.

"Well I'll be, you're as easy to pin down as the blue rose," he said as I made my way to the patch of counter he had claimed as his own.

"Good to see you again. And dapper as always. Why on earth aren't you betrothed to a smart city girl I'll never know."

J tipped his hat and glanced at the menu. "Don't like pie," he said eventually. "I could never devote myself to a girl who ate less than I did. I'll take the bilberry and a coffee if it's not too much to ask."

"I'll see what I can do."

We chatted aimlessly for a while, filling in the silences more than anything else. I pushed myself further and further towards the counter, pressing towards him - so desperate to touch - like a schoolgirl inching closer to the television set as her pinup strums his guitar. I wanted to know him inside out, I wanted him for myself. Part of this was his mystery, and what a mystery, Jonah! J gave himself away in scraps, in torn pages with missing dialogue. Even minus any ulterior motives I suspect this has always been his manner.

"I still don't get what you're doing about here, save making the most of our delicious facilities. This town aint exactly a thriving hotbed as I'm sure you've deduced."

He wipes a thin stream of fruit syrup from the corner of his mouth and pushes his plate away from him, informing me that my services are required. I take the plate and leave it on the counter beneath me. The washing can wait. I am audience and performance all at once, and I plan on making every second count. "Something was taken from me. Something real special."

"That's established," I say.

He pauses and checks his inner pocket for an item I cannot quite make out. He looks around and notices that the cafe is all but empty save the two of us. "My Daddy was a rich man. Only he got himself into some, shall we say, difficult situations. Situations that started with his heart and ended with his wallet."

"Some mean old girl stole from your Daddy?" I asked, feigning concern. In my fantasy he was immune to matters as lowly as money or status. We were to be free and liberal, sustained by only nature and one another. I felt part of my dream evaporate as he went on, though not enough to break my infatuation entirely.

"You could say that. Whatever the case I intend to get back what's mine."

"And you think that girl's here?" I ask, topping up his coffee whether he wants it or not.

"I followed a smell, led me right to this town."

"How intriguing."

After that his visits became more frequent. I'd spend half the time I should have spent sleeping readying myself for the shift at the coffee shop, determined to look my best and disguise any traces of fatigue caused by my questionable moonlighting. J seemed to have a sixth sense as to when we might be alone, and before long these interludes became the highlight of my days.

"Sunny side up, sugar?"

"You know me. God damn it Valerie," he says after a long and pregnant pause. "I just want what's mine. I got a family to feed," one tear shrivels back into the reptilian slit where his eye should be. I tilt my head understandingly. "There was a time we could have ordered this whole damn state for breakfast and still had change for lunch."

"It's a funny waltz the Lord has us dancing," I say as I pass a cloth over the crystallised sugar on the Formica at which he sits. "And that's a lesson you only get to learn the hard way. The only thing you can know in this life is yourself. And even that's on shaky ground."

He smiles and it nearly kills him.

Unknown to me this is no longer an amiable encounter. There is darkness beneath those wet waffles and dry eggs. And in hindsight that really was a gun in his pocket. He was never that pleased to see me. One bullet has a name etched into its chrome base. But which one?

"... and she hit the ground running the second the cheque cleared. It's enough to make a man sick... " Every day the same conversation. Always different. But always the same. " ... it's not about the money. It's my pride that's hurt. I was raised a man of principle and I intend to die that way too... "

Even at this stage in our relationship I have to stop myself from laughing.

"You know," he says one afternoon, for reasons known only to him. "I remember when we were kids, and he'd take us out to the park, we were happy then. He was a real good Dad. Real good. But when he sold the company, that's when he changed. When he started taking in those cheap girls like dogs without collars... "

This is a lie. He does not remember this. For whilst it may well have happened these are not the things you remember. These are photographs taken, around which you build a story. Edit. Redraft. Tint. These events drop from your memory like pennies in a handful of notes. The things you remember are those that change you, the encounters that leave scars. The man in Chicago who said I love you only when you had your back to him. The husband who went out for milk and cigarettes six years ago. The smell of your father's cologne still clinging to your skin as the police car pulls onto the drive. These are the things that make you; that you remember and that are true. The rest is just fiction, or some variation of.

"Tell me something, Veronica," he says one lazy day over a scant feast of dry toast and black coffee. A jukebox changes its track. I lean back on the cash register and flex the arches of my feet. "How come you always answer to a different name?"

"What's that, honey?" I say, picking an imaginary ball of fluff from my apron.

"I must have been coming to this diner every day for two weeks now and you never once corrected me when I got your name wrong. I do it on purpose now, see if I can't catch you out."

"Because between eleven and four I'm whatever you want me to be, so long as it's upright and behind this counter."

He laughs to himself, standing up. "God damn Verity, you can't know anyone in this life can you?"

"Amen to that, honey," I say with a smile. A careful smile. Not too certain. Not too sad. A perfect smile. A novel of a smile.

"So," he says, now heading to the exit. "That's my story, what about yours?"

I do everything in my power to stop myself from blushing. "What's that?"

"You know all about me."

"I know what you tell me."

"Clever girl. How about we go out one night, under less... commercial circumstances? We can get to know one another properly."

"I'd like that a lot. Only night time's tricky for me."

"A dark horse?"

"Something like that."

"I bet you've got the boys lining up round the block," he says, now out of the door.

"More braying mob than orderly line."

He chuckles and lets the weight of the door press against his mighty chest. "Well you just rearrange some dates and find a night for you and me. I could do with a friend in this town. And you may well be a valuable girl to know."

"I'll see what I can do. But like I said, I'm a busy woman."

He shakes his head and looks to the floor, and I can tell that he enjoys how difficult I am making the whole situation for him. "Until next time," he says quietly, with his back to me, as the door closes behind him.

He doesn't leave a tip.

"What's that you got there?" I ask back at the trailer. Eve is crouched on the floor at the side of the bed, studiously rifling through her suitcase. I walk towards her to try to get a better look.

"Nothing. Just some of my things," she says, slamming the

lid and throwing the case deep beneath the bed. "Well, well, well Verity you're positively glowing. You look like a satisfied woman if ever I saw one." I kick off my shoes and swoon onto the bed. Eve sits beside me and begins braiding my hair. "Don't tell me it's love?"

"No!" I yell, turning onto my back to stare up at her, fully aware that were our roles reversed Eve and her poor Labrador heart would very much consider what J and I have to be some version of love.

"Well then?"

"Like," I say, finding myself suddenly embarrassed. "Like... with a boy from the coffee shop. He wants to take me on a date."

"VERITY!" she yells, standing up on the bed and running to the drawers at the farthest corner of the room. There is the sound of a mess being created, clothes being upturned, something knocking against wood, and then Eve skips back towards the bed carrying a half empty bottle of scotch and a full packet of cigarettes. "Who? When? I want to know all."

"Don't know yet. He wants to take me out one night."

"And... "

"And night time's too profitable to be squandering on lust."

"Lust?"

"You know what I mean!"

"Love's worth any price," says Eve, glugging her first sip of scotch.

"Rent's not though. Which reminds me... "

Eve gives me an old fashioned look and pushes her hands into the back pocket of her jeans. "There," she says, handing me a fistful of crumpled fifty dollar bills. "Consider it paid. Now, you and I aren't moving until this bottle's empty and I've been given every last detail of this handsome stranger that's given you a blush. But first - " she said, leaning over the bed and pulling a package from the floor, " - this arrived for you this morning."

I tore open the package - tiny, magnolia, bound with red ribbon - and pulled out a small printed card, which read, simply:

*Sometimes it takes more than the bottle. Let it not be said girls like us aren't prepared. With love.*

At the base of the envelope, still swaying with the weight of its package, was a tiny pewter pistol, heavy with bullets.

All my love,
Verity

Dearest Verity,

The days leading up to my meeting with Michael seemed to pass in spurts; dreamy stretches of the most basic undertakings during which I found myself silent and distant, followed by long periods of contemplation as an acidity swamped my stomach until all I could do was lie, sleepless and anxious, watching the moments pass by until our arranged reunion.

"The coffin dodger been sniffing around my girl again," said Harlow as we walked back from work. "She says she's giving thought to moving in with him. Said he has a spare room. Odd jobs need doing around the house and the like. I have a fine idea as to the sort of jobs he needs doing, and it's no work a lady should be receiving payment for if you catch my drift."

I muttered a nonsensical noise, if only to prove I was listening. In truth I couldn't bring myself to care.

"Says she thinks is could be true love. God help the girl, she's as clueless as I don' know what. Just worry where it's leading is all. Those scars on her arms weren't no household accident if you catch my drift."

"I guess I could talk to her... " I said, scanning the horizon blankly.

"You okay boy? Been on a different plane best part of this week. Hope two jobs isn't causing you bellyache."

"No sir, not the jobs. I'm just distracted."

"You can say that again. I don't think your brain and your mouth's been in the same room since weekend gone."

"Sorry."

"You don't need to apologise, not to me." Harlow began shifting his weight awkwardly as he walked. His face, usually kind and welcoming, became a kaleidoscope of sharp folds and angry reds. "Hope you don't mind me suggesting as much... " he said slowly, as if treading on cracked paving. "But would I be right in thinking you've not always lived such a righteous life?"

"Excuse me?" I said, still not entirely engaged.

"What I mean to say is... God damn boy you are somewhere else today. What I'm trying to say, Jonah, is am I right in thinking you've served time?"

My thoughts snapped to the present like whiplash and I felt my knees weaken beneath me.

"Now now," said Harlow, patting me on the back. "I'm not here to judge. Far as I'm concerned whatever went on, you served your time, this is a clean slate you're working from. With me at least."

I carried on walking, my head hung and shamed.

"All I meant was that I assume in such instances you make contacts. Acquaintances and such, of likeminded persuasion."

"I tended to keep my head down."

"Well knock me down with a feather boy you sure know how to surprise me," Harlow laughed to himself. "What I'm asking, I suppose - " he said, shiftily checking to see that the workers' frogmarch was dispersed enough to allow at least basic privacy between us, " - is whether or not you'd know of anyone who might... I don't know... voice my displeasure to a certain gentleman about the company he's keeping... should the situation ever arise."

I caught his drift and dismissed it in case it was a trap. "Why don't you just try talking to him?"

"If you say so. I'm not a violent man Jonah. Never have been never will be. But I'd give my life for those girls. I'd certainly give my freedom if it meant keeping them safe."

"It won't come to that. He seems a reasonable enough old man. Besides, at his age he's working on borrowed time as is. I doubt you'll have a care in the world come winter."

"Let's pray you're right," said Harlow. "Let's pray you're right."

I met Michael when he was sixteen-years-old. Already by that point his face was beginning to crack and break into the bloom of adulthood – his jaw line becoming defined where previously it hung loose and gormless, his eyes deepening into their sockets, his forehead only just learning the art of worrying. Though still he was little more than the bare foundations of himself. Enthusiastic, certainly, and as excitable as he is now, only with the benefit of youth, which diluted the menace his impulsiveness now seems to imply. At first his manner bemused me and postponed our inevitable friendship for quite some time. Of course before long I came to find it endearing. We were so different, he and I. Michael was excitable, enthusiastic, erratic. I was reserved, suspicious, demure. He was just so damn happy all the time, no matter how hellish his past or how dire his actions; throughout it all happiness spread like veins through cheese until you couldn't help warming to him. I suppose to me that's the main difference between people, the universal which fundamentally separates them. Some people are predisposed to happiness. It is their default setting. The walk through life with a sense of wonderment; each new experience an opportunity for joy, for fulfilment. Others live in a state of constant anxiety and uncertainty; they tread more carefully, as though being forced to live life carrying a priceless and delicate vase that belongs to someone else. They, too, have the ability to feel happiness - they have a capacity for it - but it must be presented to them through some external source; they must be shown something, provided with something, which they then consider and, if lucky, decide to allow themselves to enjoy. I suppose the difference between people is whether they are a dog or a cat. Whether they jump through life wagging their tails until given reason not to, or whether they stalk life's perimeters, shunning and shying from others and themselves until provided with an enjoyable and fleeting excursion from their usual state of mild depression. I myself am of a feline persuasion. Michael an eternal Labrador.

'Boy's a liability,' said Jack to me the day he became part of our circle. 'Only reason I let him hang around is he's crazy as I don't know what. Like some damn kamikaze pilot or some shit; there's nothing that boy won't do.'

Jack was a large man with few morals and a steady aim. He had grown into his own legend almost tacitly, riding the crest of his lineage without ever actually proving his worth as any sort of mastermind. His family's dealings within the town I had arrived at were legendary and longstanding. He sat atop a heritage of blood and mug shots, and was considered the most volatile of the bunch; his prominence a result of a mass court case two years previous which had culminated in just about every male relative's temporary incarceration.

Of course by the time I arrived on the scene Jack and his kin had taken a backseat when it came to direct involvement in any of our jobs, and so he became the pied piper of fallen angels; taking in us lost boys and training us in ways of speedy acquisitions. We were initiated as couriers. Unmarked packages were to be exchanged for cash in alleyways, toilet cubicles, backseats, and bars. Our cut was paltry but enough to survive on. If we proved our worth, or indeed survived unscathed, eventually we would rise through the ranks. We'd graduate to driver, lookout, fall boy, red herring. And then, how proud, we'd become armed.

After this our involvement became vital and our egos massaged to the point where we'd fly so close to the sun our wings could melt clean off and we wouldn't even notice. Jack would arrange the jobs, mark maps and plans. Each of us a coloured pinpoint on a shoddily drawn diagram. There were stores, bars, houses and the like. Nothing sacred, everything gained. Like most of the boys working with us I had little to lose, only difference was I didn't care about myself, and so I soon became Jack's favourite ammunition; fine china removed from its shelf for only the haughtiest of occasions.

Michael entered our upper echelons almost two years later. By this point I must have been circling twenty-one and he was barely scraping adulthood. We'd served one or two jobs together, as part of a group, sometimes individually. Nothing spectacular. We'd pull down our hoods and change into shapes, into fear, into memories that would cloud each life we touched forever, brandishing guns, sneaking through shadows, always leaving heavier than when we arrived.

It was a cold night in November when everything changed.

The Mayhills' farm was a rumoured goldmine. Mr Mayhill was a wealthy man whose land was for entertainment value only. He'd made his fortune through crops and now tended to plants for he knew no different. Mostly they went to charities, occasionally he would sell them when the mood took him, but on the whole his wealth was established and everything else was just cream.

They were to be an easy and profitable target, and like most things where Jack was concerned they had been carefully selected as if winners of some bastardised lottery. Their lure was that along with their fortune they were but two generations removed from the Amish way of life, yet their sensibilities remained steadfast. Everyone knew Mr Mayhill seldom troubled the bank. Whatever he had was in that house, and according to Jack it was enough to retire from several times over.

We drove three miles out and carried our tools as close to the house as we could get without leaving the mask of the hedgerows that hid us so perfectly. Myself, Michael, Herman and Pete sat and watched as one by one the house lights grew fewer, until we were staring at a black shape in a black night.

As we arranged ourselves into our established formation, Pete strolled to the side of the house, slicing two wires with a hunting knife causing the porch light to buzz loudly once, and then fall dark. We entered the cellar door, which opened so easily our elaborate tools seemed ostentatious, as though we'd arrived at a child's party in tuxedos. The basement was a basic games room – table tennis, billiards table, a broken old television holding a coat hanger aerial in the crown of its head, and a bar, which on further inspection, Michael declared 'drier than a nun's cunt'.

We walked in uniform up the stairs towards the ground floor of the house. The rooms were cavernous and utilitarian even in the dark. From the hallway we dispersed, each taking a different room. I found a locked door, which I would later find out in court was Mr Mayhill's study, and the source of all that we sought. Herman continued in the living room, tapping floorboards and checking for submerged handles behind the iconography that hung on each wall. Across the hallway Pete took each key from the rack in the kitchen on the off chance they may be of use. Michael stood in an open doorway silently. I saw him enter the room without warning. Curious as to his unlikely restraint I followed him through the door, which had closed silently behind him.

"Found me some treasure of my own," he said, staring at a small cot in which a girl of no more than ten lay, pristine and oblivious. He made his way towards the edge of the bed and was stopped by my hand, which gripped his shoulder so tight I thought I felt it crack beneath the pressure.

"Oh come on Jonah," he hissed. "Can't a guy have a little fun around here? Call it a reward... candy for the boys."

I gripped his shoulder tighter still and he grimaced in pain, his body jerking for release.

"Alright," he said eventually. "But we already given away our reservations with St Peter. Don't see what difference it makes."

I was careful to shut the door behind me as we exited the room.

The cavalry had regrouped in the living room whispering plans when we heard the first shot. Mr Mayhill must have been silent as an assassin as he descended the stairs. The bullet streaked past Pete, taking his ear clean off, and jammed itself into the wall behind my head. Pete fell to the floor. Michael yelped and fumbled for his gun. Mr Mayhill remained stoic in the doorway, his shotgun glinting in the stolen light of the living room. There were more gunshots. The doorway where his daughter slept opened and then shut again. Michael rushed towards him and tried to wrestle the gun from his arm as Herman bent down to check on Pete's injuries and relieve him of his surplus weapons.

"Woah, Tiger that's some kit you got there!" yelled Michael, holding the neck of the shotgun as Mr Mayhill struggled in the doorway.

Another bullet flew past me and caused a draft of cold air to blow over the proceedings as a window pane shattered to the ground. Herman stood up and then fell again at the sound of the third bullet, slumping over Peter like a winter blanket.

I ducked behind the couch and pulled my pistol from my pocket, firing blindly into the air. Shrapnel and glass showered me as ornaments erupted into fragments that snagged on the skin of my face. The white innards of the sofa began protruding like boils as something else hit the floor, and then silence.

I stood up slowly, my gun still poised. In the doorway Michael lay groaning on the floor, his face halved and weeping blood. Mr Mayhill pointed the gun at me. In the seconds that followed I noticed that from my stomach a trail of blood ran steadily to the floor as though I were a burst pipe. Then, without words, one final shot rang out.

Mr Mayhill hit the ground still clutching his shotgun, as peaceful as he'd ever be.

I felt myself fall to the floor, grasping desperately at my exposed entrails with one hand as though trying to retain each diminishing ounce of myself. My hands soaked and my head became light.

My final conscious act was the one that still haunts me to this day, and one that save the only other survivor of that doomed night you alone are privy to. God help me Verity, I crawled over to where Pete and Herman lay and with some difficulty swapped my gun with Herman's, doing my best to wipe the streaks of blood and fingerprints from both handles.

I woke two days later, handcuffed to a hospital bed.


So this is how I know Michael. And now, as well as yourself, he remains the only person who knows the true extent of my cowardice, and the sheer scope of my own wickedness.

Of course I was not without blame, even within the manipulated evidence I had created. And if, when barely out of your teens you are shot, you are forever held as a boy, though if at the same age it is you found holding the pistol you are deemed a man and tried as such. So for the sake of a few days, I, a grown man, was tried in what became one of the most prominent crimes of the decade.

Luckily I was able to rise from the ashes of my own misdemeanours. The crime itself became further reaching than even I could have contemplated. Jack's family circle was disbanded and the extent of their wrongdoings examined forensically, until just about every member of his family was held behind bars. The newspapers ran pieces on the dark heart of America, of the world us boys inhabited. And then the magazines latched on. We became symptoms, metaphors, the dark heart of the American Dream. Press coverage grew like tumours until more ink and paper was spent on us than any movie star in the world. The highest lawyers were flown in, fuelled by prestige and publicity which - we were told repeatedly - was worth tenfold their waived salaries. Suddenly both Michael and I found ourselves at the centre of an ugly drama in which the death of two broken boys and one innocent man took a backseat to a national debate on the nature of guilt. It seemed that the whole world became a philosopher during the months of that trial; every moron with access to a pencil had their own idea as to who was to blame, and bar the odd exception it was seldom those with hands of red. We were the media; we were our parents, our upbringings, our incomes, our area codes, our blood types, our diets... just about every single contributing factor was aimed squarely at us like shields, until we became shrouded and immune to the glint of the limelight; surplus to our own carnage.

It was odd, I can tell you, reading back over my life as I awaited my fate. Odd when they'd got things just wrong - my age, say, when my mother was killed, or the year I finally left school for good. Odder still when they got things right that only I could have known.

As someone who'd never even seen his own birth certificate, let alone a payslip or a bank statement, it was as if for the first time in my life I had proof of myself; like I had been written into existence by excitable strangers. I can't say that a part of me didn't enjoy the attention. Either way I felt like suddenly I had been invented by the whole country that seemed to have a better idea of me than I did. The inevitable upshot being that by the time our stories had been stretched and woven on the media's loom our sentences were lowered to just twenty years apiece.

Herman was nineteen when he died. Pete twenty-two. Mr Mayhill a grown man of forty-five; nothing if not halfway what he deserved. I can't say I'm proud of what I did, but then again I can't say I don't feel as though I've more than paid my dues.

On Friday morning, unable to sleep, I took coffee alone in the cafe amidst the nightshift workers who chewed the fat before returning, soiled and exhausted, to their daylight beds. Halfway through my second cup Mary was readying herself for the start of her shift as the lights inside became nullified by the rising sun. A man in overalls went to pay his bill and left a five-dollar note on the counter.

"I'll double it for your phone number, precious," he said, the 's' of precious catching on his chipped front teeth.

"You could triple it and add six zeroes and you'd still be no closer to my specifics. Now if that's all I can do for you... " she scowled, placing the money into a communal tip jar as her paramour left, face red and ego bruised.

Mary's indignation towards the male gaze was now silently respected by almost all who frequented the diner. The lonely truckers who politely requested a private dining experience were met with a steely dismissal, and one morning not long after I'd moved here I was served coffee in a cup dotted with blackened fingerprints. I stared at Mary quizzically - like recognising like, though she was not to realise this - and she shrugged as if to say 'it was all I could do'. Eventually when we were alone she began talking. Turned out a gentleman on her bus ride home had allowed his hands to wander suggestively against the nylon of her overalls. After her polite request for him to desist went unnoticed, she had taken a fork from her handbag with which she ate the same lunch every day (cottage cheese and pineapple, with a single wheat cracker) and tore four skid-marks of skin from his forehead to his chin. Thankfully the gentleman turned out to be a prolific and still-at-large sexual predator, and so the charges of attempted murder were dropped. But, as Mary told me proudly:

"My Daddy was a hunter and his Daddy before him. I could pick a bird clean off a power line with nothing but a fork and my steady aim. If I'd attempted to kill him he'd be dead."

"You sure got a fine line in letting a guy down," I said as she poured herself a small cup of coffee, which she took black and gulped hungrily.

"You could drop most of these log-heads from a high-rise and they'd still climb up and try again, dumb sonsofbitches. Say, you're an early riser today, honey," she said, topping up my cup. "Though we don't see all that much of you these days. Got yourself a little lady?"

"No ma'am, grafting like an honest man. Got myself not one but two sources of income."

"Well you don't do things by half, huh? We miss you around here. Don't give us no hassle. Not like some."

"I'll try to make the effort," I said, before remembering my promise to Harlow.

"Levi?" she said, surprised that I had asked, "Oh he's a card alright. Hasn't been in as much these days. I guess it's getting too much for him, what with his age and all. Last week he forgot his little notebook. I made sure it was returned. Boy, I tell you, it was something to stop myself from reading it. I think more than anything I just didn't want to ruin the surprise."

"So he's harmless enough?"

"As the next man who needs a stick make it to the restroom. Though you'd be wrong in thinking he's as dumb as he acts. The man's a copper bottom genius, has the money to prove it too. They say he has over three million dollars in paintings alone. 'The bard of small town America' that lady from the magazine called him when she came round sniffing. Funny that a place where nothing happens can get people so damn excited. Suppose there's a lot to be said for recognising your own. He writes the little people so well you see, that way everyone understands."

"I heard he was a writer."

"You heard? You mean you haven't read it?"

"Read what?"

"Oh you must! He wrote us all so beautifully. We're all in there. The coffee shop, Main Street, the town fair. Of course he changed it all just so, you know, I daresay he wasn't so keen on the town taking him to court... or running him out with pitchforks for that matter. Some of the stories he made up... " she laughed. "Phewey, he's got him an imagination. Had the sheriff shoot a man and bury the body. Have you ever!"

"Can't say I've come across his work."

"Oh he doesn't write as himself. Uses a... what's the word?"

"Pseudonym?"

"Penname. That's it. Here, I'll write it down, you can check him out next time you make it to the library. That is if you still do, now you're a corporate big shot and all." She scribbled a name on a napkin and handed it to me. "You really should read the books. He wrote us all so beautifully. Especially you."

"He wrote me?"

"Well, here and there. There's always a stranger, always handsome, always full up with secrets... always gets the girl in the end too, even when he don't deserve her, which he usually doesn't."

"Doesn't sound like my sort of thing."

"Oh but it would be. How can you not? Don't you at least want to know how it ends?"

"I've survived this long without his clairvoyance. Can't say I've suffered as a result."

"You know you are like him. The character I mean. Boy has he got you good."

"What's he like though, character wise?"

"You?"

"Levi."

"Oh, an old fool. Hasn't spent a penny he doesn't need to. Wouldn't tell by looking at him the man was worth more than the rest of this town put together. Has an eye for the ladies too... I say ladies, some of them are barely much more than girls. And don't they just eat up his promises! Sweet really. Why do you ask darling?"

"No reason," I said, and paid my bill.

I arrived half an hour early to meet Michael, partly through nerves, and partly due to an eagerness to claim the shadiest booth available in the entire bar. As is turned out the latter was overkill, the bar was empty save for the serving staff, yet still I felt the need to locate the darkest table in the room.

One hour and three beers later Michael entered, his shadowy associate trailing behind.

"Well aint this quaint," he said, taking a seat.

I nodded.

"So Jonah, now that the shock's worn off, how's life?"

"Quiet. I keep myself to myself."

"Not much changed there then. This boy... " he said to Ed, "... this boy quieter than a praying monk. You never seen cash handed over as quick. Never so much as raised his gun. Silent but deadly, huh pal?"

A waitress in tight blue jeans passed the table and Michael extended his arm to block her path.

"Two more beers when you're ready, darling."

"Sure thing," she said, making her way back to the bar.

"So Jonah, what's your line of work?"

I told Michael first about the sideline with Caleb, and then moved onto the details of my main source of income, carefully omitting the names of any allegiances I had managed to make over the previous months.

"Well I'll be!" he yelled as the waitress placed the drinks on the table. "You're part of local folklore. I been in this town nearly three weeks and it's all anyone seems to want to talk about. They say that money's ill-gotten gains. Though we'd hardly be in a position to judge now would we buddy?"

Michael slapped Ed on the back to little avail.

"Don't ask don't tell. I do an honest day's work and to my mind I get paid an honest day's wage. Whatever goes on behind the scenes don't matter to me. It's as if it doesn't exist."

"Well that is one mighty philosophy you got there my friend. So, how much you earn?"

"Enough to get by."

"Putting some money away?"

"A little."

This is a lie. Having survived for so long on next to nothing I am now perturbed as to what exactly I am supposed to do with excess income, and as such the majority of my salary now goes into a savings jar which I store beneath the loosest floorboard in my bedroom.

"So you're no good for a loan, huh?"

"Not unless it's for a down payment on a coffee. Even then I'd be needing interest."

At this Ed made a brief exhalation, which I took to be an embryonic laugh.

"How many people working on that site there Jonah?"

"Nearing sixty."

"And they pay you cash?"

"So far."

"Well that's a lot of dirty money passing hands," said Michael. "A lot of dirty money."

"You working?"

"Not as yet. We have ourselves one or two avenues we're looking to explore though."

"Where you based?"

111

"Wherever I lay my hat as the saying goes. This is a nice town Jonah, plenty of opportunities it would appear."

"Don't be fooled. Took me best part of a year to find a job and even then I'm being paid to move dirt onto more dirt. And believe me when I say I use the term 'paid' loosely."

"Now now, you're too modest. Besides, I'm sure that between us we'd be able to enterprise, as the saying goes. What do you think?"

"Too busy with what I got, but thanks all the same."

I left little more than half an hour later. Michael's voice rose higher and higher with each passing inch of his glass. He tipped that beer down like it was water until his roving eye became a glass marble in a pop bottle, spinning and twirling in the scorched socket of his face.

"... and then this one time Jonah and I, phewey I don't even like to say it as much what with ladies in earshot and all, we found us some women - well, I say women... "

As he continued with his stories I made an elaborate show of securing my wallet in the vain hope it would indicate my imminent departure, though experience had told me that such subtleties were wasted on Michael.

"Oh now don't be getting all coy Jonah," said Michael, feigning concern. "Ed here's in no position to judge. I'm just messing with you. It's sure nice to have someone to waltz through the past with; especially given every other face must be near enough dust by this point. Say did you ever find out where they buried the boys?"

"Can't say it was a subject I researched. Best leave them in peace. We were different people back then."

"You can say that again."

I made to leave but Michael's hand shot forward and grabbed hold of my arm. Ed inched forward gently and I felt the echoing barrel of a handgun press into the base of my kneecap.

"Just hold your horses there friend," Michael hissed. "You took half my face and all my best years, now you'll show us some civility or things are going to get real ugly in here, you understand? I decide what goes and what doesn't. Way I see it I got a royal flush and you're not even in the game. I'm playing win-win, if you catch my drift, so sit the fuck down."

I did as instructed and Michael removed his arm from mine. The gun remained in place.

"Now why you got to go and upset everyone like that Jonah? We were having us a nice evening. Good company, good conversation. All we wanted to do was chat."

"And we did."

"Nah, we didn't chat. We skimmed the surface. We touched base, if you will. I was hoping we could talk the way we used to."

"Those times are gone."

"Not entirely. God damn Jonah this isn't you. Digging for a living. You got class boy, you got brains. And I... I got balls. Together we could have anything we wanted."

"Didn't work out so well the last time."

"We were boys. The benefit of maturity and so on and so forth. We made mistakes and boy did we learn from them. I bet there isn't one night you don't wake up in cold sweats remembering what you done? Remembering that feeling in your stomach when you got up to see just what a little finger action can do to a room... to a face."

I didn't respond.

"A town like this is just crying out for villains Jonah, and we're the best of the bunch, don't you forget it. No leopard ever changed its spots the way I see you making out like you're some God damn reformed character. We watched you, all sad eyed and slumped shoulders like the wronged gentle giant of the lowlands. It as good as doubled me over laughing Jonah, really it did."

"People change."

"Not for long. The past stays with you whether you like it or not," he pushed himself further across the table, his face protruding like a Bloody Mary emerging from a mirror. "I could remind you the way you did me, if you think it'd make any difference?" At this, with a rested elbow on the table, he lowered his hand towards my face, pointing the tip of a switchblade towards the corner of my eye.

I shook my head and stood up. Ed returned to a more upright position within his seat and looked at Michael as though awaiting instruction. Michael appeared strangely calm, though I could tell that his skin was only just containing the rage that rolled like lava beneath his strange, unreadable surface.

"I'm real sorry for the way things turned out Michael. But you're part of me that doesn't exist anymore, like it or not. I wish you all the best, and I wish things could have been different. But they're not. You see I've nothing of interest to you. Least you can do is leave on good terms."

"Well," he said as I walked towards the bar, my back to him the whole time. "I can't say I'm not let down Jonah. I saw big plans for you and me. Big plans. Still, I might remain within earshot for the time being, in the hope you do change your mind about reinstating our alliance. Opportunities are abundant for two boys like us out there. And if there's one thing I had plenty of practice of it's waiting. It's an art you and I are both black belts in, huh buddy?"

"Goodbye Michael."

"Until next time, friend," he said as I mounted the stairs and left.

I walked home in the dark along with a bottle of scotch that I had purchased at the 24/7 liquor store whose main custom came from swatted barflies still thirsty after closing time. I no longer feared the worst. I knew it was to come. Michael's warning was characteristic and prophetic. I never saw a boy so concentrated on revenge as Michael when he set his mind to it. Soon after we became acquainted he was short-changed in the sort of bar where customer service was not considered paramount. After a brief exchange of short words and minor blows we were expelled from the premises on the end of the owner's foot. Three weeks later Michael noticed said barman queuing at the bank. When they found him his jaw had been ripped so far down he is still, to my knowledge, being fed through a tube. And though never so much as encroached as a subject, the fact remains too that the twin daughters of Michael's second foster family went missing shortly after his seventeenth birthday. Had they ever been found they would be celebrating their thirtieth birthday this year.

I sat and sipped whisky by the side of the road. Main Street was a glowing hum to my left; the suburbs closed and dark behind me. As I drained the life from the bottle two police cars trailed indigo smudges straight past me into the heart of the town centre.

I stood up and made my way home.

With all the love of a heavy heart,
Jonah

Dear Jonah,

Sometimes I forget to wake up at all these days. I always was a heavy sleeper, whereas Eve slept the way stupid people read; skimming the surface, barely touching the bare essentials before declaring herself done and moving onto another, more worthy task. As if by being observed going through the motions she might somehow absorb at least a fraction of its intended purpose. "But, Verity don't you get bored?" she'd say to me, fussing and clanking about the trailer as I pressed my face back into the pillows.

"Don't you ever get tired?" I'd usually try, in an attempt to initiate one of her monologues during which I hoped to nod back off.

"Hell no! Life's too short for rest. There's a whole world out there needs discovering. Besides, I couldn't even if I wanted to. Princess and the pea, that's me. The slightest thing just knocks me for six."

In truth until I had Eve in my life the majority of the time I slept because it seemed to be the only time anything happened of any interest. My imagination would take hold as I sunk into oblivion, and away I'd go. It was my waking hours that appeared lacklustre. I'd attend work, I'd pay my bills, and then nine times out of ten I'd cocoon myself deep within the down and cotton, the springs worrying beneath me as I drifted into the unknown. For the seasoned napper - or the outright narcoleptic, which I sometimes feared I was becoming - to sleep during daylight hours was the greatest luxury of all. Nothing thrilled me more than the artificial chill of a darkened room, and the way that sunlight would peer slyly beneath the black square of closed curtains as if spying on some godless act.

This morning I was woken from such a slumber by a gentle

115

knock at the door to my room. I went to answer and was faced with Rosalita - one of the child maids - holding out a package. "Someone leave this reception, miss. For you." She walked away without further elaboration. I watched her disappear along the corridor and down the old wooden staircase leading to the vending machines and the reception area. I went to open the box that had clearly been tampered with. I suspect many packages don't reach their intended recipients at this particular hotel, so for all I know you could have joined the FBI by now Jonah and I'd be non the wiser. Either way this little gift seemed to have survived the hazing process intact, so I carried it inside.

I placed the box on my bed. Excited, I have to say, that it may have been a keepsake from your good self. Another carving, perhaps, or something equally thoughtful.

Alas, it was not meant to be. On opening the box I was elated. The posies were a dusted pink and the roses not much darker. A tad old fashioned for my liking, but the sentiment remained the same. And their perfume! It shot up and darted about the room like a new kitten. Amidst the damp of the room that fragrance, those colours... it was my first taste of life in weeks.

Only it wasn't life Jonah. Quite the opposite in fact.

I suppose that's always been my trouble. I zoom in, closer and closer, until I like what I see. And at first I did like it. But context maketh the gesture, and I suppose even flowers need context. It was only after a moment of bliss that I realised what exactly I had been sent.

It was a wreath, Jonah. No two ways about it.

I managed to make it to the bathroom before I threw up. Then, true to form, I dug deep within my blankets and went back to sleep.

Back at the cafe J became a more regular fixture. Hovering over uneaten mounds of food until it was just he and I, alone at last. "They work you too hard in here," he'd say as I turned the sign on the door to 'closed' whilst allowing him to sit for as long as he liked.

"Only as hard as I deserve. Besides, I don't mind so much."

"In it for the love of the game, huh?"

"In it for the diversion. Besides, we got one or two regulars who make it all worthwhile."

"Well aren't you on the charm offensive tonight?" he said as I poured him a complimentary coffee and refilled my cup.

"So, what's your story then?" he asked one evening.

On nights like these, when my services were not required at the club, I'd let him sit for hours and hours. He had a sense of loneliness about him. Beneath the staunch veneer which could, by a more callous soul, have been read as ignorant, I thought I sensed a man just crying out for company. And so I'd let him sit and talk. J was a natural talker. Selective, always. But a talker nonetheless. Though I would hate to make these nights sound in any way selfless. I was more than happy to sit there opposite him, taking in that handsome face of his, drinking his half-truths like a hungry dog.

"You know mine by now," he said. "Hell I done nothing but bend your ear since I met you."

"I don't mind. I like it. I know my story, anyway, yours is a lot more interesting."

"Not to me. Truth be told there's not much more I'd like than to get to know you more."

I felt my stomach flutter but forced myself to maintain the icy indifference I had adopted since meeting J. All that hard work was certainly not going to be sacrificed at the altar of one smooth line, that was for sure. "Well I'm an ongoing project."

"Aren't we all?"

"Why don't you help me out with some headers, and I'll see if I can't fill in the blanks?"

J smiled and shifted in his seat as though about to take aim. "Alright. Where did you grow up?"

"Here and there."

"The game only works if you play properly."

"Forces baby. I never lasted more than eighteen months in any one town."

"You ever make it abroad, you know, growing up?"

"No siree, I'm the product of these fair soils."

"Alright. College?"

"See name-badge and swollen ankles," I said drolly.

"Good point."

"Live?"

"Nearby."

"Favourite food?"

"Cigarettes."

"Earliest memory?"

"My father."

"Doing what?"

"The bare minimum."

"Favourite colour?"

"Blue."

"Drink?"

"Scotch. Though only ever after midday."

"Midday?"

"Before midday I'll settle for a beer," I said, breaking a piece of his soggy pie crust in my fingers and pressing it into my mouth.

"Brothers, sisters?"

"Only child."

"Boyfriend?"

Silence.

"Alright then," he said, eating the final piece of pie left on the plate. He offered me a cigarette from his packet and I accepted, bending down towards his cupped hand and sucking in the flame of the match. "I feel like we're nearing even ground now, you and I."

"Glad I could be of assistance."

"So... what else?"

"That's about the size of it," I say, suddenly lightheaded from the cigarette.

"Girl like you must be full of stories."

"One or two."

"You sure like to make a man work for his payment."

"Call it a test of will." Another silence and then, feeling generous, I began. "Alright. Something interesting. How long you been here, exactly?"

"About a month."

"You drive?"

He nodded.

"Ever drive out, past the last buildings, into the desert?"

"Never had reason to. Yet."

"Well if you did you'd find a place... "

"Now I'm gripped."

"A bar, The Iguana Den. You heard people talk about it?"

"Can't say I have."

"Can't say you will either. It tends to attract a, well, let's just say a more discreet type of customer."

"I think we're on the same page."

"Well, would you believe me if I told you I danced there sometimes?"

He looked at me and smiled, lighting a cigarette. I told him everything. Well, almost everything. I told him about finding it by accident, about Eve, about the characters and the customers and the dreamy glow I got from doing what I did. J sat silently, chain smoking and hanging on to my every word. It gave me a kick, to tease him the way I did. At every key detail I'd make sure to hesitate somehow - drag on a cigarette perhaps, or take a sip of the now invisible coffee from my cold cup - and then continue a little after the detail I had omitted, causing him to wince though, ever the gentleman, never correct me or force me to backtrack.

Sweet, I thought at the time, how easily led a lonely man can be.

"Well you are a dark horse. I always knew you had it in you."

"I try my best. You want any more coffee?"

"No thanks, I'm good."

"I hope you don't think I'm a fallen women J. I went into this with my eyes wide open."

"Just like those boys pushing dollars into your garters."

"I wouldn't take to the pole for anything less than twenty."

"A woman of principles."

"So, you any further forward with your quest?"

He cleared his throat and became visibly less comfortable. "I got one or two leads. Why, you want to help me for a cut of the profit?"

"I don't think I'd make such a good detective."

"A spy, maybe?"

"Why's that?"

"Well here you have us thinking you're such a sweet girl when all the time... "

"All the time I'm hawking my flesh for an honest month's rent."

"I wouldn't put it quite like that. You could help though."

"I thought I was helping."

"You are. You are. Man needs a friend no matter how focused he is."

"Well here's to friendship," I said, raising my empty cup.

"To friendship," he said, raising his cup. "Seriously though, you could do some listening for me. Sort of place you're working is exactly the sort of place this girl sets her traps, if you catch me."

"I promise I'll try. How's that?"

"Good enough for me," he stubbed his cigarette out into the saucer we'd been using as ashtray and as he extended his wrist I caught a glimpse of his heavy gold watch.

"Good God! The time!"

We hurriedly ordered the remnants of our night. J threw the contents of the ashtray straight out of the open window as I piled the plates and cups into the sink with an ominous cracking sound. Out back behind the counter I went to take my coat from the hook when I felt two hands on my waist.

"Want me to drive you home?"

I picked up my coat and turned to face him. "I brought my car," I said and watched his face fall. "But that's the only reason. How about you put me on a promise? I'd like to see your quarters sometimes."

"A promise. I like that," he said with a twitching smile.

"You a man of your word?"

He bent down and kissed me hard on the lips. I kissed back, dragging my hands across his face. He must have been freshly groomed that very afternoon, as when I ran my hand through his hair, stray follicles stuck to my skin like iron shavings, as though he were disintegrating before my eyes. "I'll see you around, dark horse," he said with his back to me as he waltzed cockily past through the flapping jaw of the service entrance.

"Not if I see you first," I whispered, though couldn't be certain he heard me.


Back at the trailer, Eve was sitting on the bed mending a hole in her nightgown whilst still wearing it. A cigarette jigged beneath last night's lips as she carefully drew the pin from her skin.

"Morning," I kicked my work shoes across the trailer and flung my bag onto the couch before joining her on the bed.

"Verity, don't tell me you been out all night long and didn't even think to call. I was worried sick. Barely slept a wink."

"Sorry," I said, the thought having never once crossed my mind. In truth it's been so long since I was anyone's responsibility, even their concern, that my regression into cohabitation slipped my mind completely.

"I'm just joking with you. I got no tags on you girly. I couldn't sleep for excitement. I want to know everything."

I lay back on the bed and felt myself immediately start to doze. "Nothing to say."

"Nothing doesn't take all night," she looped and knotted the thread before snapping it with her teeth. Then with the pin safely secured in the fabric of the lampshade lay down beside me. "That same boy?"

"Yeah. J."

"Where'd he take you?"

"Coffee shop."

"He took you to work? Darling you need to find yourself a man with some money. Or at very least one not too shy to rob for the woman he loves. I got me a little black book just full of the type if you're interested."

"It wasn't a date."

"It was something."

"We talked."

"All night?"

"Didn't realise what time it was."

"So you talked... " she said, leaning in and over me, straddling me with her legs.

"Yes."

"That's it?"

"Yes."

"Nothing more?"

"No," I said, pulling a pillow over my face.

"Verity, you aren't telling me something, and instinct tells me it's exactly the sort of details I like hearing the most."

I pulled the pillow from my face and pressed the hair from my eyes. "He kissed me. Said next time we'd spend the night somewhere more comfortable."

"So you didn't even sleep with him?"

"NO!"

"Don't sound so shocked!" Eve said, climbing off me and returning to her side of the bed where she lay, pressing her head against mine. "I think it's a shame, is all. I don't think you can know anyone until you've been to bed with them."

"For all the good it did you," I said lazily, and within seconds a pillow launched lightly across from Eve's side of the bed and hit me in the face. I laughed and so did she.

"That's for besmirching my good name! Besides, it did me plenty good. Meant I got to know they weren't right on day one." She curled her legs up and lay her arm across me. "You tired?"

"Exhausted."

"Me too," said Eve.

And for the first and only time she slipped to sleep before I did.

As I lay there neither asleep nor awake I thought of Eve's sweet way with words and couldn't help but smile. Each person I've ever come close to knowing I've shared a bed with in one way or another, though more often than not in the biblical sense. But where does that leave you and me, I wonder? The ancients said love was a mystical force, completely separate from matters as lowly as those of the flesh. Perhaps that's us Jonah. We transcend the carnal.

Yet there is something to be said for closeness Jonah, and not just of mind but of body too. We could protect one another, of that I am sure. Given my recent downturn and your current predicament I never met two people more ready for a fresh start.

Of course my worst has already happened, though I fear yours is yet to come. You need to take any measures necessary to get rid of those men. I know you don't need to be told as much, but to risk everything you have for some shadow of the past seems ridiculous. You are always in my thoughts, Jonah, even when I don't say as much, and think of just how unlikely it seems that the two of us should now be as lonely as we are, on what feels like separate sides of the world.

So here's what I ask. Let me love you. Let me worry for you. Let me protect you where for all these years you've protected me, which you have Jonah, you keep me safe from sorrow, from self; keep me out of harm just by being there. You're the warm shadow whose outline I conduct myself by. And each time I try to grasp hold I'm held in complete indignation over my apparent gall. But why? You're a free man, so you tell me. Your past crimes were upsetting to read but only because I hold you so dear. And though fey and fallible I am far from dim, and had suspected that such a lengthy incarceration was not the result of some missed tax payment or minor automobile misdemeanour. So please don't let shame inhibit you. I want every part of you, good and bad. I don't wish to make you uncomfortable. It just seems that for some time now we have been moving forwards hand in hand, but towards what? Where exactly do we go with what we have? You're the most important part of my life and I've never so much heard you speak a word. How do you speak? Is your voice light and lyrical as your letters would suggest? Or is your penmanship the exception to the rule? Which side of your face do you prefer? Are your scars as evident as you'd have me believe? Do you allow yourself to smile freely, or try to maintain a sense of propriety where emotions are concerned?

Though only ever a fleeting notion I sometimes fool myself into thinking I don't ever want your reality. That your letters provide me with everything I could ever need. It's the fear Jonah, the chance of having to dispel something I hold in such esteem. But this is a lie. I want proof. I want more and more. I want you all. Perhaps this would be my undoing, and you are accurate once more in your reluctance. Maybe when faced with the old man behind the sheet I will become disillusioned and alone again. But I doubt it. To me it would be a risk worth taking a thousand times over, just for that fraction of a chance that you may in fact be everything I imagine you to be.

Think about it Jonah.

I don't think you could ever disappoint me.

Eve had requested a couple off days off in pursuit of a gentleman who'd caught her at the coffee shop and wooed her relentlessly ever since. This was her preferred line on the subject and to correct her would have been unkind. In truth she'd followed him around town like a stray cat until he tossed her the driest bone of conversation in an attempt to rid himself of the swooning shadow that had cast itself to his routine. Eve's version was that his wit and warmth set the world on fire and she knew the moments their eyes met that he was the one for her. In truth I doubt his input was little more than the most basic of greetings and a one-liner on the weather. Either way it was love once more.

"And I just know he's the fathering type... " she told me for the thousandth time that morning, sitting cross legged on the floor, ironing pleats into her miniskirt in an ongoing bid to appear homely. "I just got to show him I got the sort of eggs he wants to scramble. Do you think I could tell him I got kids already? You know, just to show willing."

"How fast do you want to see him run?" I said, applying lipstick using the back of a CD's reflection.

"He's sure the honourable type, I bet he'd take those children in and raise them as his own."

"Eve?"

"What? Say, will you check on my cookies? I'm going to bump into him on the way to drop them off at the hospice. I bet he'd be swayed by my generous spirit, don't you think?"

"You do realise you haven't actually got any children?"

"I don't know why anyone would say such a cruel thing to a woman."

"The way you talk I sometimes wonder if it's him or you you're trying to kid."

Eve rolled her eyes. "Jealousy is an ugly thing," she said, stepping into the skirt and pulling it up around her waist. "God damn cotton's hotter than summertime in hell. How's my cookies?"

I checked through the glass and turned the gas down three settings. "Five minutes and you're good to go."

"Not quite," she said, pressing her hands between her legs and pulling down her underwear which she flicked onto the laundry pile that now acted as third party in our sleeping arrangement. "There, that ought to do it," she sashayed to the mirror and marvelled at her transformation. "You sure you don't mind picking up my money? I just couldn't bear to risk letting this one getting away."

"It'll be a pleasure," I said, halfway out of the door. "Say, you really want to impress him try telling him you're a virgin. That'll do it for sure."

"Verity, I can steal me some pretend children, but some things can't ever be faked, and believe me when I say that's one of them."

I arrived at the club for our monthly instalment. In the main room Miss Jemima sat in the shade, a lone candle flickering at her table, as she berated a shoal of new looking girls who were becoming more jumbled with each elaborate move.

"Darlings we want them to cheer, not call an ambulance. Ten minute break then back on your marks."

The girls filed out to behind the stage, limping and moaning. Many accusations were levelled at Miss Jemima whilst I was at The Iguana Den. Some said she was a dictator of the worst kind; others hailed her as nothing more than a jumped up Madame. More often than not tales came thick and fast of the innovative ends her husbands had met whilst the cruellest implied that she had been born a man and shifted gradually over time to her body's natural instincts. I'm not saying some of them weren't true (even Chinese Whispers have a nucleus I suppose). Eve, half a bottle down, would often swear blind that they had all been the case at one point or another. Personally I never found her anything but warm and loving to us girls. I suppose I was just privy to her best version.

"How's Eve?" she asked as I took my seat.

"You mean Doris? She's just swell. Off to bump into her latest beau with some homemade cookies."

Miss Jemima swivelled towards me on the hump of her skirts. "You come for your money?"

"I'm doing the rounds. Eve told me to catch hers too, said given the choice between love and money she'd pick love any day of the week."

Miss Jemima reached into a fold of her skirts and pulled out two rolls of notes, bound individually with a bow of red ribbon. "Won't pay the bills though."

"Eve lands on her feet no matter how high she's thrown."

"Like all the best dancers." Miss Jemima pulled back her shoulders as out of nowhere a waiter conjured two glasses of crème de menthe. She picked up her glass and knocked it against mine. "I do hope you girls stay for a while. Life's more interesting since you came along."

"I could say the same about you," I said, taking a tiny drop of the too-sweet liquor, which disappeared in my mouth before I had a chance to swallow.

"More profitable too, you're our star attraction you know. I put in an extra few dollars, to show my gratitude."

"You're too kind."

"Kindness has no place in business. I like to think of it as a shrewd investment."

"Truth be told I'd do it for free now I've got the taste. Which I suppose is the wrong thing to say to an esteemed businesswoman such as yourself?"

Miss Jemima laughed and tipped the glass towards her lips. By the time it hit the table it had shed its green entirely like trees in fall. "We'll make a corporate mistress of you yet."

"Here's to hoping."

"To hoping. You take care. And if there's anything you ever need, just you say."

"I will. Oh and Jemima, what did you mean, sending us that gun?"

She spread her fan and blew three cool drafts across her face. "Ask me no questions and I'll tell you no lies. Be prepared for any eventuality, that's my motto. You girls just make sure you look after one another," she said as her protégées began to flutter back onto the stage.


Back home our front door was closed. This struck me as odd as whilst resigned to life as an eternally single female, and all the fastidious security checks that it entails, Eve was more free spirited on matters of home safety. Lamps would be left on at all times, taps left running. Once I came home to find a smoking blender still spinning a margarita as Eve sprawled on the bed, unconscious and suckling the teat of a tequila bottle. She felt that to shut the door was rude.

'What if someone wants to come by but thinks we're busy?' she'd ask, tacking the door wide open with a piece of g-string elastic.

'They could always try knocking. Besides no-one ever just drops by these days, except Doloris, and then you hide under the bed, so you can cut the Stepford Wives routine.'

'That was once! Besides people don't like to knock. Best this way then everyone's happy.'

Eventually I managed to ease her in principle on the subject. Of course she agreed with me in theory, yet the practice still eluded her despite her promises that she would try her best. Obstinate to the last she still recoiled in horror on the occasions I suggested actually locking the door as we left.


Inside all was quiet save for a rustling in the bedroom, like a groundhog scurrying across dry leaves. "Hello?" I called, on the off chance our visitor held the gift of speech.

The scurrying grew quicker, more hurried. I called again but there was no answer.

"Is anyone in there? I got a gun," I said, my voice bending in the middle as I spoke.

As the rustling grew quieter I slid my feet towards the bedroom door, keen not to alert any intruders with my clod footsteps. With my ear pressed against the door I stopped breathing. The sound had died down, and all that was left was the final reveal.

I flicked the handle and kicked the door with all my might.

It flew open and revealed an empty room. I felt my body relax when a figure burst from behind the door and smashed me onto the floor. I fell backwards with it on top of me and flung my fist into its face.

Eve jerked backwards with a scream and began crawling on her elbows towards the farthest edge of the bedroom. Her eyes held in them a fear so succinct it made me dampen with a feverish sweat. I would see that terrible look once more during our time together.

"Oh... " she said, holding her hand to her face as she relaxed onto the floor. "Verity, you scared me half to death. God damn it I thought my days were over."

"Eve, what the hell are you doing? I thought you were trying to kill me!" I rushed over to her and dragged her to her feet. She crumpled onto the bed, her arms wrapped tight around my waist, as I stroked her hair and examined what, I am slightly pleased to relay, was a rather impressive shiner below her left eye.

"Sorry for scaring you," she said.

"You're the one looks like you've seen a ghost. What were you thinking?"

"I was thinking I got to sort out my problems before they get to be yours too," she started to cry. "You're the best friend I ever had, and I can't even be straight with you."

"What you talking about, Eve?" I said, wiping away the tears with my bloodied fingertips. "There's nothing we can't fix."

"You'd be surprised," she said through gentle sobs. "Look." Eve nodded towards the bathroom door.

I laid her head gently onto the mattress and stood up, again noting how my bones now jarred with each exertion, as though already I was the type of lady who could be rendered incompetent for days after one measly fall. "Nothing going to jump out at me from in there is there?" I said only half joking. Eve shook her head and then buried it into he blankets.

The bathroom was as it should be which in itself seemed suspicious. After such a dramatic build-up I expected a porthole to another dimension, or at very least a maimed corpse to verify my worst fears.

As it was everything was in its place. The sink was caked with eye make-up and the wastebasket overflowing with the red-ends of Q-tips and the dead ends of lipstick. Bottles of scent and suds lined every upright surface and a vanity case sat on the window ledge, open, like the window itself. I was about to turn back to Eve and ask where exactly my attentions should be focused when it caught my eye.

Beneath the window, surrounded by its own halo of lunchtime light, the bathtub was full. Eve's suitcase was open. This I could only tell by the leathery tips of its edges jutting out from the deluge. For surrounding it the entire tub was full of dollars - twenties, tens, the occasional five - scattered and unfurling like we'd reached the end of the rainbow.

I closed the door and sat back down on the bed. "Eve... Eve, quit playing the ostrich and look at me will you."

She shook her head at first and eventually rose to my level, her face red and her features hidden beneath smudged lipstick and puffed skin.

"Eve, there isn't anything you and I can't work out. But you're going to have to talk to me, okay?"

She nodded.

"So why don't you go bring us a fresh bottle, and we can start from the beginning."

I heard the clink of glass against glass as Eve tried to situate a bottle that hadn't been skimmed or outright downed by either one of us. I felt my knee twitch and my head moving towards the bathroom door despite my best attempts to maintain a steely and proper pose. But I'm nothing if not a slave to curiosity and before I knew it was back outside the door, gently peeling it open to make sure that in my surprise my mind had not magnified the true extent of our riches.

Fortunately there were no such worries on that score. And as I surveyed the thousands upon thousands of dollars growing damp in the un-wiped bathtub of my comfortable little trailer I felt a smile trace across the length of my face.

With love,
Always,
Verity

Dear Verity,

It seems that you are not the only one to be presented with death in such elaborate form.

It began three days after my meeting with Michael. I had decided, en route to Caleb's, to stop for early morning coffee to try and extract any further information Mary may hold on Levi. I had scanned his books in the library. And, as foretold, in each novel a stranger appears, initially glimpsed from behind - the way Levi might have seen me as I sat at the counter while he scribbled in his log - before taking centre stage to the cookie-cutter dramas that unfolds.

The circumstances shift from book to book, but whether he's the traveller, or the salesman, the charlatan, or the thief, the climax is always some passionate embrace in the most unlikely of surroundings. A kitchen counter, the backseat of a car, billiards tables, alleyways, the forest floor. In the most memorable - and least likely, I have to admit - this very character tail ends a novel by ravishing mother and daughter on separate occasions at two otherwise nondescript family funerals. The things I've gotten up to would turn your hair white, I can tell you. I skimmed the novels for the bare essentials, as to get a taste of what exactly all the fuss was about. I suspect they were crafted with little more ambition than as a stopgap between domestic chores for the bored and lonely and, on the whole, female readership. I personally wouldn't use them for kindling, so decided against checking any of his tomes out of the library lest they mar what is up to now a somewhat impressive anthology.

The car lot was empty. The sign had been turned to open, yet the door was jammed shut. I peeked through the gaps in the dusty window assuming that Mary had skipped the most basic of tasks in favour of more strenuous activities such as mixing the batters and patties that she would spend her day flipping and frying.

I knocked twice and there was no answer.

The windows were fogged from the inside and something was steaming on the hob. I moved round to the side entrance where floor-length windows dressed in red lettering flanked the family tables. Between two letters I pressed my head to the glass. A coffee pot was cracked and spilled on the counter. Two pans smoked, one blew steam gently from its copper base, the other a more choking fog that rushed towards the ceiling and bloomed towards each corner of the room. The after-hours lights shone just enough to allow visibility, though I couldn't say what I was staring at until I caught sight of a small patch of white at the foot of the counter, from which a bloodied hand curled tightly around itself.

I returned to the front door and kicked as hard as I could. The doors dented but gave nowhere near enough to enable me to enter. Towards the back entrance a muddy dollar bill lay trampled into the concrete and a chain had been bolted around the interlocking handles. Again the door wouldn't budge so I ran back to the side of the building and selected the smallest window I could find.

My foot passed through the glass with ease though the jagged edge cut straight through my jeans and gifted my ankle with a near perfect bracelet of ruby dots. I kicked the most threatening shards from the empty void and made my way inside.

The air was hot as hell and slick with oil. I leapt over the counter and turned off the gas, which provided a minor respite. Broken plates scattered the floor and were drizzled with red like some intricate art installation. Mary lay on her back, her arms outstretched, her apron pulled up over her head. Dark red had begun to pool around her. I knelt down and pulled the cloth from her face.

How long she had been dead I can't say. And details within the press are being kept to a minimum while investigations are ongoing. I made my way behind the counter, trying not to slip on the blood and scattered sugar that coated the floor, and managed to call 911.

I sat alone with Mary while we waited for the police. All the while she seeped gently further and further across the floor, her Technicolor diminishing with each passing moment in a tidy circle, which shifted in size and hue like a slowly turned kaleidoscope.

The usual questions were asked. Initially with sympathy, then with a thin air of suspicion, before eventually the two officers arrived at a tone somewhere between officious and jovial. "You did everything you could, sir, I'm sure," they said, I assume taking my naturally distant demeanour for some sort of emotional response to the morning's events.

"Everything except get here five minutes earlier," I replied.

Back home I turned the faucet to its most scalding setting as I worked the suds into my skin. Scouring red welts that lingered long after the blood, which I so desperately wanted to be cleansed of. As the water dripped slowly to a stop and all that was left was steam, I found myself playing over the previous months in my mind, considering the catalogue of minor incidents that had dominated the town's gossip in the preamble to Mary's murder. Whether or not I can fairly blame Michael for each crime I do not know. All I can say is that despite the heightened vigilance of the usually lax policemen, a sense of unease pervaded the town as a wave of similar incidents took hold. Bricks shattered shop fronts. Lone women arrived home tearful and shaken after being trailed by dark, driverless cars. A fire engulfed the school kitchen though only after the majority of its supplies had been relieved. Two masked gunmen took the day's takings of a small but profitable hardware store and a pellet from the window of a passing car had blinded Maxwell in one eye mid-speech. His sight could have been saved, they said, had his writhing not been initially ignored as his tendency to reiterate utmost devotion by speaking in tongues.

I did manage to make it into work that day. A little after twelve, but present all the same.

"We were beginning to worry, boy," said Caleb as I made my way to the workshop at the farthest edge of his garden. "Thought we'd scared you off."

"Just been an odd morning is all."

I told him about the diner, and about Mary's murder. The whole time he sipped from his coffee cup, immune to the horror.

"Well, aint life a bitch," he said as I finished and had changed into my overalls. "Chances are we'll be full to bursting come the day of the funeral. Folk like to see off those that make the news. Can't say it's right. But facts are facts and coverage makes custom, chances are you'll be drafted in to make her coffin too... "

I felt myself blanche at the prospect.

"... well, only if you feel you'd be up to it, having seen what you've seen of course... "

"I'm sure I'll be fine to do it, if needs be."

"You're on your own today too, did I say that already?"

"No."

"Richard's taken ill. It's his heart you see. He was never a well man, I'm sure he will have told you as much."

"He mentioned it once or twice."

"I'll bet," said Caleb. "We've got a special one for you today son. Real special. Never known the like in all my life." He placed his empty cup on the bench and led me towards the back of the workshop.

"What is it today?"

"We have," he said, pulling a white sheet from a pile of beautiful mahogany. "An advanced booking. A reservation if you will."

"How so?"

"Someone's been gifted with foresight. Sadly for them it don't end so good. Ending quickly if the diagnosis is accurate. Small mercies and the like I suppose."

"They're planning their own funeral?"

"Right down to the dimensions. The measurements are on the side there." He pointed to a sheet of gilded paper on the counter, which held a rich blue ink perfectly detailing measurements and outlines. "Even given us a diagram of where the chairs got to be come the big day, though what use it is to him I don't know. He'd be none the wiser if we took him down to the scrap yard in a potato sack," he laughed and made his way towards the doorway, picking up his coffee cup as he left.

"Can't be the happiest of jobs, orchestrating your own funeral," I muttered, expecting no reply.

"I don't know. Might help to take your mind off things."

"It's hardly a diversion from the point in hand."

"Suppose so when you look at it that way. Then again it's second nature to me, I got my details as crystal clear as I can make them. The little lady, she gets confused by fuss. It's more for her sake than mine of course."

"And they know for sure they're dying, I mean sometimes they make mistakes, doctors. Gonna be an expensive coffee table if they end up seeing the year out."

He shook his head. "Nothing's certain in this life kiddo, but this poor bastard's direction is as near as you're gonna get."

"Do you know him?"

"Can't say personally. I heard of him okay. Everyone round here has."

"Who is it?"

"The writer."

I felt my heart skip a beat. "Levi?"

"Only one I know. Unless you count those monkeys down at the *Evening Post*, which few do by general consensus. Last year they mixed up the birthday dates with the funeral dates. A person's got to be trying to screw up like that."

It felt odd to say the least to be arranging, for all intents and purposes, the death of someone I had come to know over the past few months. Perhaps know is too strong a word. But even the fact that he had registered on my consciousness seemed to make my work somehow more sacred, as though I was offering my services as a gift to a friend. It was only as I began to wind up for the day - peeling off my overalls, now damp with perspiration, wiping a hand across my basalt brow, pebble-dashed with the grainy residue of chopped wood - did the significance of my knowledge truly dawn.

Of course Aimee would be devastated. However she interpreted life through that Escher staircase of a mind, one thing I did not doubt was the sincerity, and authority, of her feelings. But all I could really seem to focus on was that thought that I would be the one who got to deliver the news to Harlow. Undoubtedly he would feign sorrow at the circumstances. I could hear him in my head: 'Didn't like the man, son, but can't say I'd have wished this on him... ' yet he knew as well as I did that Levi's health, or lack thereof, was a blessing in disguise. And that soon, however traumatic initially, his relationship with Aimee would reach its most natural conclusion.

The thought of being Harlow's bearer of mixed news carried me home in relatively good spirits as the evening light began to muddle and fade. Outside of the cafe, cellophane sentiments had already begun to sprout in bouquets and wreaths at the borders of the police-tape. One or two officers still hovered uncertainly, more engrossed with one another's' conversation than anything else. A female officer ducked beneath the yellow tape that surrounded the entrance and placed a box of doughnuts, which I knew belonged to the cafe, on the hood of the car. Her colleagues dove in with an undisguised zeal, chewing down on the round pastries as red and purple globs smeared their chins. The mourners, of which there were few, had lit candles around the building where cards and lilies had been strategically placed, and seemed oblivious to the crassness of the officials' behaviour.

I paused for a moment and, forgetting the tragedy that had taken place, found myself wondering where I was now to get my quick fix of caffeine and fried goods. I shook the thought from my head and carried on my way.

Out on the porch Mrs Pemberton rocked gently on her chair. I had every intention of ignoring her tonight though she had other plans.

"The po-lis been asking about you this afternoon. Asked if I knew when you might be back. Told them you come and go as you please, seldom so much as a *good day.*"

I pushed my key into the lock and opened the door. "I know. There was an accident, at the diner."

"Mmhm, someone cut that lady up good and proper. It's a tragedy is what it is. Miss Violet called me on the telephone, said the poor woman'd been stabbed six times in the heart."

I didn't correct her. "Well, goodnight."

"You weren't involved, were you boy? Folk from this town aren't known for such behaviour."

"No ma'am. I found her. Called the police, she was dead by the time I got there though."

"Fine shame you aren't an early riser. Chance she might be telling the tale herself otherwise."

"I suppose we'll never know."

"I spoke to the po-lis myself. Said that man's been sniffing around your house for weeks now. And mine. I went to run some errands the other day, when I came back my kitchen window's wide open for all to see."

"Which man?"

"Don't play me no fool," she said, grinding to a halt on the seat. "I know you're up to no good. Can't pull no wool over my eyes. I had sixteen dollars in the jar when I left. Got back there were only six. Police weren't so quick to answer my call, no siree. Guess you have to have a knife in the heart before anybody thinks to stop by these days."

"You think you've been robbed?"

"No think about it. Unless them raccoons started chewing on dollars it's the only explanation for it. Someone been in my house and taken my money. And I intend to find out who."

"Well, good luck with that. Goodnight."

"You make sure to tell those po-lis you're back home. They still want to talk with you. Can't pull the wool over their eyes either. None of us blind in this town boy, none of us blind."


Work the next day was unsurprisingly solemn. As I laboured beneath the relentless sun I felt my skin prickle with untoward sweat and, to my embarrassment, caught frequent drafts of evaporating whisky as it rose from my pores. That sun felt like a vice being tightened as the day went on, and the whole world seemed somehow crueller through my tight, bloodshot eyes.


"Someone had a good night," said Emmett with a tap on my shoulder as he made a rare venture into the dirt-pit. Mercifully he did not hover long enough to warrant a response.

Though the hangover played the starring role in my day, its gloom was further accentuated by the constant mutterings surrounding the murder. It seemed that the only thing any of those boys could talk about was the crime and its aftermath. Some of the younger boys claimed they knew the culprits though, unsurprisingly, could not name names through fear of retaliation.

"Y'all don't know who we know," said Steven as we carried debris to the farthest edge of the site.

Most of the men dismissed his ramblings. In fact I think I was the only one really listening, and that in itself was a triumph of proximity. In my tender state I was less agile than usual, and had been forced to operate at the same slovenly level as the clod-kicking youths who frequented the site only when they had little else to do.

Lunchtime offered little respite. The rumours grew bigger and faster.

"I heard it was a gang," said Chris, picking the tomato from his sandwich. "Whole group of bikers swarmed the place and bashed the lady's skull in."

"No way – she was shot."

"... heard it was a knife that done it in the end."

"... panties were found jammed in her mouth."

"... head cut clean off... "

"... Daddy said he saw two foreign looking sorts... "

"Worst part is they only got away with thirty dollars in coin... "

It didn't seem to occur to the tragedy's chorus that given the police's complete lack of footwork on the crime their proclamations held little to no value. I suppose in such instances the truth is surplus to requirements. Eventually when the talk went from casually disrespectful to the outright grisly I stood up to leave.

"Mind if I sit, or were you hoping for silence?" said Harlow, casting his shadow across the ground on which I sat.

"Feel free. Your company's always welcome. It's the banshees I'm better off without, today at least."

"I know that feeling." He sat down beside me and opened his tin lunchbox. Carefully placing the wrap back in the box, he broke a sandwich clean in half and handed me the larger of the two pieces. "That wet bread you were poking at didn't look so fun."

"You noticed."

"Couldn't not. That's the problem with the bachelor way of life. The food. It'd be the death of me."

"I get by okay on the whole, it's just... " I took a bite from the sandwich and continued with my mouth full. "Been a funny weekend is all."

"What you need is a nice little wife. Someone to take care of you."

"If only it were that easy."

"Heck you can borrow mine if you like."

"It'd be an honour. She's a good woman."

"Pain in the ass more like," Harlow chuckled. "Nah I'm jus' kidding. Wouldn't have her any other way. Damn it boy you make it with a brewery last night?" he said, sniffing the cloth of my work clothes. I shrugged and felt the food hit my stomach like a penny in a well.

"Sometimes it's all I can do to get to where I want to be."

"And where did you want to be?"

"Somewhere outside my own head."

Harlow sat silently chewing, digesting the situation, before continuing. "So, you want to tell me what's bothering you?"

I thought for a moment and almost began when I felt the sandwich make itself known inside of me. My eyes watered and I felt myself drain.

"Whoa boy you got it bad!" said Harlow "Here," he pulled a hip flask from his pocket. "Now I'm not encouraging it, but this'll sort you out."

He unscrewed the cap and handed me the filthy silver goblet. I'd sooner have bent down and sucked up the mud beneath my feet than amended my rift with alcohol of any variety. But I was touched by the gesture (though dubious of his methods all the same) and took it with an unsteady hand.

"You sure?"

"Only thing that'll get you back to human."

I gripped the flask and tipped it to the sun. The whisky poured down my throat without so much as greeting my tongue, and for a moment all was well. Then it kicked inside me. I gripped my hands into the ground as my stomach writhed and bucked. My eyes stung and my throat tightened around itself.

"That's it boy," said Harlow, taking another bite of his sandwich.

I stood up and ran to the furthest oil drum, my hand pressed against my mouth. The moment I stopped I felt my body turn inside out. Specks of food cascaded with an embarrassing echo into the bottom of the tin. Yesterday's sin stung my lips and my head felt like it was ready to follow suit into the bottom of the barrel as every spare ounce left my body and pooled into a foul smelling moat.

"There you go boy, get it all up. Sooner it's out sooner it stops hurting."

Eventually I drew to a halt, my stomach aching as though I'd been punched a thousand times. As I sat back down I felt shaken, though within seconds my newfound lightness seemed to catapult me back into a form I almost recognised as myself.

"Better?"

"Surprisingly."

"Here," Harlow handed me an apple. "To take the taste away."

"Thank you."

"So," he said eventually. "Now that one weight's off your mind - or your belly, depending on how you look at it - you want to tell me why you walking around like the living dead?"

"I had a bad day yesterday is all."

"We've established that much kid. I don't want to push the subject if you don't want to talk about it, but the way I see it a problem shared is a problem halved."

"Or doubled, depending on how you look at it."

"I like to think of my glass as half full."

"I don't think I'll be troubling the glass for some time yet."

"Well there you go, you learn a lesson. I bet it almost seems worth it now."

Harlow patted me on the back and for a while we watched the sun trace the endless amber glow of the dust. "I found the lady, Mary," I said. "At the coffee shop. Had to break a window to get in. It was too late though. I was too late."

"Well I'm sorry to hear that, I guess that sort of thing stays with a man."

I bent down and pulled back the foot of my jeans to allow it some air.

"Ouch, you do that on the window?"

"Yeah, hurts like a bastard."

The cuts around my leg had spread and darkened. Dirt had mixed with blood and formed a grim tattoo around the entire length of my ankle as though I'd been shackled.

"Promise me you'll have a doctor look at that, don't look too pretty."

"Will do. Just got to make it through the day first."

"You'll be fine. Worst part's over. You know, you ever want to talk, I'm here. Am I right in thinking you don't have much family around these parts?"

"Don't have family full stop."

"None?"

"My mother died when I was younger. Dad's been on death row for most of his life."

"I take it the two are related. Sorry to hear that."

"It happens."

Harlow took a sip of coffee from his thermos. "I always wanted boys. Seem to know what you're getting with boys."

"Ignorance is bliss."

"Oh now you can't have been all that bad."

"Believe me when I say you don't want to know."

"Thing is, with girls, and I love them, God I love them, but there's no in between. Either they move away and come back Christmas and birthdays like strangers, or they stay so close you wonder why they ever bothered cutting the cord in the first place. Boys, they hang around, in touching distance, maybe stay in town, maybe move to the better side, but they're there... just as much as you need them. Boys get it just right."

"Say," I said eventually, keen to dispel Harlow's suddenly sombre tone. "Yesterday wasn't all bad. Got some news that might cheer you up."

Harlow nodded as he processed the information. He screwed the lid on his thermos and placed it with a click inside the top section of his lunchbox. "Well," he said eventually. "I can't say I'm sorry. Way I see it nature's just taking its course. He's lived his life, and now it's his time. And whatever it makes me I'm just pleased he won't be worrying my girl anymore." Harlow shook his head and wiped his face of the emotion, which was beginning to spread like damp. "God damn it I know how I sound Jonah. I know how I sound and I don't like it. But there's not one thing I care about more in this world than those girls, and if them being safe means some old man's got to plan his own funeral then I won't be sorry. I won't ever be sorry for that," he stared out into the sun and then, as though a switch had been flicked, snapped back into his usual persona. "Well, that'll be time by my watch."

He offered me his hand and I dragged myself up against his steady weight. "I don't think less of you - " I eventually managed, " - for thinking like you do. In fact I think it's something special that you love those girls enough to talk that way, to care that much about them. I think had someone thought that way about me my life might not have taken such a dull course."

Harlow slowed his pace so that he was side by side with me as I walked. "I appreciate that kiddo, I really do. You know, you can't choose the hand you're dealt in life. All you can do is play it best you can. And I know you got a trick or two up your sleeve. I can't claim to know you well but I know I'd like nothing more than to see you make something of yourself. And I know you got the goods to do it."

With love, (and please take care)
Jonah

Dear Jonah,

Eve's confession was what I believe they call a two-bottle job.

"I'm so sorry V, I should have told you. I could have made our lives better from the word go... " Was her preferred mantra throughout the lengthy explanation as to how my bathtub came to be swimming with dollars.

"Just start from the beginning and end with you trying to knock the shit out of me Eve," I said, taking another swig of wine to steady my nerves. I was listening. It was hard not to, given Eve's aptitude for volume. But throughout it all I could feel myself slipping in and out of fantasy. I pictured us bashing champagne glasses down, howling at our good fortune. Then we were dressed in furs, pirouetting down a freshly swept avenue tossing bounds of notes at salesgirls in exchange for silks and patterns that we'd never wear. We dined on lobster and sent rounds to the tables of men who caught our eye, all wowed by our beauty and abandon. I buy a one-way ticket, once Eve has absconded with yet another lover, and you and I are together forever...

"V!" Eve mewled. "This is serious. In fact it's just about the worst thing that I've ever done. Quit daydreaming and listen."

"Sorry. It's just a lot to take in, is all."

"You're telling me. I don't even know where to start."

"The beginning usually helps."

"That's too far back. God knows what went wrong to make me the way I am. Oh Verity I'm sorry... "

She began weeping again. The routine was beginning to grate and already our first bottle was nearing empty, so I grabbed her by the arms and sat her bolt upright. "Eve, you just got to pull yourself together now darling and start talking. You understand?"

She wiped her face and nodded. "Well, I suppose it started when

142

I turned up at a town not too far from here after one or two incidents that I'd sooner forget. I was a rich woman again after that kind Mr Hounslow left me his estate and then I met... I mean... " her throat tightened but she forced herself to go on, "... oh it could have happened to anyone, Verity. I mean of course you share everything once you're married. What was mine was his. We were going to share the rest of our lives."

"You got married?"

"No. I thought I did. The priest turned out to be his cousin and four million dollars turned out to be a big fat zero before I'd even had the chance to change my name at city hall. He didn't even stay long enough for Bermuda. I'd packed rose petals, handcuffs. We'd been waiting, see, to make it all the more special. And he left me sitting on top of that suitcase for six hours before I realised something was up."

"Oh Eve, some cruel man played you?"

"He wasn't playing Verity. He broke my heart and left me penniless all over again. Only positive I could draw was that I never became Mrs Eve Gooberman nee Lubbock. I mean on paper, in person I'd been introducing myself that way since the first time I set eyes on those beautiful lips."

I rubbed her shoulder for support and poured the rest of the bottle of wine down her throat.

"So, anyway I was broke and homeless and cradling my heart like a bird with a broken wing. I didn't think I was ever getting back to life again. So I skipped town. All I had was debt, bad memories, and a pair of tits that could get me a ride wherever I wanted to go, so I hitched with this old man in a big red truck. He had a picture of the Virgin Mary in his cabin and a copy of *Playboy* in his glove compartment. He told me his destiny was to win *Jeopardy* and you know what? I think it'll come true. He was smart, and kind."

"Eve," I said, popping the cork of a second bottle. "You're straying, sweetheart."

"Sorry, so anyway I get to this town a broken woman, cold and hungry, and then I met Mr Parker and it hit me all over again."

"Not another millionaire? Eve, darling no-one's that lucky."

"No, he wasn't a millionaire. Far from it. He lived by his wits though. Minor investments. Worked in delivery and distribution, with a sideline in the hospitality industry. So we started going together, dates and the like. He was real gentlemanly. Set me up working in one bar of his. I good as lived with him from that very first night. Only it didn't last so long."

"How come?"

"Well, Mr Parker and I, we had our love, and that was that. But food don't come for free, so after some negotiations I agreed to expand my facilities within the outfit. I became more active in my role as hostess."

"He had you turning tricks?"

"I was no whore. I was an escort. Most of the time it was my company they wanted, that's what Mr Parker said. Of course at first I didn't know how it'd work, what with us being so madly in love, but he said that it wasn't personal, just business. So long as I knew where the line was in my head then there weren't no issue. We were exclusive in our hearts V, that's what you have to understand."

She spoke with such certainty, as though privy to some higher truth that I wanted to take her in my arms and never let go. Life could never be as sweet a place as Eve's own mind. It seemed so tragic that she ever had to step so much as a foot in the real world.

"Only I was under the impression that my... dalliances... were strictly for profit. We were going to buy ourselves a hotel one day. Somewhere real nice, with a pool. That was until I walked in on Mr Parker riding Cindy like a bronco."

"Who's Cindy?"

"She was our treasurer."

"Then what happened?"

"Not all that much. Cindy spat the billiard ball he'd jammed in her mouth so far it broke the bottle on the bar. Poor thing."

I lit a cigarette and passed it to Eve in the hope that it might calm her into a more coherent train of thought. "So how did you get to the money?"

"By accident of course. I don't need money, long as I got a roof over my head and enough for the occasional bottle of wine I'm the happiest girl there ever was. But I stormed out of that place madder than hell and twice as sad."

"Then what?"

"I got in his car and left him in the dirt screaming for me to come back. See I'd grown stronger since Mr Gooberman. Learnt the hard way. I was nobody's fool by then, so I took his car and went to the house, grabbed a suitcase for my necessities and fled. I sold the car. Kept the bracelet he gave me though, look." She held out her arm for examination and a gold chain of charms and talismans that she had, without me realising, been wearing the whole time I knew her, shuffled around her bony wrist.

"It's pretty."

"Damn right. Only by the time I got myself sorted and unpacked the suitcase was still heavy. Turns out it was one of his work-cases. He had them made special, you look inside and it's like there's nothing there. But if you really look there's a whole other world behind that cloth – you just got to know where to pull. And if you find that then all the secrets fall out like glitter."

"His money?"

"And the rest."

"What?"

"Oh Verity let's not play dumb," she said, drying her eyes once and for all. "Mr Parker was not what you'd call by the book. I found me a gun for insurance and met some nice boys who promised to turn my little bundle into cold hard cash, and boy did they make good!"

The next morning we rose slowly and without words. Eventually, having splashed my face and slurped a gallon of water along with a fistful of white pills, which I took to be medicinal, took hold of Eve like I was readying a Heimlich manoeuvre.

"So, we gonna talk about what we're going to do about our little dilemma?"

She groaned and turned over to face me. "Yeah, I guess. Just let me sort myself out first," she stood up unsurely, before gambolling her way to the bathroom.

I sat and smoked three cigarettes to the nauseating sound of her retching. That vomit slapped the bowl like the tide crushing the bow of a ship over and over again. At first it made my own stomach churn, as well it might. But before long I got used to it. And then she came back, red eyed and revived, like a woman reborn.

She got back into bed and curled next to me. A stringent peppermint blanketed the sour bile of her breath.

"So, what now?"

"Those boys will come after me, and I don't want to be anywhere near you when they do. You're the only person I've ever known won't break my heart."

"It'd break my heart for you to go," I said, channelling maternal authority as best I could. "Whatever will be will be, that's my motto. And for a long time it was yours. I mean you've been living with this since the day I met you, seems silly to start getting nervy now."

"I didn't know you when I met you. Now I'd die if I knew anything I did were to hurt you in some way."

"You got nothing to be scared of," I stood up and pulled her by the arms until she was facing me. "I never had a sister, but I sure would like one. What do you say?"

At this Eve smiled and gripped my hands tighter and tighter.

"So, from now on it's us, you got that? Wherever you've been, I've been. Deal?"

Eve nodded furiously, wiping her eyes with the cuff of her gown.

"Now," I said, edging my way towards the kitchen. "How about you clear up that tub and run me a bath. Nothing like a hot soak to clear a girl's head."

"And then what?"

"Then? Well then we start enjoying ourselves."

So that was us for the foreseeable future. Eve loosened up the moment she realised just how much fun two girls like us could have in a town like this. Of course the couture was not exactly abundant, so we became more and more elaborate with our spending. That's the beauty of going from no money to big money in an instant I've found; you'd sooner see it disappear within the day than spend one second worrying about it. We waved goodbye to those dollars like they were the worst houseguests you could ever meet.

First we were cunning, though. Eve was still fussing about those boys coming back to claim what was theirs, so we split the bundles in case of emergency. Handfuls of notes were stuffed into every hiding place we could think of. Each fissure in the couch was cemented with a tightly wrapped stack of twenties. The oven - used solely for storage anyway - was scattered with discarded fifties. Into the backs of drawers we pressed hundreds and hundreds of dollars, and slept giddy and restless atop the crunching mattress now engorged with Eve's nest egg. Of course she was careful to keep a small amount aside, which she kept in the suitcase.

"That's the exact amount I found in there. The rest is just profit. If they ever come back they'll be none the wiser."

I shrugged and continued jamming notes into the urn that once held my mother; a tragic loss twice over, thanks to one overzealous vacuuming route and a less than stable plinth.

Before long we began to tire of the boutiques and salons. Eve and I were never the pastel types. Didn't have the figure for one thing. Those two-piece and pearls never quite sat comfortably on our hourglass bodies, no more than the tastefully neutral make-up the lady at the brightest cosmetic counter hawked. Eve and I were built for vivid hues; a green swathe here, a touch of blue there, two beautiful scarlet smudges to X-mark our lips. It was as if we weren't painted every colour of the rainbow we were scared we'd disappear forever.

Our favourite trick was the hotel. We'd march right up there, sometimes still dressed in work's clothes, (or lack thereof as was more often the case) and book the biggest suite they had available. We'd always choose pseudonyms. This was Eve's idea though it thrilled me too. We had no reason to lie. It was all just part of the game. We'd decide as we approached what roles we were playing that day and behave accordingly. First we were the rock-star spouses seeking refuge from the tour bus. Then we were landscape artists exploring new vistas. There were the happily married couple on the look out for a surrogate, ruined somewhat by an impromptu demonstration by the bellboy as to his capacity for the job. There were more, of course – the merry widows, the gay divorcees, the Sapphic supermodel and her controlling partner, the lottery winners, the undercover officers...

The funny thing was we'd only ever spend a few hours in our rented suites. We'd order enough food to feed a small army. Unravel in the bathtub as bubbles popped and tickled our ears. And then return, rested and replenished, before the dusk had so much as a chance to settle.

"We hope you enjoyed your stay ladies, and look forward to seeing you again."

In those strange, halcyon days with Eve I got to know her as well as I've ever known anyone. For a girl who went to such lengths to appear open she was surprisingly full of her own troubles, which she doled out in manageable chunks. Her lovers' names were relayed like a nursery rhyme. Give her a drink and she could work her way through the alphabet twice over without ever having to pause for thought. But her life before that was as cloudy as a poem and not nearly as lyrical. From what I gather her parents had been as neglectful as two people can be without input from various authorities.

'It was no hardship, though,' she'd tell me, combing her hair in the giant orb of the mirror in the presidential suite. 'They had their lives and I had mine. It worked just fine for all involved. I guess you could say it did me good. One thing's for sure, I'm all my own invention. Never had no-one tell me what to do from day one. If anything I'm more myself than those kids whose backgrounds were peeled straight off a Christmas card.'

I found glamour in the poverty of her upbringing; the scavenging for food; the endless days and nights when her whereabouts was not once called into question. I myself experienced no such hardship. I neither went without nor grew to expect life handed to me on a plate. Jealous, too, that she seemed to know her own mind so well. Eve *was* her own creation, right down to the bone. Whereas I suppose I always felt like somewhere along the way my character became consumed by the rest of the world, like I was translucent, taking on any hue that shone my way. I was a mousy child. Round faced and long limbed, with a shyness that bordered on chronic when faced with strangers. Pretty, I suppose, if I ever thought to make anything of myself, though I seldom did. It was like I'd been made just that little bit too diluted, in my mind at least. As a result I began to take on scraps of others as if to make myself whole, to calcify what I had into something resembling a personality. Not in a sinister way of course. I'd affect an accent I picked up from the more exotic girls at school, or declare undying love for the preferred foodstuff my favourite cartoon characters. Only on occasion would it grow to extremes. One summer I was hospitalised and observed by the finest psychiatrists my mother could find when I limited my intake solely to chocolate chip cookies and root beer. And there was a minor furore when I took not just the hairstyle, but the boyfriend of my high school best friend.

On the whole it was harmless, though. In truth I still feel myself doing it. With Eve, with J, even with you. Somewhere between introduction and maintenance of any relationship I feel myself altering to the rhythms of my chosen other. My speech shifts in its pattern. My manner morphed so slightly it would be unnoticeable to anyone but me. Stripped to the essentials I suppose I'm little more than a collage of each and every person I've ever come across in my life; I paste on their attributes, good or bad, until I begin to fit the mould. Of course the problem comes when alone and not always so sure as to how I ought to act. What would X do... I find myself thinking, in supermarket lines when I realise my wallet's back at the trailer, or when answering the door to bible salesmen. Eve had no such issues. She was herself and could be nothing else. All I can hope is that a little part of her lives on in me, whether she knows it or not. The world was a better place with her in it. Or my world was, at very least.

As we continued spending like sailors on shore leave Eve's presence at The Iguana Den became less and less.

"You sure you don't want to come? Even just to watch?" I said halfway to the car, thirty minutes late and appropriately harangued.

"Maybe tomorrow," she said, unfolding the sheets of paper with ink stained hands. "What do you think of these lonely hearts ads? You think they ever lead to real love?"

"I think you've had dumber ideas, in the grand scheme. Why won't you come?"

"I'm just nervous is all," she said, reaching for the bottle.

"Eve, those boys were going to come after you they'd have done it by now."

"You don't know them. These boys are real rattlesnakes. They'll sit and wait until you're in licking distance. That's when they strike."

"I think you're thinking too much about this. The hard part's over. Now it's just up to us to enjoy the aftermath."

"Well I'm taking no chances. I want you to pack that pistol. And come straight back home afterwards."

"I promise. See you in the morning."

Eve nodded though did not respond.


That night J was in the audience. This I did not realise until I was up on stage, half blind by the lighting and suddenly aware of the owl's eyes that twinkled in the darkness.

He sat on a table with Kingpin, I noticed. Kingpin was not what you'd call the most welcoming of hosts. Nor was he the type to encourage spontaneous guests. This seemed to pose little issue to J. The pair sat quietly, as both were inclined to do, occasionally whispering to one another. Kingpin's eyes remained glued to the stage. J was edgier than I'd seen him before. His eyes scanned the room like he was searching for a needle in a haystack. It was as the sound of the crowd dipped and the music rose that each and every piece of the puzzle began to fit into place, and I felt my two lives collide into one another with such a violent jolt that both were irrevocably damaged. Those long nights, the gilded ache of courtship, that sweet, handsome face and the future that existed only in my head... it had all been a lie. He was here for Eve. Proof was redundant. You've said it yourself Jonah – some things you simply know.

I felt my heart break on that stage and it is yet to be fully fixed. Lust does terrible things to you Jonah, and love? Love eats you alive and tells you it's what you wanted.


I snake my way to the centre of the stage. All I know is that I have to move and I have to make it believable. The rest will fall into place, of that I am sure. But for now I have to perform and I have to do so for my life.

The music rises and I know it's now or never.

He watches me as I wind down the silver pole; my knees scraping into ugly marks that no-one can see through the blue haze. J sits back in his chair and pulls his hat over his eyes as I pour wax down my body. It stings, but only for a second.

What feels like only seconds later, I make my way from the stage to the sound of their applause. The noise heartens me, but deep down I remain forlorn that I was unable to clock J's exact reaction.

In the dressing room Miss Jemima flounces over to me and I allow her to kiss me on the cheek. "Darling, you did it again!"

I grab my belongings as quickly as possible. "I have to go."

"What in the world is wrong? Here, sit down," she says, pulling a cushioned chair from beneath the laced derriere of one of the new girls.

"No," I say, wrapping my coat around me. My eyes beginning to water, my voice breaking. "I got to go. I'm so sorry Jemima, I don't know what's come over me."

"Girls like you know exactly what's wrong. You just think it's impolite to say as much. I'm right, aren't I?" By this point she has taken my arm gently and led me into an abandoned corridor through which the noise of the crowd plays out like a scream underwater. "You're ever in trouble you know I can help."

"I know," I say, wiping all traces of emotion from my eyes. "I know and thank you, but I really think I just need to go home. Eve's still sick and, well... "

"Darling there's nothing in this life worth ruining your make-up for," Miss Jemima coos, touching the edge of my eye with her embossed handkerchief. "And you know where I am, ever you need me. We take good care of our girls here. Good care."

I nod and kiss her once on the cheek. "Thank you."

And with that I am gone.


Outside a breeze picks up and the dancing sands stick to the oil on my legs. A hand touches my shoulder as I reach the car. "Come back to my place," he says, sheepishly, as though he had never been with a woman before.


I contemplate killing him. I swear to God, Jonah, the thought crossed my mind and lasted longer than it should in any sane woman. The gun's cold weight presses heavily against my thigh and I feel my hand stroking its outline. That would have solved our problems, though I suppose it would have been as useful as covering house mess with a filthy sheet.

I also want him to fuck me. To tell me he loves me too, that for all the wrong he's done, for all the lies he's told, he's found himself drawn to me like no other girl he ever met. I feel frightened and for the first time in my life I know how it feels to truly hate myself.

"J," I say as casually as ever, opening the car door. "What in the world is a nice boy like you doing in a place like this?"

"Just following a hot lead. Good friend of mine recommended the establishment. I think it's exactly what I'm looking for."

"Well now you've found it I'd hate to distract you. You take care now."

"What's this?" he grabs my arm, gently, but with a strength that suggests I may need backup if I decide to elaborate on any notions of murder I might have had. "You spend weeks and weeks teasing me, now I get the cold shoulder. God damn it, Verity, I don't know you at all, do I?"

"It's late, is all," I say, trying my hardest to ease my arm from his grip without him noticing. "And I'm sure you'll attest to my claims of a strenuous evening. These legs don't dance themselves."

"You looked real beautiful up there tonight."

"Thank you, you are sweet."

"So quit fooling. Come on back to my place. Let's finish what we started."

"I think I've had quite enough excitement for one night. Besides, I like my epics long and drawn out. I'm afraid I'll need a little more wooing before we get to that part."

"Not what you said last time."

"People change."

"I think I got me a lead as to where my money went."

"Your Daddy's money."

He shrugs. "Think I might pay a visit tonight. If that's the case you might never see me again."

At this my heart became a caged beast, thrashing against its enclosure. Whether it was the truth or a line he'd feed a girl to see her insides I don't know, but it was not a chance I was going to take.

"Well," I said, suddenly melting into his touch. "If that's the case then the least I owe you is five minutes of my time. Why don't you get in the car, we can have us a talk."

He looks around at the empty lot, and the endless desert in every direction.

"I got a quart of whisky and a radio that almost works," I add. "Don't know if that'd sweeten the deal."

J nods and gets into the passenger seat of my car. We sit for a moment and he leans in to kiss me. I let him and do everything I can not to enjoy it.

"So," I say as he returns to his side of the car. "You think you found what you're looking for?"

J lights a cigarette and the smoke's thick plumes begin to hurt my eyes. "Why?" he asks, cracking the window open and flicking ash onto the dirt below. "You think you know something that'll help me?"

"We're not paid to talk in that place. Nor to listen. Unless Ida has a suitcase full of dollars somewhere I don't think I'm the girl to help."

J drops his cigarette. His hand curls around my neck and he pulls my face towards his, then presses down until my forehead is resting on his upper thigh. I run my hand up around his leg as he unzips his flies. Above his waist I feel the handle of a gun pressing against my head. As I jerk back and forth, working to the sound of his growl - deep and assured, like a Harley trailing the sidewalk - I wonder whether my stealth would outweigh his brawn.

But, alas, it was not meant to be. By the time I sit back and he is buttoning himself up, shuffling in his seat, any chance of atonement on behalf of Eve is momentarily gone. "I don't know what I'd have done without you."

"I'm just another girl in just another town. We're ten a penny. You'd have found someone."

"Now I know that's not true. Come on," he says, with a note of urgency previously absent from his voice. "Come back to my place. We can talk. It'll be nice. No menus."

"No strobe lights," I say, patching my lipstick in the car's mirror.

"I'd like you to. I want to talk to you properly. I got things to say."

"Well," I try, slipping the keys into the ignition. "I'm not so sure I wish to be associated with a man who frequents such establishments."

I laugh. He does not.

"God damn it, Verity, what's the fucking problem? We've been circling this same patch for weeks on end now. You're hotter than a dog on heat one minute, next thing you're some God damn ice queen. You scared of something?"

"I'm scared of nothing."

"Well then there's no harm in it, is there? You can come and have a drink with me."

"And I could marry my first cousin, but I won't," I turn the key. The ignition kicks in and J steps out of the car to the sound of mechanical coughing.

"To be continued," he says over the clunk of a weary engine. He watches me as I flicker and blend into darkness.

I pulled over not too far from the trailer park. I dipped the lights and silenced the engine, and then, only then, did I hold my head in my hands and cry.

I'm not entirely sure what I wept for. For a broken heart, I suppose. For a whole lifetime over before it had even begun. It seems heartless now to admit such sorrow in the face of what was to come, but I felt a loss at my future that never was. I cried, too, at the thought of change. For the first time I could remember things had been not just bearable but enjoyable. It felt strange, then, knowing as I drove onto the gravel, watching the car's lights flash and dip on my front door, that we would be leaving so soon, never to return again. But no-one ever said life was linear Jonah. It changes, whether you like it or not. All you can do is follow the current and hope you don't get swept under forever.

I took off my clothes and put on a nightshirt. For the first time in living memory I cleansed the night before from my face in the bathroom mirror; wiping thick gloop across my eyes and lips until I was as blank as nature intended. All the while plans of our escape rose in my mind like a sapling in spring until it became the only thought left in my head.

Eve groaned as I got into bed and turned over to face me, though allowed herself to remain in the lull of a light doze. I edged into the curve of her body and felt her chest move to the beat of her heart.

Her arm pulled me tighter towards her once and then relaxed as I felt myself fall to sleep, mimicking the soothing rhythm of her breath.

With love,
Verity

Dearest Verity,

It seemed like the whole town had turned up just to watch. Girls from the coffee shop sat sobbing into their prayer books; one or two of the regular customers clustered together and seemed bemused, as though still waiting to be asked how they preferred their eggs. Towards the beginning of the service a lady collapsed in the third stall and two men cussed at the top of their voices, damning the still at-large culprit.

The mood settled as the procession continued. Three rows ahead of me, Aimee held tightly onto the arm of Levi. She had no reason to be there, and I found myself wondering whether or not she was simply observing how one behaves in such situations, preparing herself so that, if emotions failed her that day, she could method act her way through the imminent funeral of her dearest compatriot. She rested her head on his frail shoulder, her blonde hair bobbing up and down as she struggled silently for breath between sobs. Levi seemed unmoved, though he did find time to scribble occasional musings in a discreet notepad he had tucked within the central pages of his hymn sheet.

I was the only man from the site in attendance. Harlow said he hadn't known the lady and the rest seemed to have shifted their attentions to other atrocities. This seems to be a common trait of the masses. Their devotion to a disaster cools with the corpse. The kinetic burst of tragedy can captivate an audience like little else whilst the long, grey aftermath holds no such sway over those not directly involved.

I stayed for the burial. Having known Mary in life as well as being the first - or, more accurately, second or third - to experience her death, there seemed an obligation on my part to complete the cycle.

A flock of starlings dimmed the sky above us whilst the final prayers were spoken before parting, as the sun rose sharply through two mountainous clouds, tracing Mary's descent with fierce blade of light.

"Earth to earth... " he said with his head bowed. "Ashes to ashes... " I felt a hand touch my arm and then link me from behind. "Dust to dust... "

Aimee pressed her head into my arm as the coffin lowered into dirt. Handfuls of mud showered the wooden lid and then instinctively the congregation dispersed like steam through a window.

"You'll walk me to the wake though?" she asked, as though the culmination of a long and fruitful conversation that had gone before.

"I'm not going that way. Got the impression it was friends and family only."

"I thought you were her friend," she said, pulling her arm from mine. "Daddy said you found her body. Said it'd been so horrible it'd messed your head up real bad."

"I knew her to talk to. Couldn't tell you a thing about her though, except where she worked. Fact is I didn't even know her last name until half an hour ago."

"Me neither," said Aimee, shaking her hair so that it covered her face. "I only came along because Levi wanted to take some notes. Then he went and ditched me with those nurses he's been getting friendly with," she shot a stony glance behind her and then returned to me. "You sure you won't come with me?"

"I'm sure. Think I'm going to take the rest of the day to myself. You take care though."

"And you," she said, gently pressing her lips into my cheek. "I'll be seeing you at the fair."

I walked home alone. In the centre of town, Maxwell was back to his old tricks. He was manning his soap box with particular zeal for a weekday afternoon, perhaps in part to show indignation towards recent attempts upon his person. The only evidence of his misfortune was the oozing bandage where his right eye had once been.

"Ladies and gentlemen I beg of you to heed my call," he cried. "For the devil has come to this small town!"

Even those who could afford the luxury of an afternoon stroll didn't care to process his wisdom. I continued on my way, as he grew more animated with each syllable.

"He walks among us, upright and presentable. He has no forked tail. He has no cloven hooves. But rest assured that Satan's work is being carried out right beneath our very noses... ladies and gentlemen I have felt the devil's wrath and lived to tell the tale... "

The next night was the state fair. It had taken all my energy just to rise to the occasion. The whole day I had been sanding my new structure, now almost complete. The roof had been tacked to the shed and the wood treated as to protect it from the elements. I had even managed to dig out the most shoddy of foundations in case a winter breeze carried it swirling into another world so it stood staunch and unmoveable. Inside I arranged my pristine tools and accessories. At first by size, then colour, and finally I just pushed them to the farthest edge of the tiny room and sat quietly, on a creaking sun lounger, proudly observing my masterpiece from within.

I must have dozed off as when I came to, the light had begun to dilute and a cool breeze had caused my breath to steam.

I showered and changed as quickly as I could, and grabbing a four pack of beers from the refrigerator began my trek to the transformed fields just south of Harlow's yard.

You could see the fair for miles around. Lights every colour of the rainbow flashed and spun. Children's cries and the insincere screams of those who rode the rickety old rollercoaster made the air seem thick.

It was already in full swing as I entered. Along the entrance, leading towards the main deluge of lights and energy, a small petting zoo bordered the walkway. Children pushed carrots towards the mouths of restrained beasts. Baboons howled and shrieked as they pounded their paws against the bars of their world. Two baby lions snarled and jerked, as their muddy tethers grew looser by the second; a horse arched its hooves as though cursing the skies.

There were the usual additions. Cotton candy stalls. A game in which an eager adult was dunked into an icy pool once a beanbag had hit the giant red button. Two fortune tellers sat in Romany caravans opposite one another. A girl in angel wings sitting on a cushioned throne turned and growled at me with drawn on whiskers and tiger stripes as her young transformer clouded a jar of water with a fine paintbrush.

I flinched as I felt something touch my ear.

A man in a top hat spun on the spot, brandishing the King of Hearts. "Well look what we have here!" he yelled to the dispersing crowds, all shuffling in unison towards the rides at the heart of the fair. "Let's see what else we've got in here... " He placed his hand to my head once more but I picked up my pace, not entirely comfortable in my position as glamorous assistant.

Beside the funhouse, which shuddered against the heaving mechanism of the rollercoaster, various offshoots were free for those not willing to pay the minimal entrance fee. Children trailed red-faced parents through hanging beanbags which pinged and snapped on the elastic which held them in place, knocking you to the cushioned floor. I walked through a darkened dome of mirrors, each one showing a different version of myself. One moment I was grossly huge, my edges uncontained by the reflection, then I was long and lean, stretching up like some nursery rhyme monster. I was wavy and curved and blurred and shrunk. As I stepped out, twin redheads pushed past me to reach the teacups.

"Those brutes nearly had you flat on your ass," said a pretty woman, wearing a glued-on moustache and a top hat. Her velvet jacket trailed in the mud and the paintwork of her kiosk was beginning to fade around her.

"I'll have my revenge," I tried, half-heartedly. It's been so long since anyone showed even the slightest bit of interest that my default setting is now suspicion.

"Dare to enter the house of mirrors?" she asked with a raise of her sculpted eyebrow, in no way enthused about the mystic treats on offer.

"I don't know, just how magical is it in there?"

"Those who live to tell the tale have never been the same again," she said with a sly grin. "Also," she said, this time more hushed, "you give me one of those beers you can walk right in there for free. God knows I can't do this sober much longer."

"Well, I admire your nerve," I said, handing her the full pack. "Help yourself. I'll pick up whatever's left when I make it out."

"If you make it out alive!" she said, cracking open a can and taking half of it in one gulp.

"Here's to hoping," I said, stepping onto the wooden step and peeling back the curtains.


My eyes took a moment to adjust to the matinee dark of the labyrinth. I stepped forwards with my hands pressed, groping for safety, until I reached the first mirror. As I grew accustomed to the light my image came at me time and time again. I stretched as far as I could see in synchronised clones. I moved forward to what I thought was an alleyway but found myself bumping headfirst into another pane of glass. I heard the laughter of two invisible children.

I slid forward and sideways, multiplying and dividing as I went. The toe of my boots clanking on the enforced glass each time I took a wrong move. More footsteps echoed around me. I walked forwards three paces before reaching a dead end and wished I'd kept at least one of those beers on me.

I heard the sound of cheers as a separate group of players must have reached their destination. I turned three times but became more and more agitated despite the structure's implied enjoyment. To my far right, at the final version of myself before I curved into a vortex of blurred shapes and light, I saw a glint and the shadow of an arm touching mine. I turned but no-one was there.

I pressed onwards. Footsteps grew closer behind me. Wood creaking in every direction. I took a sharp left turn and saw Michael's scars, magnified and swirling they zoomed towards me before retreating. My movements became less controlled as I forced my way forward. Ceiling length mirrors began shifting and scratching against the floor as they stretched on their hinges. The sound of breathing behind me, so close it warmed my ear. I turned to face an empty void. I jammed my way in a diagonal stretch as my reflections became distorted, my body circling in and out of itself over and over again. A cool breeze on my face. My palms began to sweat. I saw his body come towards me a hundred times over like determined cavalry. I pressed myself backwards against a mirror and felt it shift as I saw him moving forwards, the scrape of his knife dragging in a painful screech across the mirror. I felt something give and I tumbled backwards towards a shaky wooden barrier and felt the night air surround me.

The mirrors turned black the moment I escaped, as though they had never been there at all. Inside the maze was silent. No footsteps, no shouting. I steeled myself and walked shakily towards the stand at the front of the enclosure.

"A brave man," said the moustached woman, pointing at me with a magic wand. "Who has survived the horrors, but will he ever be the same again?" A gang of colour coded children laughed and ran inside, followed less enthusiastically by two begrudging parents. "You were a while inside. I had two. How'd you like the house of mirrors?"

"Well, two probably won't cut it."

"That bad?"

"You could say that," I cracked open a beer and drained the can right on the spot. "You see the men who followed me inside?"

"A magician never reveals his secrets," she said, tapping me on the forehead with the tip of her wand, then, dropping back to her own voice. "But if you scout any more supplies I'll swap my company for a can any day. Fucking kids make me want to torch the whole damn place. It's no work for a graduate. Not a sober one at least."

"You'll be the first to know if I do," I said already fleeing the vicinity, the second can inches from empty.

I made it to the nucleus of the fair. Those places were designed to spook you, I told myself. Already the biggest attraction had been the medical tent, where faint women dipped their heads into buckets as though freshly guillotined, and children lay delirious from an influx of sugar and speed.

It was all in my head.

I followed the scent downhill towards a hexagonal cluster of food tents. Escaped balloons floated high overhead and the ping of the strong-man bell sounded triumph as fathers shrugged no-big-deal shrugs as they discreetly massaged their torn shoulders. The smell of fat off the hot dogs overwhelmed, the grease of onions coating everything like ash after an eruption. But through it all that gentle buzz of chilli carried me to where they were, my throat scratching and tickling with the heat as I grew closer and closer.

Somewhere in the distance a bang exploded like a car backfiring as a rocket shot up to the sky and scattered its innards in a deafening waterfall of reds and greens.

"Well I'll be! Come on back here and sample the fruits of our labours," said Harlow, edging Barbara to the edge of the counter as they scooped angry red slop into paper cups for the masses.

I skipped the line with pride as opposed to the shame such dupes would usually elicit. The hungry mob didn't seem to mind, focused as they were on the ever nearing promise of sustenance.

"How you doing, darling?" asked Barbara, unable to look up as she changed notes for coins and passed steaming bowls to the wall of grasping hands.

"I'm good thank you. I see business is booming."

"You bet your ass it is, best damn chilli in the state. And don't let no-one tell you any different. People sniffing around here with their suggestions and their tips... "

Barbara continued on her rant as she spread sour cream on tortillas and flicked cindering squares of onion from the gas rungs. She was a woman who could fill even the deadliest silence and make it seem like a pleasure. It's not my fault. I try, really I do. I just find myself unable to flow when it comes to conversation; the moment I could articulate the point that has weaved slowly from brain to mouth always seems to pass by without me. To some people it comes so easily, and for their gift I'm always grateful. For me it has never been anything but unpleasant. I've gotten this far on the kindness of strangers and those that mistakenly interpret shyness as depth or mystique. It's one of the few things that have actually taken a nosedive since I met you. My conversation has become even more stuttered and sporadic as our exchanges have developed. I suppose I just save the best of myself for the page, these days at least.

Harlow passed me an unopened beer beneath the counter with the gentlest shake of his head.

"So I've heard. You think you'll stretch it to last the night?"

"No," replied Barbara as the crowds began to ease off. "Sooner run out early than trick on the portions. It's just the way I am."

"Quite right too."

"You been on the rides yet, kiddo?" asked Harlow, opening a beer and taking a welcome sip.

"Just getting the lay of the land for now."

"First timer, eh?"

"That's the one."

"Oh we been here every year since the year dot. Know the place like the back of our hands. Nothing ever changes. Even recognise some of the hot dogs."

"You just ignore him," said Barbara, now entirely free of her customers. "It's a good night had by all. You enjoying it so far?"

"I'm just finding my party spirit."

"Oh it'll come, sugar, don't you worry. Say, I'm sorry to hear about your news... "

"Barb... " Harlow warned her but she slapped his hand as to silence him. It seemed to do the trick and she edged past him towards me.

"She was part of my knitting circle for a while."

"I never really knew her."

"No-one did if you ask me. She seemed lonely, truth be told. I think she only came for the conversation to start with. Didn't bother me, I was always one for the gossip too – "

"You don't say," interrupted Harlow, though Barbara ignored him.

"Gave up soon enough, Lord knows the poor thing could barely cast on without breaking a sweat. Some of the girls though, they take their yarn real serious. I think that put her off. But I used to stop by, sometimes, to the diner, and we'd chat and say we'd arrange lunch dates. Of course, between this one and that, I never had time. But I'd like to think we might have, one day."

"I'm sure she'd have enjoyed it."

"A real tragedy. And those men are still out walking free. I tell you if there is a God he's got one fine sense of humour."

"This really where Jonah's party spirit is?" asked Harlow.

Barbara considered his interjection for a moment, and visibly gave thought to challenging his appeal. Though eventually her face fell and she shook her head. "You're right, I'm sorry. You don't want me raking up all that old dirt. Here," she handed me a bowl, "get something in your stomach before you fall down drunk as a preacher."

I walked around the fair having promised that I would return to help disassemble Harlow's food stall and aid him in the removal of any remaining refreshments. Rainbow lights spun and shone like luminous organs as machines rose and fell for the shrieking pleasure of the masses. A wave of yells came and went as a circular seat shot a crowd up into the air then stopped, momentarily, before plunging back down to earth. A juggler tried in vain to secure an uninterested group of schoolchildren who sat glued to a puppet show as socks dressed as princesses and crocodiles played out muffled fantasies behind a wooden stage.

"Come sir, prove your worth at the Hercules challenge!" yelled a muscled man by a shining tower, brandishing a sledgehammer in my direction. I dipped my head and continued on my way.

I cocked the long neck and rested the heavy wood on my shoulder as I took aim. I never thought I'd hold a gun again in my life, let alone pay for the privilege. But after some cajoling by the tattooed salesman and five dollars of my own money I found myself staring with one eye down that slim metal pole, silently calculating the likelihood of a tin duck's head against the paltry firearm I had been granted. Around me, pellets blasted off the dartboard, pinging the failure of a thousand red-eyed fathers, already into double figures for stuffed toys which would have cost no more than a dollar a piece in the first place.

"Close but no cigar my friend," said the man on the stall, carefully removing the rifle from the hand of a man as his daughter kicked her disappointment into the base of his shin. "You got a steady hand," he said to me, moving between the putting guns. His arms were beaten and speckled with dozens of purple hearts from a lifetime of overconfidence in the face of friendly fire.

"Just getting my money's worth," I said, firing my first shot and feeling myself grimace as it swooped past the beak of a duck and embedded itself in a serpent's tail on the jungle mural.

"Three to go. Good luck," he offered before moving past me to take a single bill from an outstretched hand.

"God knows I need it." A pantomime puff of smoke drifted across my line of view, the faint scent of gunpowder lingering like tyre marks as I moved my aim gently to the right, steadying my hand as best I could.

"Two rounds, good sir."

I heard a voice behind me and thought nothing of it. The man on the stall stuffed the dollar bills into the leather pouch dangling across his crotch and passed a gun to my unseen hunting mate.

"Paying money to shoot, well blow me if that's not irony, huh buddy?" The voice became familiar, crisp and hot, a whisper straight into the lobe of my ear. I turned to face him and the gun moved with me. There was the sound of a ping then a deep holler.

"Fuck, damn it!" The man behind the game crouched down, a bloodied ear cupped in his hand.

The crowd inhaled courteously and then returned to their targets as the injured party stood up, unscathed save for a trickle of blood no more elaborate than a requested piercing would produce. I could feel Michael's body jig up and down behind me as he almost choked laughing.

"Sorry," I offered.

The man with the pouch walked towards me and picked a dirty cloth from beneath the counter, wiping the final traces of blood from his ear. "Had worse, let's try for the ducks this time, there's no bonus points for killing the steward," he chuckled and moved to the farthest edge of the game.

"I don't know about that," said Michael, readying his gun. He moved his body so close that our barrels were as good as locked. "Care to take me on? For old time's sake?"

"I thought I told you to go," I said and pressed my finger to the trigger. My shot rang out but caused little indent.

"And I thought I chose to ignore your request." Michael shot once and missed.

"This isn't a game anymore. This is my life."

"Who's playing?"

"You kill that woman?"

"No," he turned to look at me and blindly pulled the trigger. The bullet hit the tin duck straight between the eyes and sent it falling rigidly to its side. "You did."

"Good shot," the man said, his minor wound now clotted and black. "Take your pick!"

He held his hand out to an array of toys and tat. "I'll take the rose," said Michael, pointing at a plastic flower with red, glittered petals. "For the little lady."

"One rose." He handed Michael the flower and he trailed off, merging with the crowd. I ditched my weapon, still one shot heavy, and attempted to follow his lead.

"Michael... " I tried. He ducked towards the barn-dance tent, which played the same tune over and over again. "Michael, come back." I pushed my way through the crowds until finally all that remained between us were twenty paces and a dozen paper cups jewelling the mud. "Wait," I grabbed him by the arm and spun him to face me. Just beneath his left eye four tiny fork prongs had pierced the skin and dragged down towards his cheek. Inside the tent the band paused for applause and then sprang back into action. "You can't go around saying things like that."

"Ah Jonah. Don't play dumb. The way I see it I'm owed some compensation. Now, being the genial soul I am I was all for the nice way. But you've changed my friend, you've changed."

"What are you talking about?" I said, dipping my voice as an elderly couple in tracksuits and gold sneakers marched past us towards the tent's entrance.

Michael considered me for a moment before something over my shoulder caught his eye. He craned his neck to see then returned to staring at me once more. "Well would you believe I found me a little lady?"

I turned to look as Aimee bounded towards us, a stuffed animal dangling from her arm. Michael waved and smiled past me.

"Michael, listen to me. You leave that girl alone. She's no good for playing with."

"Here," he said, his eyes still somewhere in the distance, "take this." He pressed something into my hand and instinctively my grip tightened. It was the handle of an unopened switchblade, rusted and worn. I tried to pass it back to him when I felt Aimee's hand brush the base of my spine. I jammed the knife into my pocket and loosened my shirt so that it hung over any trace of the weapon.

Michael held out his hand, which Aimee took and sunk into the embrace of his arms.

"You two have met?" she said, kissing the good side of his face.

"No," I replied, beads of sweat tickling my upper lip.

"Ah now that's not true now is it? Me and Jonah been bonding over some target practice. Got me a girl and a friend now. What are the chances?"

"Jonah works with Daddy," Aimee said to Michael, who handed her the rose.

"Well small world, darling," said Michael in mock surprise.

"Edward's a businessman," she told me proudly. "He owns a factory and two movie theatres."

"Edward?"

"Edward," said Aimee, gripping him tighter.

"I thought it was Michael."

"Must have misheard my friend. No offense taken."

"How long you known each other?" I asked.

"Nearly twenty-four hours," said Aimee.

"We value quality over quantity, isn't that right, precious?" Michael added, squeezing Aimee's waist.

"Edward's been helping me through my grief, what with the funeral yesterday and, you know, the other... "

"How is Levi?" I asked.

Aimee looked down at her feet and shuffled on the spot. "Dead man can't love you."

"Damn right, darling," Michael added. "And he sure as hell won't be writing you in no book, not in his condition."

"Seemed alive last time I checked."

"Only a matter of time though," Michael shot back. "Say, darling, why don't you go in there and get us a table? I'll be there before you can blink."

Aimee smiled and made her way slowly into the tent.

"Sweeter than candy," he said, his tongue slithering over the crooked yellow of his teeth.

"I'm not joking Michael, I don't know what you got planned, but leave the girl out of it," I went to take the knife from my pocket as another group passed between us.

"Now just you remember what it is you owe me, friend," he said. "The moral high ground doesn't suit you Jonah, the sooner you realise what you are the better."

"And what exactly is that?"

"You're one of us. It's not your fault, some people are just born that way."

"Some people change."

"No they don't," said Michael, moving away from me. "They just act different. Scratch the surface and you're rotten to the core."

"You killed that woman, didn't you?" I said as he pulled back the flayed entrance of the tent, causing a crescendo of sound to cloud our conversation.

"I'm not the one holding the knife, nor am I the one in possession of a morning's change."

"Why are you doing this?"

"I just want a moment of your time, Jonah, that's all I'm asking. Atonement if you will. Now if you don't mind I have a little business to attend to."


Michael led Aimee to the dance floor. I made my way to follow them but found myself tangled in a mass of bodies, as the crowds closed around me like a wave.

"I want you guys to hold on to your girls real tight now," said the conductor as the band's beat increased in pace. "This is going a be a fast one."

The notes grew denser as the dancers attempted to establish a communal rhythm. Michael spun Aimee around the wooden floor so hard she looked like she was going to twirl up into the air and be lost forever. She didn't seem to mind as much. She allowed herself to be led, her head flung back and smiling as his hands wound her further and further into a daze. I became lost in the milieu, in no way attempting to dance I simply manoeuvred myself in accordance with the increasing frenzy around me, aware that were I to trip I'd no doubt be trampled beneath the hooves of the masses.

"That poor boy's dancing all alone," I heard a lady say as she spun past me on the arm of her suited husband.

"Watch it kid," said a large man as his wife's elbow caught me on their way past.

I ducked and swerved the arms and legs as the music became faster and faster, eventually I made it towards where they danced and held out my hand to Aimee who instinctively took it. "Hope you don't mind if I cut in," I said as she left Michael's arms, which were promptly filled by a plump woman in a cartoon tshirt who had been following me blindly on my voyage, keen for nothing more than a stranger's touch.

"Well I never had two boys fighting over me before," Aimee said, regulating her limbs to my more sombre movement. "You boys won't be duelling over me I hope."

"The night is young," Michael said, as he was spun to the centre of the dance floor by his somewhat forceful new partner.

"I guess it's true what Daddy says about still waters," Aimee said, pressing her head into my chest as we spun around the floor, the whole time her eyes remained glued to Michael.

"What?"

"I never knew you were such an accomplished dancer."

"I've been called many things in my time but never that."

"I think you'd make a fine husband one day Jonah, just fine."

"You barely know me."

"I know what I see."

"You'd be surprised."

"You think Edward would make a good husband?"

"Who?"

"Edward, you think he'll treat me right."

"I think you deserve a good husband. But I don't think he's it."

"You got evidence of that, stranger?"

"I need you to listen to me, Aimee," I said, edging us as subtly as I could towards the tent's exit.

"That sounds awfully serious."

"I need you to go, now, you understand?"

"Not entirely."

"I want you to go now and I want to know you'll never see Mich... Edward again."

"Why ever would you say such a thing?" she asked, suddenly resisting my attempts to exit the tent. We began spinning more and more to her movements, I felt myself being led back into the ebb and flow of bodies whose enthusiasm was beginning to far outweigh any skill in the coordination department.

"He's bad news."

"You only shot ducks with the poor man, he can't help the way he is... the scars and all. I'd have thought you of all people would understand."

"I met Edward's type before."

"Edward doesn't have a type."

"Believe me when I say he does."

"You going to have to stop speaking in code one of these days stranger."

"God damn it Aimee no-one in this whole world's been as nice to me as your Daddy has, and no-one deserves happiness the way you do. Edwards bad news, please believe me."

"I'm not so sure I do."

"He hasn't even told you his real name."

"How would you know?"

"I used to know him."

Aimee looked up at me and began to slow her rhythm. "In another life?"

"Something like that. Please just do this for me."

"How did you know him?"

"We were the same, he and I."

"And now you're not."

"Now we're not. He's dangerous."

"*Mysterious,*" she corrected me.

"Aimee just listen to me, just don't see Michael anymore you hear me?"

"You're serious about this, aren't you?" she said, looking up at me, a tear beginning to take shape in the corner of her eye.

Before I had a chance to answer a scream sounded out from behind the band. The music stopped and the attention of the room shifted to the rear of the tent.

The flames started small at first, teasing up the canvas like it was being spilled back into itself. Then it began to crawl along the rope that held the lights. It seemed as though no-one moved in those moments, though my memory may not serve me entirely correctly. The bulbs began popping like tiny little fireworks, pieces of glass showering the band and the dancers closest to the stage. Then the flames grew up to the dome of the tent, the chill around our ankles becoming more pronounced by the tingle of warmth that dripped from above.

Another scream. Then another. Before we knew it the crowds were rushing around us, tripping on tables and upturning folding chairs in the rush to escape the tent.

"Where's Edward?" cried Aimee, battling against the bodies towards where the fire was at its fiercest. I grabbed hold of her wrist and dragged her into the suffocating heart of the crowd in which she had no choice but to move towards safety. We were carried almost without effort towards the exit where some of the elderly couples were already sprawled on the grass, exhausted from the excitement. From outside the tent black smoke crept beneath the gaps in the awning. "Where is he?" said Aimee, pulling against my hold. "I have to find him." The flames grew over and around the roof of the tent like a cake being iced.

"I'll find him," I said as she struggled against me. "Just go."

"You don't even like him."

"Just trust me I'll find him, now go," I pushed her into the crowds, which swallowed her whole and seemed to carry her to a safer distance. I turned and stood my ground. Around me people rushed in hazes of colour and warmth, children's feet levitated as their parents took either arm and double-stepped away from the mounting heat.

The tent became more and more furious, roaring towards the sky as though in competition with the commotion below.

"Where's the girl?" said Harlow, grabbing hold of me in both arms as Barbara hovered, jerking from the bodies that pushed past her.

"Went with the crowd, should be waiting for you at the front," I said, forced to shout over the din.

"Come on," Harlow took my arm and began dragging me backwards.

"Friend of mine's back there," I said. "Just need to make sure he's okay."

"It's not safe."

"I'll be out shortly, just go."

Harlow hesitated before thinking better of entering into discussion on the subject, and, taking Barbara by the hand, joined the hourglass of bodies that flowed seamlessly towards the edge of the field.

I walked into the masses - breaking and muddying everything in its path - shoulders bashed and bruised against mine. A boy following his father's footsteps bumped into my leg and then picked himself up again.

Through it all I saw him moving towards me, an unlit cigarette clamped between his teeth. He picked a lighter from his pocket and lit it as bodies rushed all around him like a flooded dam. "Well won't this make for a fine story," he said over the noise of the fire, already wilting into itself.

I walked towards him and grabbed him by the shoulders, driving my knee into his stomach. I felt him double over and fall back.

"Well now, that was far from a clever move my friend, far from a clever move."

"What the hell do you want from me Michael?"

"An apology for start."

"I'm sorry," I hurried. "I'm sorry, God knows I'm sorry but please, please just go."

"Well I don't think you really meant that. I want you to beg."

"I'd sooner die."

"Second time lucky. I don't think you'll be swerving the injection so easily this time," he said, pointing to my stomach.

I reached down and felt the bony handle of the knife protruding. I pulled it from the fold in my denim and went to throw it.

"Now just you hold your horses," Michael said, walking closer to me, wincing slightly as he moved. "This day and age a man has to be careful what he leaves lying around. You're all over that blade like stink on shit. I think - " he said when I found myself unable to respond, " - I'm going to hang around these parts for some time, get acquainted with the little lady, maybe start me a family. Can you imagine that? My looks and her brain, it'd be the most backwards son of a bitch there ever... "

His speech stopped as I took his head in my hands, pushing the blade of the knife towards the lowest edge of his lip.

"Now I don't want to have to ask you again. I near as killed you once, nothing stopping me getting it right a second time. You either go or I'm going to cut the good side of your face clean off, you understand?" There was a moment of stillness, that stinging second where the audience contemplates its reaction. I allowed Michael to work his face free from my hands before stepping back, returning the knife to my pocket. "I won't ask you again," I said as I began to walk away.

He made no attempt to follow me, and it was only when I was some steps away did I hear him begin to chuckle to himself.

"Well, you're as succinct as ever, big guy. But if you ask me you're gonna be grateful for a friend like me once those police start sniffing around your house. There isn't one thing I left to chance my friend. And folk round here won't be so kind once the fingers start pointing."

"I'll take my chances," I said, still not turning to face him.

"It's just incredible what you find when you go sniffing around someone's house. Five minutes in that old bedroom of yours I got a direct line to your soul, wow! I tell you you're a man of hidden depths, I never knew you had it in you." I heard him move, and a rustling of papers. On the horizon car lights veined the brow of the hill as towards us six flashing eyes of cobalt grew larger and more vocal with each passing instant. "'My Dearest Jonah... '" he began, in a whiny, pitying voice. "'Please excuse my lateness in response, for there have been developments... '"

Before even I was aware of my actions I had knocked him to the ground and was sat on top of him, my fist working into the dried flesh of his face. Eventually he was still, his hand limp beneath him. I took your muddy letter and folded it neatly into my pocket.

"Well wouldn't you know," he said through damp, swollen lips. "Looks like I found your Achilles heel."

"You so much as talk about her I'll kill you. You understand? One word Michael... all it'll take," I moved towards him and, still bent doubled, he raised his hand to stop me.

"Now don't be getting all excited there, friend. Of course I took her address, for insurance... " I grabbed him by the throat and held him tight at arm's length. "... and I'm sure that both you and I would hate to hear of any such accidents happening, so how about you reconsider my terms? That's all I'm asking. Just an evening of your time and skills, then it'll be like I was never here." As he spoke he freed himself from my lessening grip, smoothing his shirt now speckled with blood.

"When?"

"I'll come to you, friend. You old romantic." I turned to leave. "Oh," he said, when I was almost out of earshot. "If I were you I'd dig up that money the second you get home. That old sack of coin's a one way ticket to you know where."

"Where is it?"

"Now," said Michael, standing up. "Where'd be the fun in that? The old Jonah'd have known exactly where to look. Think of it as a test of your skills. I'm gonna need you sharp as ever," he patted me on the back as he passed. "Happy hunting. I'll be seeing you soon partner."

I will sit and I'll wait for Michael's call. It's all I can do. You have to understand that I'm doing this for you, Verity. However bad things get - and I can feel doom building like a snowstorm - you have to believe me when I say that at the back of it all, however misplaced, is my love for you, and only for you. And I will do whatever it takes to protect you from harm. The world's a more interesting place with you in it, and I intend to keep it that way.

Always,
Jonah

Dear Jonah,

Eve's murder arrived like a plague. It grew impalpably, silently - crawling and multiplying beneath secret, unturned stones - before combusting into something grotesquely irreversible.

"What do you think you'll be when we get where we're going?" I asked, contemplating three half used lipsticks on the bathroom counter. "Blood Roses, Honey Blossom or Candy Frosting?"

Eve yawned as she came into the bathroom, sitting down on the toilet as her head drooped between her legs. "Aren't they some of the girls at the club?"

"This is serious Eve, we got to sort ourselves out and fast."

"Just take them all," she said, pressing a gesture piece of tissue between her legs before standing back up.

"Eve I'm not your damn mother, you have to cut me some slack here. We need to get this sorted."

She sat up and began to tease a nail with a dull file. "I don't see what all the fuss is about. I don't have one thing I need except you and that cash. I say we start our lives fresh as mountain snow, let all of this turn to dust."

I sunk onto the sofa next to her and took a cigarette from her packet. "Life's not that simple."

"It is for me."

"And thank the Lord there's only one of you. I say this out of kindness you understand."

"I'll miss this little life," she said, relaxing into her third glass as I picked over the jewellery that scattered the coffee table. "We didn't have it so bad."

"We could have it so much better if you'd help me pack."

"I told you, I got it covered. All I need are the clothes on my back and a few dollars to see me straight. I'll charm the rest."

I bundled the jewellery in two tangled handfuls - mock gold, cubic zirconia, all brown edged and rusting - into an empty shoebox beneath the couch.

"You think we could go back to the club, just to say goodbye?"

"No!"

"Well you don't have to yell," Eve said, attempting to squeeze the final drops from the spent bottle. "I just think after all Miss Jemima's done for us it's be rude not to say thank you."

"We'll write her."

"You're a cold woman, Verity," she said, reaching into a crevice within the couch and pulling out a handful of bills. "Why don't you go get us some more resources, so we can celebrate our last night in style?"

I took the money and located my car keys. "I swear to God, Eve... I don't find you here when I come back there'll be hell to pay."

Her hand rose from the sofa and waved lazily, before slumping back onto her stomach.

In the store I made my usual gesture of scanning the brands as if to imply I had any idea what I was looking for. In truth such trips were always born of the same incentive – maximum effect with minimum outlay.

The lights above me shone sullen and iridescent making even the most menial tasks feel like a living, breathing headache. I selected the three cheapest bottles of burgundy grape I could locate, unperturbed by the triptych of languages which formed its elaborate description, and placed them on the counter.

"This all, miss?" asked the man on the desk.

"No," I said, walking back down the aisle towards the less heady luxuries. "I won't be long."

"No worries. You just take your time."

I pressed my hands against the shining foils of the chocolate. Outside a group of teenagers sat on the roof of their car, a radio booming loudly from the doors, opened wide like aeroplane wings.

"I'll take these too," I said, placing a bag of potato chips and three bars of chocolate on the counter.

"Bad week, huh?" asked the attendant as he placed my questionable feast into a brown paper bag.

"Something like that."

"Well you have a good night. We got aspirin, in case you're interested."

"I'll man it out," I said, leaving the receipt on the counter.

"Hey lady, hey miss!" one of the boys yelled from across the lot.

I looked up but did not stop walking.

"You buy us some hooch? We got the dollar if you got the time."

"Sorry boys that's one thing I'm short on," I said, fiddling for my keys.

"You want me to take that?" he said, his hand reaching beneath my bag.

I jumped and felt my face redden. "Thanks," I said, as J held my shopping bag, leaning against the car.

"You with the squad over there?" I asked, suddenly unable to process my own thoughts.

"No ma'am. You see my lady friend went awful quiet on me so I took to prowling the streets like some lonely old drifter."

"Sorry," I said, now urgent for my keys. In the hurry, and my overriding attempt to appear calm, I pushed my fingers clean through the lining of my jacket pocket. The keys dropped down my leg and onto the floor. "I've been busy is all. It's not personal."

"Well that is a relief. I'd hate to think I'd scared you off. Say this is quite the night in you got yourself here," he said, prodding his fingers into my grocery bag.

"It's a leaving party, for a friend," I took the bag from him and placed it on the back seat.

"You never mentioned no friend. I thought you were that cat that walked alone?"

"My charm prevails."

"This friend going far?"

"She doesn't know yet."

"It an open party?"

"Invite only - " I said more abruptly than intended " - sorry, I'm late as it is J. It was real good to see you. We should meet up soon. I'd like that."

"Well," he said, pushing himself upright against the roof of the car. "That ball's in your court now isn't it darling? You're as hard to pin down as I don't know what."

"I'm working this week."

"You gonna dance for me again?"

"No. But I'll pour you a real good coffee, if you're lucky," I said, shutting the door.

J bent down to the window, the rim of his hat edging towards my face. "Well you really do know the way to a man's heart."

"Straight through his back with a nine inch blade... so the saying goes."

He laughed and leaned further towards me. "How about a little kiss, sugar, something to remember me by?"

I parted my lips and allowed him to work his way towards me. The emptiness of his open mouth suffocated me and I sat, motionless, hating every passing tingle that trickled up my inner thighs. His tongue tasted dry and bitter, like a thousand and one nights of whisky and regret. I swallowed hard to destroy any evidence of him.

"I'll see you around J."

"Not if I see you first, darling. Not if I see you first."

Back at the trailer I stepped out of the car shaken but not entirely displeased at having seen J. I hated him and hated what he had done, what he was still doing. But, God help me, I couldn't help but feel a fleeting pleasure at the thought of him still pursuing me, however misguided he may have been. I walked inside with an added spring to my step, the bottles of wine clanking against one another in my bag.

"Three of the finest bottles sixteen dollars'll get you!" I said, placing the carrier on the floor, "And enough crap to kill a diabetic. You packing?"

There was no answer.

"Eve?"

The house was still. No movement, no sound. I dashed into the bedroom and flung open the bathroom door.

"Damn it, Eve!" I said, making my way back to the sofa to open the wine.

On the coffee table a note had been written in her girlish writing:

*Sorry V, I couldn't do it. You know where to find me!*

Each 'i' had been haloed with a love heart. Three X's marked the bottom of the page.

"Fuck!" I kicked an empty tumbler the full length of the living room: its dregs - a particularly astringent Shiraz - splattered the wall like a burst pimple.

Something hit my foot as I jigged across the dirt roads out of town, and I found myself unable to brake. Beneath the pedal and the floor a stray bottle of wine had lodged itself awkwardly. I let the car guide itself on the lonely road as I bent down and retrieved the little miracle, all the while grovelling to the god of screw tops.

Inside the hallway was empty.

"Well aren't we blessed," said Violet, the doorman, not entirely sincerely. Miss Jemima's unabashed favouritism had erected somewhat of a divide amongst us girls. We weren't to blame, of course, we were simply held accountable.

"Not tonight, Violet. You seen Eve?"

Violet shrugged and began counting dollar bills beneath her desk. "See everything, say nothing. That's our motto," she said coldly.

The chorus line kicked and dipped, their tassels twirling like a hypnotist's watch. I stood towards the back of the room, searching for Eve. At the bar a man had already passed out and was slumped, dead to the world, across the table as two old men flicked peanuts towards his hanging jaw.

The crowd had been whipped into a controlled frenzy and I felt frightened, as though suddenly dropped into the lion's cage. I made my way farther into the room, still unable to see Eve.

J had his back to me, and his arm was so close to Kingpin's that they seemed joined at the hip. J sat upright, whispering something to a waitress. She nodded and made her way to the bar as he sunk lower in his seat, pulling his hat down to the edge of his eyes.

I ran back out of that room and slammed the door behind me.

"Well you look like you seen a ghost. There aint gonna be no trouble tonight, is there?" asked Violet, lighting a cigarette.

I made my way past her and towards the backstage entrance. "No trouble. Oh and Violet, anyone asks you haven't seen me here, understand?" She did not respond so I chose to reiterate the point. "I found out you did otherwise I'm gonna knock you straight into next week. Now I need to know we're on the same page here."

She nodded and looked down.

Backstage clothes strewed the floor like shed skin. The music played on in the background and the sound of the crowd, rapt for the most part, built at intervals to a communal groan of longing. I peeked past the curtain, my hand tight on the brushed velvet, and watched Eve in her natural state. She bent and dipped, the other girls merely served as her shadow as she wound the audience tighter and tighter as though stretching them on a rack. I pushed forward, past the velvet curtain, and saw J sitting at his table, his eyes disguised by the rim of his hat, the rest of him merged with the candlelight. He leant towards Kingpin and pointed towards the centre of the stage. Kingpin nodded as J stood up and made his way to the back of the bar room, out of sight.

Within seconds I heard his footsteps grow closer and I ducked behind the door. I felt him beside me, breathing steadily but deeply. The door closed and we were face to face.

"J," I said, taking the first coat I could find from the rack and putting it on. "This here's private quarters, no place for punters."

He smiled and walked towards me, taking my arm in his hand. "Let's quit fooling, sugar. You're the biggest disappointment I've had in a long time. And I've had my fair share let me tell you."

"J don't do this," I said, freeing myself from his grip and falling back into a vanity mirror.

"You knew all along, didn't you?"

"I didn't, I - " My cheek made the sound of a snapped twig as his hand graced it so suddenly. "I didn't know J!"

"Bull... shit," he said, one hand working inside of his pocket. "Now my way of thinking is that little bitch got something of mine, and I'm going to get it back. But what we have here is an unfortunate twist of fate."

"Let me go," I said, standing up only to be knocked back down to my original starting point

"See, I liked you a lot darling, liked you a lot."

"I liked you too. I wish I didn't but I did."

He slapped me across the face once more. "The problem - once you've learned not to interrupt me - is that I now feel I'm owed something from the both of you. Between her and my money and you and my feelings. I'm a sensitive boy, Verity, and you hurt me real bad. You never can know anyone in this life, sugar... aint that the truth." He grabbed me by the nape of my neck and dragged me to my feet.

"You weren't so pure yourself. Those sad stories about your Daddy."

"The specifics aren't really the issue here. I want my money, and I want that little whore to realise the error of her ways."

I spat in his face and within moments felt the weight of his body concentrate into a fist, which sent me spiralling to the ground. I screamed as he climbed on top of me, his hand holding my chest as he unbuttoned his trousers.

"God damn it girl I'm gonna show you just how bad you hurt me."

I dug four nails into the skin of his forehead until I felt them pierce his flesh. Four tidy crescents of blood rose to the surface as he dragged me up and pushed me flat on my stomach.

"Now this is just a little reminder of what could have been, sugar."

"J - " I was barely able to breathe. I fumbled between the two coats as I felt him raise his waist inches from my back, but the gun became nothing more than a suggestion of itself beneath the cloth and the zips. "Please don't do this J," I said as I heard the quiet jingle of his buckle unfastening.

"Oh my, you're gonna know about this."

I screamed once more and then stopped, shocked, as the weight of his body pressed down on top of me and then lay, stuck like an anchor. I turned my head to see Miss Jemima standing above me. J groaned and pushed himself onto the floor as he made an attempt to sit up.

"Get the girl and go," she said, dropping a broken stool to the ground and walking straight over J's body. She helped me to my feet and reached behind the stage curtain, flipping a switch. Suddenly the stage lights dipped. The audience moaned and yelled. Then with another flick of a switch the room went dark save the candles that lined the tables and bar. "Go now."

"Verity, why you ruining my dance! Feels like I got nearly two hundred dollars in these garters and fully intended making more," Eve hissed.

"They're here," I said, taking her by the arm.

"What you talking about?"

Men from the audience, blind as moles, yelled into the darkness. Chairs shuffled and glasses clanked.

"The men, they're here and they want their money."

I felt Eve grow cold against me. "They're going to kill us," she said matter of factly.

"They're going to try," I said, leading her to the edge of the stage.

The girls around us clustered together as invisible hands began to crawl across the lip of the stage. One slipped on a patch of oil and the rest flocked to her assistance. We were inches from our escape when J appeared, upright and recovered.

"My God - " Eve said, quietly, " - this isn't happening."

"You bet your life it is baby," J said, walking towards us.

We turned and ran towards the edge of the stage, jumping into the scrum. Kingpin stood up and fired a round into the air. Men started hollering, making their way towards the door. We joined the mass of bodies and dashed towards the exit. More bullets sounded out. Paul, now barely much more than a decorative torso, rolled to the floor and scrunched his eyes tightly as limbs ran over and past him as mocking as they were painful.

Outside, boys flew in every direction like spilled marbles. Grown men hid, frightened, in sandy ditches that surrounded the club like a moat. Most jumped into the closest cars to hand regardless of ownership. We reached my car and climbed inside.

It was almost a mile before either of us could speak. "They'll find us," said Eve, still blank, still certain. I reached my hand out and held tight onto her arm.

"We'll be okay. I just need you to be strong for me now, you hear me? This can work."

"I love you Verity, no two ways about it."

"I love you too."

"I'm so sorry."

We made the remainder of the journey in clinical silence. Back at the trailer I unlocked the door with a wavering hand and made sure that the gun was, this time at least, in touching distance.

The moment I stepped inside something jerked me by the neck. I stumbled to the floor and Eve followed. A light was turned on and the door closed as Kingpin stepped towards us. Dollar bills marked the carpet like footprints. The couch had been upturned, the oven door snapped from its hinges. J made his way from the bedroom as Eve began to weep. "Welcome home ladies."

"J, you don't have to do this." Eve shot a dumfounded look in my direction and I felt my heart break.

"I wouldn't be troubling myself if this were not a paramount concern," he said, taking Eve's head in his hand as he bent towards her face. "Hey darling, long time no see."

Kingpin moved towards us so that we were kneeling on the carpet between them.

"J, just take your money and go, please."

"Now, I want to know where every damn dollar is, and I want to know now," he said, picking something from the side of the couch.

From high above a cool ointment doused our heads. Eve began to whimper and whine as the smell of the fumes became overbearing.

"There's some in the oven - " I said.

"Found it."

"And underneath the bed."

A further trickle poured over us, soaking and stinging through our clothes.

"J, God please... "

"Keep talking darling, it'll be over soon."

"Behind the bathtub - "

"That's a good girl," he said, splashing short bursts of fuel across our bodies like babies being blessed.

"God, J... "

"Not long to go darling, you just keep up the good work."

"There's some out back, underneath the power box - " I became more frantic, my words jumbled and stuttered. Eve started to whisper something softly under her breath, occasionally choking as the fuel caught and dribbled into her mouth.

"What's that you're saying, precious? Is that an apology I hear?"

"Our father who art in heaven... " her words began to take shape through the fracture of her voice. "Hallowed be thy name... "

"There's a whole bunch in a suitcase beneath the bed... please J don't do this... " I tried as more and more liquid cascaded around us, pooling between my splayed fingers.

"Thy kingdom come thy will be done... "

"The last should be in the mattress, J, please, that's all of it, just look, it's there... " I pressed my hand to his ankle and felt it soak through the fabric of his trousers towards that strong, lean calf.

"And the rest," he said.

"On earth as it is in heaven... "

"That's it."

"I know that's not true."

"Give us this day our daily bread and forgive us our trespasses... "

"Bullshit!" he slammed the can into my face and I felt blood cut through the coolness of the petrol as it snaked its way down my chin.

"She sold it J, it's gone, the money's all there, just about, God J you can't have what's not there - "

He upturned the canister and raised it high so that the torrent became steadier, gushing down on us like a waterfall.

"As we forgive those who trespass against us... "

"Oh baby, it could have been so much better than this. We could have been so much better than this."

Even when dizzy with the fumes I found myself wondering which of us he was addressing.

"And lead us not into temptation but deliver us from evil... "

The final drops echoed out as they merged with the pool around us.

"J, please don't do this."

"For thine is the kingdom and the power and the glory... "

I tried to stand up, half blind and leaden with fear. "J, God, please listen to me, I will do anything, I mean anything. Just let her go, please, please don't do this."

With the palm of his hand he pressed me back to the floor, my face hanging low so that all I could see were my bent knees and Eve wringing her hands in the fold of her stomach. "Darling, it's not personal. It's just business."

"For ever and ever... "

I heard a match roar in his hand. There was a moment of still as the sulphur's cackle dipped; its combustion merging smoothly with the steady burn of the narrow stick; the whole trailer suddenly illuminated by its amber orb.

"Amen... " Eve finished and raised her head gently. Her hand jutted out and wrapped itself around Kingpin's leg, the other curved smoothly as she pressed a nail file into the soft skin at the back of his knee, driving the metal blade all the way inside. "Verity go!" She gripped me by my arm and dragged me to my feet while she remained on the ground, working the metal farther into his skin as Kingpin roared in agony, tumbling to one side like a felled giant.

I stood up, propelled by her force, and ran to the door. Kingpin grabbed Eve by the hair and drove her face into the ground. J cupped the match, which extinguished in the palm of his hand, and made his way towards me. I felt air, the world, clear as rain in the desert, blow sweetly across my face before the door slammed shut. He pulled me back into the trailer and struck me so hard across the face I lay motionless on the floor.

Kingpin rose, doubled over, and passed something to J who took Eve's head in his hand and whispered something in her ear. She nodded and looked him straight in the eye as he pressed once into the centre of her stomach. The whole time she didn't flinch, not once.

Eve fell backwards gently, peacefully. Around her stomach a perfect rose began to bloom, its ruby stem trickling down between her legs. Her face turned towards me as she unfurled and relaxed; shades of scarlet gilding the pale curve of her body. A tear rolled down my face as she closed her eyes and was still.

I heard Kingpin groan and slump in the corner of the room. Footsteps fluttered past me and then grew louder until I could feel the tip of his sole at the side of my head.

I turned to face Eve, certain only that whatever he took he would not be granted the gift of my scream. Any fear I felt I held on to like treasure. I felt my body double as his foot thrust into my stomach, and then a second time as I snaked around myself. He knelt on top of me, my arms spread out and pinned beneath his knees. With the dull edge of the knife he traced my jaw line all the way to my breastbone, popping my buttons as he went. Then he stopped and looked down. He pressed his hands into the pocket of my jeans and pulled out the pistol.

He smiled at me as he placed it carefully on the floor, next to which he rested the knife.

When I heard the sound of the match I seemed certain of my own death; certain that after a brief agony all would be lost. I suppose somewhere in the back of my mind I had always assumed that the world ended with me; that with closed eyes darkness really was all that remained. But in those seconds, those long and frightening seconds, reality swept over me like a wave. If I were gone then the world would carry on. If I did not turn up for work then someone else would. If my taxes went unpaid the economy would adjust accordingly.

But what if I stopped writing? Would my memory remain acute, Jonah? Or would it fade with the ink and the paper until years passed by and I became little more than a forgotten amusement? What am I, I suppose is what I'm asking, and more importantly what am I to you?

I was granted no great epiphany as I closed my eyes and prayed that whatever came next would be as immediate as could be. There was no one moment that forced itself to the fore of my mind's eye, enlightening me as to my function, my purpose, my origin. It was as though a movie was playing behind a screen, and all I could do was piece together a narrative from the glimpses of light and sound that flickered at the edges. Images grew and shrank, as strange and alien as another person's photographs. I saw my mother, her face changing from rage to regret as was ever the case, and my father asleep in the dark, cooled by the television's cold light, an empty glass falling from his unconscious grasp. I saw flowers in summer, the gentle snow that pre-empts the blizzard, a swing set, ribbons, I saw my lovers pass through me one by one, their faces shifting with each thrust; the wallpaper of my first home, the envelope of my first paycheque, someone's coffin, Eve dancing on that very first night I laid eyes on her, a hospital bed. And then you, somehow, your presence as real as all those things yet a thousand times as vital, like a dark glitter scattered across all that went before and after.

I don't know how many hours passed by after that. Whether they dismembered Eve before or after locating the money - almost all of which was gone when I returned - or whether Kingpin remained lame, or died haemorrhaging from his injuries. I don't know how badly I was beaten, or how the decision to spare my life was reached. Most devastatingly of all I don't know what became of Eve's remains. I pray she is somewhere beautiful, somewhere quiet. Somewhere people may one day leave flowers, even without realising the significance. I pray that wherever she is she's at peace, and laughing, and forever in love.

All I do know is that I woke up alone and frightened, and you were all I had left.

With all my heart and soul,
Always,
Verity

Dear Verity,

When I returned I found myself tearing apart my own house in the dead of night.

I turned every stone, so to speak, upending furniture, reaching into spaces that had never seen the likes of soap and water, puncturing plaster in speckled patterns. Occasionally sanity would prevail and I had to remind myself that I was working to a remit as I began smashing holes into the walls out of sheer frustration. After an hour of scrabbling about on my hands and knees I resigned myself firstly to failure, and then thought, perhaps, that Michael could have been lying all along. The ruse would not be beyond him had he thought that it might lead to him securing my services in whatever area he had them earmarked for. But even I couldn't fool myself that easily.

I walked to the kitchen thirsty and exhausted, and took a sip of tepid water from a cup on the counter. The garden was still and peaceful, only just visible beneath the moon's dusty light. Flowers were beginning to take hold where before there had only been dirt. The soil, tilled and quenched, was now rich and inhabitable, and led in a perfect runway towards my beautiful new workhouse.

I crossed the garden in my stocking feet, dew dampening the cuff of my jeans. Inside, the space was as I had left it. I took both halves of your letter from my pocket and returned it to the box where I store everything you send me. Black fingerprints now lined the pages I had taken such care over - flexing the edges after reading so that they were as fresh as the day they were posted - and streaked down from the sentences that must have particularly amused Michael. I sealed the box and placed it back on the highest shelf.

I pushed my chair to one side and took out a hammer. The first floorboard proved the trickiest. I jammed the claw into its slim cleft and pulled as hard as I could until I fell backwards, the plank splintering into two separate lengths and jutting upwards. I reached down, too tired to so much as turn on a flashlight, and pulled a handful of weeds. I repeated the process again and again. By the sixth floorboard I was almost hysterical, as close to tearful as I think I've ever been. I reached down and patted the cold ground. Nothing. I pressed farther, my shoulder digging into the remaining wood of the ground. My fingertips brushed something soft. I inched forwards, nearly there, and managed to grasp its edge.

I removed my arm from the hole, a small cloth sack gripped tight in my fist. Coin and paper moved about inside as I passed it from hand to hand, almost relieved to find my madness denied by the horrible evidence.

I rolled the bag as tightly as its contents would allow before hiding it beneath my shirt and locking he door of the shed.

Above me a light turned on. Mrs Pemberton, dressed in a nightgown and curlers, appeared at the window like a ghost. "What's that hollering down there?" she said, still shaky from sleep.

"Nothing Mrs Pemberton," I said as I made my way back to the house.

"I heard a ruckus."

"There was no ruckus."

"Well I wouldn't be standing at this window if you'd been going about your business quiet as a dormouse. I can't hear my evening prayers."

"Evening prayers were six hours ago Mrs Pemberton. Go back to bed."

"That's enough of that smart mouth. What you doing causing trouble at this hour?"

"I'm sorry, I'm done."

"I don't like this," she said, closing her window. "I don't like this one bit."


Back in the house, or what was left of it, I sat on the floor, counting the bag's contents. There was fifty dollars in notes, and fifteen in coin. I placed the piles of silver neatly on my kitchen table. In the morning I would bury them as deep as I could dig.

I lit a fire in the front room and accepting sleep to be a missed opportunity began to burn each dollar one at a time. I watched as the ink tainted the flame and then curled around itself before disappearing to nothing but a black fly that danced up the chimney. One by one they hissed and disappeared.

I bundled the empty sack into a ball and threw it onto the flames, sitting back at the sudden increase in heat and light. I sat all night long amidst the sorry remainders of my little house and watched as the logs burnt themselves to nothing.

In the morning I didn't make it to Caleb's. I crawled into bed and lay in a daze as the seconds and hours passed, rewound, and passed again until once more it was dark. Monday came and went, as did Tuesday. I did not attend work. I did not leave the house. I just lay in wait, knowing that the second Michael walked through my door everything would change and it would change forever.

On the second day a knock sounded out sometime after dusk.

"Hey Jonah... Jonah... you in there?" Harlow yelled at the locked door.

I remained silent.

"Me and the boys been real worried about you. I hope everything's okay in there. Jonah - "

I heard a thump as he pressed his forehead to the glass pane.

"Jonah, you in there?"

I turned my face to the wall, sealing my bedroom curtain shut with an outstretched leg. All was quiet again and then a knock, this time louder, caused me to jump but did not rouse me from my daze.

Harlow banged on the kitchen window, calling my name.

"What's going on down there?" I heard Mrs Pemberton call

"Just checking on my friend there, ma'am," said Harlow, now inches from my bedroom curtain.

"I never trusted that boy. Never trusted him one bit. Wouldn't surprise me to find his face on the six o'clock news tonight."

"Well now that kind of talk's not helping no-one, is it?"

"Watch that mouth of yours!" yelled Mrs Pemberton from afar, "I'm just telling it like it is. Anyway, I have a mind to call the po-lis."

"You do huh?" said Harlow, a note of amusement in his voice.

"'All I know you could be a burglar, sniffing round other people's gardens like you got the right."

"Is that so?"

"Don't think I won't call them."

"You do what makes you happy, ma'am. I'll be back same time tomorrow, if you think it'd aid them in my capture," he said with a chuckle.

Mrs Pemberton muttered something before slamming her bedroom window shut, and all was silent.

From a crack in the curtain, behind which I sat bolt upright on a kitchen chair, a dark shadow cast across the full length of the window as Harlow pressed his body towards my bedroom.

"That what they call a neighbourhood watch?" he said, the long stretch of darkness growing and shrinking as he swayed on the balls of his feet. "Look kiddo I just want to know you're okay. I'm not mad about the work, no-one is. Caleb said he aint seen you all weekend. Truth be told - " he said, clearing his throat and resuming with a softer voice, more vulnerable in its tone, " - I want to talk to you myself, too. Barbara's close to tearing the hair clean out of her head. You see, Aimee's been gone since the fair. Wouldn't be the first time she's pulled this sort of trick, granted. Doesn't mean it don't scare the hell out of us time and time again though - "

I stood up and Harlow stopped talking, the shadow disappearing as he stepped back from the window.

"Anyway," he went on, this time from a distance. "If you hear anything, I know we'd both be grateful. And you need anything you just call us. You know where we are. I'll be back, tomorrow, check you're okay. I left some chilli out on the front porch in case you get hungry. It aint gone by the time I get back I'm knocking this damn door down, you hear me?" he said as he shuffled to the side of the house, closing and locking the side gate as he went.

For three days not a drop passed my lips. I became weak with hunger and almost delirious with thirst, my mouth parched and longing like a weaning child's. The only conscious activity I completed was to pass my hand through a crack in the doorway to retrieve Harlow's kind gesture of food, which I promptly binned and returned to my bedroom, where I consoled myself with glimpses of the outside world from the crack in the curtains.

I thought about Michael, about the past, about my life in this town; once so golden, it now pulsed in purples and greys like the first lick of a summer storm. The feeling of hope I had carried along with my measly suitcase was no more and I know I am not the only one to feel this degeneration. It is as though the elements are shifting to my very own mood the way they did so conveniently in Levi's storybooks. What had once seemed a shimmering prospect appeared danker, like a puncture had drained it of its lifeblood. This is a town that now lives in fear. Fear of the minor - the vandalism, the robberies - and of the major - crystallised by the brutal murder of an innocent woman for an amount that wouldn't even buy you a week's worth of groceries. This is a town now well versed in loss. Cellophane sentiments line the streets and the cars in Caleb's driveway have suddenly increased in quality and quantity. Evidence of the communal rot could be observed almost everywhere you looked; small businesses closed and relocated to pastures new, front doors that would once have been left gaping were locked, double locked, alarm systems were fitted and surveillance cameras now winked their glassy eyes as you entered most stores or, worse still, television monitors hung overhead so that you caught a skewed version of yourself walking in the opposite direction. The reaction was almost enough to turn a man to crime, if only to justify the irreversible slide into mistrust.

I thought about you, about you over and over again, and the terrible things that you have been through.

How could you not tell me, Verity? I could have helped. I could have tried. I'm not sure how, exactly. But if only you'd been honest with me, something could have been done I'm sure. It breaks my heart to think of you that way, and reading your post-mortem of the ordeal was one of the hardest things I've ever had to do. But why hadn't you told me sooner? What were you so frightened of? Judgement? Pity? Scorn? All I ever did was love you. All I ever do is love you. Maybe I take that for granted sometimes, maybe I should attempt to prove this to you more often. I guess I only realise how vital you are to me when I read letters detailing how close I've been to losing you, the way you only ever really remember your anniversary once the divorce is signed. All I can promise you is that someday, somehow, those men will get their just deserts. Of that I can promise you. There's nothing I wouldn't do for you. And if keeping you safe means I have to sacrifice myself to Michael's will then so be it. I know you don't understand this now. But I hope you might in time.

On the fourth day I heard a knock at my front door. I stood up on instinct, my mind snowy and unfocused, despite having no intentions of answering. The knocks sounded again and I made my way to the bedroom door where I rested my weight against the steady beams. Something slid between the lock of the door and after a brief clicking, it flew open to reveal a gentle, amber light inside of which dark shadow hovered.

"I won't lie to you friend, I begrudge the inconvenience," said Michael, walking straight into my front room as he returned a blade to his pocket. "Hey, get in here!"

I heard something small fall to the floor and break. I followed its sound, steadying myself on the walls as I went. His image still had not set, and my eyes struggled to focus on his slight, jerky movements. I sank into the couch and used every ounce of strength I had to hold my head upright.

"Well you look like the living dead, you aint going to croak on me I hope."

"I'm fine."

"Now that's a fabrication if ever there was one." Michael jumped heavily into an armchair next to the window, making his image all the more painful to look at. "What's wrong? You sick?"

"I don't know. I'm just hungry I suppose."

"When'd you last eat something?" he said, standing up again.

"What day is it?"

"Now that is not an answer that warms my heart. Myself I could go for a little nourishment. Let's see what you got." He darted from the living room and out of sight, his frenzied rustling sounded from behind the walls, marked by the creak and crash of cupboard doors. "Boy you sure as hell gone to town on this place. There isn't one damn wall you haven't kicked holy hell out of. I take it you found the deposit?"

Tins and glasses clattered across the kitchen's tiles. I nodded and felt my eyes grow heavy once more as my head lolled back onto the arm of the couch.

"Damn it that is one barren landscape you have in there. Man can't live off bread alone. Especially not stale bread at that," said Michael, tossing a bluing loaf into the unlit fire. "Here, let's try this for starters," he placed a glass of water in front of me and took a gulp of his own. "It's a cold setup you got here all of a sudden, friend. I had me finer feasts when I had but the stars for shelter and my wits for currency. Go on - " he said, pushing the glass towards me " - take a sip. You don't look so smart. In fact you weren't talking I might try to bury you myself."

I picked up the glass and cradled it in my palms.

"So," he said eventually. "You get the cash?"

"Yes."

"Seek and ye shall find."

"It took me four damn hours."

Michael smiled and widened his palms. "All part of the test."

"Did I pass?"

"Time will tell. So what you spend it on? Sure as hell didn't put it towards groceries."

"I burnt it."

"Up two rungs of the ladder and straight down the snake! Why'd you go and do a thing like that?"

"Town like this every dollar's marked."

"Still, there's other towns. And you and I are nothing if not adaptable."

"I was happy here."

"Say, you remember that old beach hut we hid out at, back in the day?"

I nodded.

"Man those old sailor boys took no prisoners. You still got your mark?"

Michael rolled up his sleeve and stroked the smudged blue anchor inches above his wrist. The ink had faded so much that you could barely tell what it was you were looking at, beyond an unnatural dark smudge on an otherwise unexceptional patch of skin.

I nodded and rolled my own shirt a few inches.

"Well I'll be... you can hardly see it at all. What do you say we refresh the memory? You got any Indian ink lying about? I'll carve real gently. You won't feel a thing."

I shook my head and returned my sleeve. "What do you want Michael?" I said, my voice hoarse and old.

"... and those girls? You remember those sisters?"

"There were no girls."

"Course there were girls. There were always girls. The Fentam sisters, that was it. Daddy owned the bar room on the pier."

"I don't remember."

"That's a fine memory to let slide. You don't remember? I tell you, those little girls they tasted sweet as honey. I was picking kelp out of my teeth all morning long!"

"I can't... "

"Where you got your name, too."

"I always had my name - "

"You really don't remember, do you?"

" - had it my whole damn life."

"Boy when that shark started circling I thought we were gonners... "

"That never happened."

"Old Melvin, dragging you onto the deck, 'well - '" Michael chuckled " - he says as he's bandaging you up, 'I guess part of you'll forever be in the belly of some whale!'"

"That never happened."

"It's right there - " he said, pointing to my stomach. I raised my shirt and looked down, playing my fingers across the pink, puckered flesh haloed with fading teeth marks.

"Where's your friend?"

"The girl?"

"Your *associate*?"

"What you talking about?"

"The man you came here with."

"There was no man."

"He was here."

"I walk alone."

"You told me his name."

"Must have been my shadow."

"No... "

"God damn it what was the name of those fish they served up at that old shack. Ugly sons of bitches... had to swallow them whole in case they turned and bit you first... "

"Michael... "

"I know, I know, I'm rambling. You sure I can't get you something to eat?"

"What do you want?"

"Straight to the chase, huh?"

"I'm tired, that's all."

"I miss us, Jonah. We belong together, boys like us. This is the nature of my visit."

"How?"

"From the day I set eyes on you I said to myself, I said there is a man after my own heart. You haven't changed Jonah, you haven't changed one bit. I see straight through you. I know exactly what you are."

"And what's that?"

"You're me, or some variation of. Now my proposition, if you'd be so kind as to hear me out, is our last chance to reclaim our kingdom, before the effort outgrows us. This is no game for old souls, I'm sure you'll agree."

I nodded and took a sip of my water. "So what did you have in mind?"

"You mean to tell me you're amenable all of a sudden?"

"You promise to leave forever I'll do just about anything you want."

"Well now - " said Michael, standing up as if readying to address an audience " - that is music to my ears my friend. Music to my ears."

After an hour of discourse during which I did little but nod weakly I stood up to see Michael out.

"I'll be in touch in due course. Glad we're reacquainted, friend. I tell you, this'll be the making of us. I can feel it in my bones."

I returned to the house and made my way back towards the bedroom when a draft crept up and around me like a shawl. I turned back to the door, my stomach churning and my head pounding. The door hung ajar and I took one step with difficulty. I reached out to place my weight on the wall and made a second step, which in itself felt like a mighty triumph. I lifted my right leg once more and felt the light from outside wash over me. I felt cushioned and tranquil as I drifted slowly towards the ground, like feather spat from an air vent. I remember the sensation, the sinking, wallowing descent. And then... nothing.

A bright light shone above me, something electrical beeped and then exhaled before the sound of scribbling became prominent. A more localised light shone into my eyes and, gently, my name was called over and over again.

"... can you hear us?" Two women all dressed in blue, their hair tied back and their aprons starched, leant over me; one stroked my forehead whilst the other removed the miniature flashlight from my eyes. At the base of my bed I felt a lotion cool my feet as a gentle hand and damp swab circled the stinging bracelet of dried blood around my ankle.

"Short round of antibiotics and it should be as good as gone," said the third woman as she applied a linen bandage to my wound before tucking both of my feet back inside the covers.

"Do you know where you are?" the blonde woman asked.

I took in the room from the slim brick of a bed and tried to sit up.

"No, no," said the other. "You just get some rest. Nasty bump on the head you got there. You must have fallen real hard."

Despite the weight of her hand pressing my shoulder I sat up and cracked my neck. "How did I get here?"

The nurse placed a clipboard into a slot at the base of my bed and stroked a crease from the sheet that had gathered and knotted around my feet. "Friend of yours found you, good job too. You were in quite some state."

"How did I... "

"Doctor said dehydration. It happens, usually to the older folk though, or the kids that think beer's the tonic. There'll be someone along in a moment to talk to you. Until then just get some rest." She moved over and turned the blinds to a half mast and left me alone in the dimmed room.

I reached for the cup of water at the side of my bed and went to take a sip, then another. The cool stream seemed to tease each corner of my body like some miracle elixir, and before I knew what I was doing I had knocked the lid clean off the jug and was pouring its contents straight into my mouth, gagging when my throat was unable to maintain the speed at which the torrents poured into and around me, soaking my chest and hands.

I slammed the empty jug down and went to stand up but found myself unable to balance, and so flopped back onto the hard mattress, cold and damp.

"Do you feel better?" said the man standing in the door. He moved towards the side of my bed and from the pocket of his white coat took out a flashlight which, without asking, he scanned across each eye.

"I don't feel any worse."

"It's a start I suppose. It's a good job they found you in time. You lost a lot of blood."

I touched my head and felt a warm liquid soaking through the sutures. "Who brought me here?"

"Didn't say. Just said they'd be here to pick you up when you were better. Left no number."

"I think I'm ready to go now."

"We'd prefer to keep you in overnight for observation, you understand."

"It's nothing painkillers and liquor won't cure."

"Not a combination we'd be in a hurry to recommend," he said with a laugh, walking over to the blinds and opening them fully.

"You were extremely dehydrated when you came in, that probably caused the blackout."

"I did not black out."

"Malnourished too - "

"I've been busy."

"You still have to eat."

"I'll know for next time."

The doctor made his way to the foot of the bed and scribbled some notes the folder which he then slid back into its holster. "You've been under a lot of pressure recently?"

"You could say that," I said, easing myself back into bed, suddenly exhausted from my three minute day.

"Things been playing on your mind?"

"I guess."

The doctor nodded as he made his way to the door. "I'm going to send someone down to speak with you."

"Who?"

"Just a colleague who might be of some assistance. Things can get on top of you and... "

"I don't need a head doctor."

"The bandages would suggest otherwise."

"You know what I meant," I said, forcing myself upright.

The doctor shook his head and placed his hand on my arm. "Take it easy. No-one's going to force you to do anything you don't want to do, okay?"

"I don't need to talk. I have to go home."

"In time," he turned and made his way back to my bed. "In the meantime there are some forms that need filling out. Personal details, insurance information and the like. Pretty rudimentary. Usually they'd have been filled out by whoever brought you in, but, well, you know. You must have some busy friends. Well, here you go. Only when you feel up to it." He left the coloured sheets on the wheeled table along with a slightly chewed pen before turning to leave.

"Doctor," I said. "The guy who brought me in here, was he... "

"Was he what?"

"Scarred? You know, his face all messed up?"

He thought for a moment, raising his head as though being fed the answer from some force on high. "Can't say I noticed. I only caught a brief glance. Besides, we tend to focus our attentions on the horizontal guests. Why do you ask?"

"No reason, just trying to whittle down my options. Process of elimination and all."

"Well you just get some rest. I'll be back to check on you within the hour, and you need any more water just pull on that cord there, the nurses'll see you're looked after."

When he was gone I lay back and felt myself drift towards sleep. Instead of following my instincts I shook myself awake and picked up the leaflets he had left me to complete. They were colour coded, with carbon copies beneath. Name, age, date of birth, address... all the usual requests and tiny black boxes into which I was expected to press my most intimate details.

I stood up and felt a shooting pain down my whole left side. I peeled the tape from the drip and ripped the needle straight out of my arm, allowing it to fall limply to the ground where it traced scratches of red across the tiles of the floor. I rummaged through each of the drawers until I found my clothes and readied myself as quickly as I could, wincing as the collar of my shirt caught on the tender bandage at the side of my head.

I made my way past the nurse's station and all the way down the hall. I had fully expected to be questioned at least once, but have come to realise that people are increasingly reluctant to ask questions when the answers will result in nothing but extra work.

I made it outside and walked straight across the car lot and onto the freeway that circled the hospital like a moat. The sound of traffic became deafening and the afternoon light near blinded me as I took a deep breath. How easy it would be, I thought, to raise my arm and flee to wherever the first kindly stranger happened to be driving, terminating at their final destination. On me I had not a dollar, but I'd survived with less before. If anything my elaborate dressings would elicit sympathy, so I was already one point up on the majority of lone male hitchhikers. I turned away from town, facing the emptiness and the cars and machines that rolled on and on until they disappeared into wherever they were going. It was doable, that I was sure of. But what would be the point? There'd be other towns, other jobs, other friends. And you, of course, I'd always have you. But Michael's shadow had cast and would now follow me wherever I went, infiltrate whatever I did until eventually - now, next week, next year - I faced it head on.

I turned my back towards the emptiness, the cars rushing towards me and through me like ghosts, and began the walk back into town.

Back at the house his car was parked on my lawn. He sat in my living room, scribbling in a pad. "You're late," he said, not looking up.

"No I'm not. I'm right on time."

"We're on a schedule here brother."

"I just need to grab a few things."

Michael stood up and slid his notebook into an inside pocket.

"You ready?"

"As I'll ever be."

He nodded and made his way outside.

We drove for over an hour to a shack out in the wilderness where Michael has been residing these past few weeks. At night I hear nothing but the animals, running in the dark, and the whistling of the late summer breeze, slowly bringing in fall whilst the rest of the world sleeps on. Michael is dead to the world from nine at night until dawn. I envy his ability to sleep at will but can't say I resent these quiet hours, when I can be alone, and think, and talk to you. I suppose all that is left is Michael's grand mission, our final day in the sun together. The plan is thus:

In six days' time the workers on the site are to be paid. Each morning on payday, cash flow permitting, Emmett arrives exactly one hour earlier than usual, this Michael deduced from his newfound ability to observe from a distance. I know the money is of a questionable source, and I know too that in order to save any embarrassing questions, the majority is kept in a safe beneath the tin shack from which the whole operation is manned. Our plan, if you can apply such grand a title to such simple actions, is to turn up precisely fifteen minutes after Emmett and quietly relieve him of his currency. Of course it is far from foolproof. Emmett is more than likely to be in possession of a light firearm, if only to complete his preferred garb. In such instances we will be forced to display our displeasure, though rest assured that no harm will come to him. Then, as Michael so duly informs me, we will have precisely one hour and fifteen minutes until even the most diligent workers are beginning to approach the sight. And even then it could be hours until someone goes to check on the poor man who will, (and this is the minor qualm I have with our agenda) be bound and gagged in his cushioned seat, thus allowing us time to have driven off into the horizon along with our gold, never to be seen again.

I can't say it pleases me to be part of this. And it just about kills me having to relay this information to you. But trust me when I say I'm doing it for the right reasons.

So think fondly of me, and pray for my safety if it's not too much to ask. And know that whatever happens, and wherever I end up, I will find a way to your next letter, if you care enough to send one.

With all the love in the world.

Yours,
Always,
Jonah

My Dearest Jonah,

The moment I opened your last letter it was as though I had been punctured. I could feel my whole body draining, the sheer effort of life's basics becoming apparent with each passing second, as if I was sitting in a tub and waiting as the water drained around me, its buoyancy replaced by my own leaden weight. And so I did everything I could to outsmart it. I became a triumph of pragmatism. Efficient to a fault. I tidied my room, placing my collections in galleried arrangements and amassing my detritus into some form of a waste pile. I made my own bed despite the protestations of housekeeping. I got ready. I painted my sallow face in the bathroom's cruel light; added colour to my cheeks, added a smile to my lips and two wide strokes across either eye. I fixed my hair and wrapped a coat around my lessening frame. With nail scissors I punctured a fresh hole in a leather strap to secure the trousers that now fall down around my curved hips. I wore heels and sunglasses and forced myself to stand upright. Then, for the first time in any number of weeks, I stepped outside. I had imagined the light would be the biggest shock, blinding me like a beast surfacing from hibernation, but the sunglasses eased the burn and in fact the chill of the late summer day caught me off guard. I tightened my coat and slipped one hand in my pocket to touch the letter - your letter, from happier times - which I had folded and secreted defiantly, determined never to let us stray too far regardless of circumstance. I walked past the derelict rooms with their windows of grime and algae, past the empty fire extinguisher and the burning cigarette butt, straight down the staircase towards the parking lot where my car sat, coloured flyers flapping beneath the rusted wiper. I was unsteady on my feet at first, having planed no distance greater than the length of my room for God knows how long. I found myself vulnerable and shaky, as though trying to control the body of another, as I made each step with care, frightened that a light breeze alone could carry me flailing and flying into the ether like a dropped dollar bill. I walked down past the strip of stores with their dimmed neon signs and their triple locked doors and eventually came to a small patch of parkland. I made my way down the winding footpath, glancing occasionally at the kept lawns and the strange trees with leaves that shifted on the breeze like a waving crowd. I began to slow my pace and noticed that some, only some, were beginning to brown and curl ever so slightly as a new season began to take root. I sat on a bench and let the warm wind blow across my face, breathing deeply and letting myself mindlessly become part of the day at large, of the world, of the sounds and the smells and the feel of the uneven ground beneath my feet. Two children ran past, laughing at first, and then becoming more frantic in their pursuit. Far above them a balloon floated on a clear path before rising and rising until it merged with the coarse lunchtime light. Mothers with babies sauntered to and fro, their enjoyment of the day overriding any impetus of route or schedule. A gang of scholarly youths lay like a pile of rope, their arms and legs tangled in and out of one another as they read aloud from a browning paperback. I breathed in deeply and let the smell of freshly cut grass work its way to the back of my throat. For a moment, the day disintegrated around me. My eyes blinked like the shutters of a slide show. I saw Eve barely able to breathe for laughter, and felt a sudden thump of anguish like the first time I ever stepped foot in The Iguana Den, alone and lost. I saw the walls of my trailer and the veiled prospect of whatever may come next. I saw your words in front of me like jewels, and my hand slip perfectly into yours; all of it seeming to matter so much more than that what surrounded me, than the here and now. How, I wondered, had each person arrived that day? What had made them come to this place, at this time? What were their intentions? Their objectives? And were they succeeding in their mission? They seemed happy enough, all of them, and placated in a way I found alien. They existed in the moment as if that in itself was of some major significance. Whilst I, on the other hand, was adrift, and frightened, one leg straddling the past whilst the other hovered over the future's murky pool. How I would have loved to ask each and every one of them whether they felt as I did, whether they were as perplexed as I by the mysterious waltz of a weekday afternoon. I began to feel more and more uncomfortable. It was as if this small stroll had been my one chance to extinguish whatever fire was building inside of me, and it had proved wholly ineffective. So I stood back up, blinking tears from behind the dark rims of my glasses, and made my way back, back to the room, back to behind closed doors where nothing seemed to matter anymore, where I could simply be, alone, and wait. You see I can bear a lot, Jonah. I can bear most things in life if truth be told. And I can certainly withstand lacking. I can go days without food, without water. I can make it, if forced, on the paltriest rations of sleep. But without you I am not so certain. It is as though even when I can't have you by my side, my entire world exists for you. Each day, each moment is there only so it can be relayed to you. Observed by you. Everything I did mattered when I knew that it was being processed by another, played out for something greater than myself. Without you I don't exactly live. In fact I seem to do the opposite of living, whatever that may be. And so now what? You make your choices, which I must assume to be correct, and you alone shoulder the consequences. But what about me? Where do I truly fit into all of this? Because I need you the way most people need food, need love, need air. And selfishly part of that means I need you to feel the same way. Is this the case? I may not always have been entirely honest with you, but my deceit was never more harmful than omission of specifics, of gilding and merging what was already there. I never once lied, Jonah, not in the traditional sense. I felt my heart slow its rhythm as I read your proposition, of the damage that you were to cause. And then nothing. No word. No news. Until, of course, four days ago. I assume you know what I speak of. You see I heard nothing of a robbery of some backwater building sight. Nothing about two ex-felons gorging like kings on the wages of one down at heel town. I did, however, hear about the famed author - the voice of small town America and he of half a dozen pennames - and his brutal demise. I heard about the way in which an octogenarian's arm was snapped like a branch and his throat slit ear to ear. I heard about his driver being shot twice in the back, and his esteemed art collection being bundled into the trunk of a stolen car. I heard about his granddaughter... my God, Jonah, she was nineteen-years-old.

She was still a child. They say it's a miracle that she survived. If you ask me the miracle is how she'll go on living after what three masked men did to her. Please tell me you had no part, in that aspect at least. I then heard about the robbers with mysterious, exotic names - names which play on the tongue like the stone of some strange fruit, names not of these shores - who fled the scene in separate vehicles. I heard about the gunshot wound that claimed the eldest, and the police chase that led to the crash and the coma into which the driver so inconveniently slid. And I heard about the third member, the one who held the knife, and his infuriating escape. I heard how a hundred eyes are now scanning his whereabouts, about the manhunt and the warnings and the bounty on his head. I heard about sightings of him in other states, in other towns, free and liberated and wanted by thousands. That was the moment this rot set in, Jonah. Was everything you told me a lie? Are these sheets little more than the ink of some poetic fantasist? Or is there some truth within? It makes no sense to me, and I'm as confused as I am frightened. Confused all the more that even as each gruesome detail emerges from my screen I find myself hoping, praying, that you were the one that got away. That somewhere you are out there and that I am tender in your thoughts. You frighten me as much as you please me, Jonah, and that is not as it should be. But still I need you, God help me that's the truth of it no matter how hard I try. But with each passing day I feel part of you disappearing and that emptiness is so great, so vast, that it starts to suffocate me. The prospect of life without you is something I am never willing to contemplate. And so all I can do is hope. Hope that somehow these words find you, and that they find you well. And hope that somehow, someday, you will find a way to respond.

Be at peace Jonah, wherever you are, and know that I will always be here, always waiting. For you, only you.

With all my love,
Always,
Verity

Come and visit us at
www.legendpress.co.uk
www.twitter.com/legend_press

Lightning Source UK Ltd.
Milton Keynes UK
UKOW050621110412

190471UK00001B/3/P